IN THE SHADOW OF WAR

BY

PATRICK M. GARRY

INKWATER PRESS

PORTLAND • OREGON
INKWATERPRESS.COM

Cover and interior design by Masha Shubin

This is a work of fiction. The events described here are imaginary. The settings and characters are fictitious and do not represent specific places or living or dead people. Any resemblance is entirely coincidental.

www.inkwaterpress.com

ISBN-10 1-59299-233-1
ISBN-13 978-1-59299-233-1

Publisher: Inkwater Press

Printed in the U.S.A.

To EAG and CJL

"Don't Call, Just Come"

No one ever thought of Ricky as my older brother. But he was.

Ricky was born in February of 1953, a year and a half before I was. My parents always said they didn't know, but they must have. They had to have been pretty determined to have another child so soon afterward. Maybe they even felt they had something to prove. They always said they didn't know, but how could they not have? The eyes were a dead give-away.

When Ricky was six years old, the doctors confirmed my parents' fears. They said he would never have more than a five-year-old's intelligence. Which was about right, I later thought. Because it was around the time when I was five years old that I quit thinking of Ricky as my older brother. Or maybe it was around then that my parents started telling me that I had to look out for him, keep an eye on him, watch over him — that sort of thing.

What I learned about having a retarded brother was that you spend way too much time trying to wring the retardedness out of him, and not enough time just going along for the ride.

✧

We lived in a fairly safe neighborhood. Not safe in a crime sense, but safe in an embarrassment sense. It was the oldest neighborhood in Willow Bend, which in the 1960s was still a small town about twelve miles outside of Minneapolis. The houses were big, with plenty of blemishes, just like the families who lived in them. The Catholic school was only two blocks away, so there were lots of large families who lived in the neighborhood. And with all those kids... well, Ricky wasn't the only oddity. Jimmy Kramer had contracted polio the year before the vaccine became available, and he was still trying to learn to walk with those big metal braces. Martha Horgan had some kind of asthma; she couldn't even go outside without that plastic mask of hers. And Bridgette O'Leary had a bright red birthmark covering one whole side of her face. In our neighborhood, no one seemed embarrassed about their families — except for the Jonkin's. When Mr. Jonkin came home drunk on Saturday nights, the whole neighborhood could hear him.

In our neighborhood, it was safe to do what you wouldn't be caught dead doing in the outside world. Even at the age of fourteen, I still played along with Ricky's martian-invader fantasies.

✧

Ever since he'd seen the movie "The Day the Earth Stood Still," Ricky was obsessed with invaders from outer space. He didn't understand the movie; he just knew that aliens were far more intelligent than earthlings and could have their way with us whenever they wanted.

I sometimes thought Ricky was smarter than the doctors had said he was. I sometimes thought his whole alien obsession was just a way of getting back at a world in which he was considered mentally inferior. And sometimes I thought the real cause of retardation was that the imagination side of the brain had completely overpowered the logical side; because when he was in his fantasy mode, which was where he was most of the time, Ricky was amazingly thorough and focused.

"Brosher Glen, I have a queshtion," he would announce. That was what Ricky called me — Brosher Glen. Ricky had trouble pronouncing his s's and th's. So for both, he ended up saying a "sh." Like the time he sat on the pet guinea pig someone had brought to school: "I didn't shee shat shitting shere," he tearfully said to Mrs. Folcrum, the teacher.

"What's your question?" I'd reply, fairly certain about the subject matter of his inquiry.

"Well, if aliensh don't have to eat like we do, how come shey have a moush?"

"How do you know they have mouths, Ricky?"

"Brosher Glen, don't be shilly. Of courshe shey have a moush. You want to look at my Shuperman book?"

"Maybe they have mouths because they're trying to look like earthlings." I always tried to see if I could answer Ricky's questions in a way that would satisfy him.

"Shen how come shey never appear like babiesh or kidsh or grandpash?"

If you let him, Ricky could interrogate you to death.

✧

On summer nights, as the sun started to go down, the neighborhood kids would congregate at whatever house seemed to be the liveliest; and what Ricky lacked in intelligence, he more than made up for in volume.

The younger kids would be the first to arrive at our front porch. And if it was a clear night, Ricky would point out to them how Martian space ships could camouflage themselves as twinkling stars.

As the sun fell completely out of sight, and the night crickets began their chirping, and the muffled lights from all the curtained windows gave a distant feel to any adult presence in the neighborhood, the youngest ones would inch ever closer to each other as Ricky described all the evil powers possessed by the superior aliens. The kids knew there was something different about Ricky — they had heard the term mental retardation — but he spoke with such conviction and in such detail. And he spoke about things that their parents had obviously kept hidden from them.

"Marshiansh have powerful transhportersh which can move shem from one planet to anosher in maybe shree shecondsh," Ricky would explain. "And shat'sh why no one can find shem — 'caushe shey don't even need to land sheir shpasheship on earsh."

"If you catch one, you can shee around sheir neck a shpeshial converter which can make sheir bodies look like anyshing, even animalsh, like a shquirel, or rabbit."

That was when I and some of the older kids would step in, once Ricky had his audience primed and ready to go. From there, it wasn't difficult to get everyone all stoked up.

"I saw some funny things going on at the Sallsman house today," I'd tell Ricky. "You think we should go check things out?"

Ricky always said yes to that question. And all the kids followed, as long as there was a big enough group.

Sometimes I would sneak away and hide behind a tree and make Martian noises. Other times I'd just throw stones, or turn up the static on my transistor radio. Ricky was retarded, but he had amazing hearing. Sometimes, though, I was more self-interested and manipulative, especially if there was another boy around who was my age. And it was fairly easy to convince Ricky that the alien collaborator was Jennifer Sallsman, and that we'd have to spy on her. Jennifer was eighteen years old; and she often left the shades open in her bedroom. "Look, Brosher Glen, she'sh taking off her Marshian shuit."

The thing about playing with a retarded brother who believed in aliens and spaceships — no one ever accused you of being a peeping-tom.

But the way to really get Ricky going was to stand him up on the top step of our front porch and begin chanting for Generalissimo Ricky to give a speech. That's what really got Ricky going — being called Generalissimo.

"We need you, Generalissimo."

"We're in great danger, Generalissimo."

"You're the only one who can lead us, Generalissimo."

"Only you can defeat the evil aliens, Generalissimo."

And Ricky would act very serious and then start waving his hands for the chants and applause to die down, just as he had seen politicians do on television. "You musht not be afraid," he'd proclaim. "I know how to beat shem. I will shave you. What we need ish a plan." That's when he'd look over at me — I was always the planning department.

Once, I suggested that the Tonneson house had been infiltrated and that we should commence a frontal assault. Mr. Tonneson was always calling our parents about us running through his yard. But most of all, he had run over our dog when I was four years old, and I still hadn't forgiven him.

The Tonneson house was set back at least fifty feet from the street, and there was a steep bank in the yard as it rose up from the boulevard. It was the perfect place to hide; it was just like a trench in which soldiers would take cover before staging their attack. It was the kind of bank I often wished had existed in front of the Sallsman house.

There were maybe a dozen of us. We laid on that bank for at least twenty minutes, spying on the house. We could see Mrs. Tonneson doing a crossword puzzle on the dining room table. We might have done nothing more — it seemed gratifying enough just to lie there in a posse and spy — but someone urged Ricky to lead us out of our trenches and onto the battlefield. He was scared, I could tell, but he gathered the courage to crawl up the hill and stand atop the bank and call out, while waving the stick he was pretending was a sword: "Onward sholdiersh, we fight for our human rashe."

And the thing was, we all did it. We scrambled up the bank, ventured a few battle cries, and then suddenly froze about ten feet from the house. We really hadn't planned beyond that. Not knowing what else to do, I ran up and rang the doorbell. And then we circled the house as if it were a wagon train, screaming as we ran, before retreating back to our hiding spot on the bank.

When the police car drove up five minutes later, Ricky was the one who flagged them down. He was glad they had responded so quickly to his S.O.S. signal. He also advised the officers to make sure their pistols were loaded. What I learned about having a retarded brother was that, even if only for a moment, he could make the rest of the world act retarded.

The older kids always pretended to be making fun of Ricky, but we still played along with his fantasies. Even after all the magic of childhood had been destroyed, after all the Santas and Easter Bunnies exposed as frauds, we still played the roles Ricky assigned us when he was organizing a neighborhood posse to root out alien invaders. The thing about being with Ricky was that we could sneak back into that world of childhood make-believe whenever we wanted.

But I also learned, the first time I went alone with Ricky to a movie, that his was a magic best confined to our neighborhood. We went to see "The Music Man," playing at the Andrews Theater. I figured he'd get a charge out of watching the boy with the stutter sing 'Wells Fargo Wagon.' There wasn't anyone sitting near us — they all cleared out after Ricky, running down the aisle, had shouted out: "I'm shitting here, Brosher Glen." But it didn't matter, we still got kicked out of the theater. Ricky insisted on singing along, even when there wasn't a song being sung in the movie.

Once I got to be twelve, I only played Ricky's games at night, under cover of darkness.

✧

Corcoran, where my grandfather lived, was a lot like our neighborhood. It was plenty safe. The whole town knew Ricky, all six of its residents. When Ricky and I went there for the summer, the population grew by one-third. Grandpa called it the summer boom.

Located in western Minnesota, Corcoran was about a three-hour drive from our house. It had virtually become a ghost town — the abandoned houses outnumbering the residents by about seven to one. My grandfather, Eamon O'Shea, had lived his whole life in Corcoran. He owned all the farmland surrounding the town, but he never got more than about two-thirds of the land harvested before the snows came. Grandpa was seventy-eight years old; and his hired man, Myron Banks, was sixty-seven and walked with a severe limp. Grandpa didn't believe in renting out his land to someone who could actually farm all of it. "If you can't work it, you shouldn't own it," he said. My grandfather would not have done well in the corporate world.

Grandpa was always boasting that Corcoran was on the verge of a comeback, that it was "on the rebound." But he was a little retarded when it came to his Corcoran. Or maybe he was just so single-minded, like Ricky was with aliens. "There's nothing wrong with Ricky," he once told me, after I had reminded him of Ricky's limitations. "He believes in this place, and belief is a lot more important than a little smarts."

Grandpa was right, I later decided. In a place like Corcoran, there really wasn't anything wrong with Ricky. And sure enough, Ricky was always better behaved in Corcoran than he was at home. But I never told my mother that. The key to living with a retard, I decided, was to give him a chance every now and then to live in a retarded world.

No one but Grandpa ever saw (or admitted to) a family resemblance in Ricky. "He's got a nose just like my uncle Thomas, on my mother's side," Grandpa said of Ricky, "and his jaw line is the spittin' image of my brother." I never knew either of those gentlemen, but I often wondered if they'd be insulted by the comparison.

Sometimes, during lunch, Grandpa and Ardelle and Myron and I would do Ricky tongue-twisters. We'd have a contest to see who could devise the hardest ones.

"Sho shew she shirt wish sheamsh shat shupply shtrengsh."

"A shenshitive and shuperchilious shpinshter shwimming inshtructor shcolded she sholishitous shpectator."

The test was that you had to say it with a piece of bread in your mouth, and straight through, without the slightest of hesitations. But nobody could ever do it like Ricky.

✧

Ever since I was nine years old, Ricky and I had spent our summers in Corcoran. It was tradition, a habit, just automatically presumed. But the summer of 1970 was different. By the time I graduated from high school in late May, I hadn't given a moment of thought to what I'd do for the summer. Not one mention of it had been made until Grandpa called that night — the night of my graduation.

"It's your grandfather," Mom said, dropping the phone down onto a kitchen chair and walking out.

"I suppose you're too educated now for the likes of me and my rundown old town," he said, trying I could tell to be funny. He would never speak that way about Corcoran if he was being serious.

"It's just high school, Grandpa."

"You're still coming, for the summer, aren't you?

There's a ton of work to do around here. And you know, this summer I thought the three of us could take a weekend jaunt over to..."

"The three of us, Grandpa? You think you can actually get Myron to venture away from Corcoran?"

"Myron? What do you mean? He'll never go, you know that. No, let's just make it you and me and..." And then Grandpa's voice dropped off, as though it had driven full speed off a cliff. And I could feel him getting flustered, the way he did when the legions of his past got all mixed up in the ranks of his present.

"I guess I haven't really thought about the summer," I said.

"I know you won't have Ricky, but there's all of us," he replied, in a voice that sounded as if he was rushing to cover-up his lapse. "And let me tell you, Glen, there's some changes going on around here. Big changes. Biggest changes in forty years. And people — we've got new blood, Glen."

"You mean living there? People have actually moved there?"

"So you'll come? When? When can you get here? Soon, I hope. Make it soon, Glen. You'll come, won't you?"

Grandpa was like Ricky in that respect: they both had their needy moments, although Ricky had a lot more of them.

"I don't know exactly when, but I'll call you as soon..."

"Don't call, for god's sake, just come."

But after I hung up, I still wasn't sure what I'd do. It always seemed as if Ricky was the sole reason for all those summers in Corcoran — a chance to give the rest of the family a break; a chance to have him spend time in an uncomplicated surrounding; things like that. And it was Ricky who had always been the glue between Grandpa and me. But this year was different. Ricky had died two months earlier.

✧

The crowd of funeral-goers had come straight to our house from the cemetery. Mom and her friends began setting out all the food, while Dad positioned himself behind the kitchen table and began pouring drinks. The mood was relaxed; it almost felt relieved.

"He's with God now," more than one person told my mother.

"At least he didn't suffer, you have to be grateful for that," others said to her.

"You mustn't blame yourself. Nothing could have prevented it. You worked miracles with that boy."

But I doubted that Mom blamed herself. She was taking my sister to a piano lesson when the accident happened. I was the one at home. I was the one who yelled at Ricky when he knocked the bottle of milk on the floor. I was the one who threw that piece of bread at him in a momentary rage, and then watched him run outside in tears and hop on his bike. I was the one who didn't go after him, or yell for him to stop.

When I finally did go out looking for him and came to the intersection of Hessler Avenue, the busy street three blocks from our house, there was an eerie quiet. Traffic had stopped. People must have been yelling — I could see their faces — but it was as if I had gone suddenly deaf.

A crowd was huddled in the middle of the street. And I knew even before I saw the mangled bicycle that it was Ricky who lay at the center of the huddle.

Afterward, I wished that I hadn't seen him. I wished that Ricky's dead body had already been loaded into the ambulance. I wished that I hadn't seen his legs spread out on the pavement like that. I wished that I hadn't seen his face, and particularly those eyes that looked like the dark waters of a cold lake on a moonless night. I had always thought Ricky's eyes were empty, that there was nothing behind them. But I was wrong. When I saw his contorted body lying there on the pavement, that's when his eyes were empty.

Later, days and weeks later, I couldn't help but think of the futility of it all. All the protections. All the special classes and chaperoning. All the child-proofing. And in the end, none of it did any good. All it took was one lousy bottle of spilled milk.

It was after Ricky's death that I began thinking about the war in Vietnam. I watched the news and tried to imagine myself fighting in those terrifying-looking jungles. I watched the bodies of dead soldiers being carried to helicopters. And I wondered if I could do it. I wondered if someone who had been afraid of what people would say about his retarded brother could fight the Viet Cong and not be a coward.

When I started thinking about the war, about what it would be like to be in it, I couldn't decide if I saw it as an escape or a punishment — or as a chance to be brave, to make up for what I had never done for Ricky.

✧

"Now you mustn't feel guilty about Ricky's death, you know that, don't you?" Grandpa said. The funeral guests were all inside the house, and he and I were sitting alone at the backyard picnic table.

"I was the one who made him run away. It was like I'd pushed him in front of that car," I said, seizing the chance to confess.

"That's ridiculous, Glen. But if you're going to think like that, then what about all the other times you rescued him?"

"Yeah, right — you mean like all those times I didn't take him to a ballgame because I was afraid of what some bully might say; or when I didn't take him to the circus because I might be embarrassed? Yeah, I was a real lifesaver." I could be honest with Grandpa. Nothing I said would ever change his mind about me. And besides, most of what I said he would forget anyway.

"Now you're just being crazy. And what about that time he got lost and sprained his ankle out past the marsh and you looked for him all night and then carried him all the way back home? Or that time you stood up to that van-load of long-hairs who'd stopped for gas? Or when you..."

"That was all in Corcoran, Grandpa. I was talking about..."

"Corcoran's no different than anywhere else."

"Grandpa, sometimes you can be so oblivious."

"And sometimes you can be so stubborn. My mother was just like that — stubborn as a mule, and you're the same way."

I could feel him trying to force a smile.

"You just don't understand, Grandpa," I said, standing up and taking a few steps away from the table.

"Oh, I think I do. Guilt is one thing that doesn't go out of fashion. And I've got plenty of people who won't let me forget about mine."

I figured he was talking about the death of his son, my mother's brother, a long time ago. But from what I could tell, what his children most blamed him for was their miserable youth in a miserable town.

Aside from when my parents dropped us off in June and picked us up in August, Ricky and I were the only family members who ever visited Grandpa. And Mom always gave Grandpa the same lecture whenever she dropped us off for the summer: Ricky needs to be watched; Ricky needs patience; Don't let Ricky wander into any deserted houses; Make sure he gets three meals a day. And then she would find a way to remind Grandpa not to treat her sons the way he had treated her. But Grandpa never seemed to pay any attention to Mom's list of commands. He was always too busy hugging Ricky and acting thrilled at the present Ricky was handing him.

Just before one of our summer trips to Corcoran, I overheard Mom talking to Dad in the kitchen. "If he thinks he can make up for everything he did to me just by taking the boys for the summer, he's sorely mistaken," she was saying. But I never thought Grandpa was trying to make up for something. More than anything else in the world, my grandfather wanted someone with whom he could share Corcoran, and I think he had decided that Ricky and I were his only prospects.

"You want some advice?" Grandpa said, as the funeral

guests inside were refilling their drinks. "No, I don't suppose you do — no one does. But I'll give it to you anyway. You can never go back to the past and fix it, so don't dwell on it. The only way to conquer regret is to focus on something bigger than yourself, something that makes your guilt seem small and irrelevant..."

I knew what he meant. The land — it was his remedy for everything. But that was when I started thinking about the war.

Summer at the Big Houshe

The changes about which Grandpa had spoken were evident, I thought, as soon as my father turned off the highway and drove down the gravel road that was still, nostalgically, called Main Street. Although, since there were only four roads left in Corcoran, and since Main Street was both the longest and the one lined with the most houses, the name was descriptively accurate, as well as nostalgic.

Main Street was also the address of what Ricky called the "Big Houshe" — the only Victorian-style house in Corcoran. The biggest house in Corcoran. The house Grandpa had lived in since 1918. It had a front and back staircase, and a wrap-around porch that was sloped on the east side because of some rotted timbers. The first thing Ricky did when he arrived at the Big Houshe each summer was run up the front stairs, through the second floor hall, down the back stairway, out the kitchen door and onto the porch, around to the front door, and then do the whole thing all over again. Grandpa called it the loop. "Let him run the loop a few times — that'll burn off some of his excitement," Grandpa always said. But I thought "the loop" was just Ricky's way of re-marking his territory, after nine months of absence.

The Big Houshe stood at the end of the road, where Main Street simply ended, disappearing abruptly into tall weeds. And a corn field bordered the backyard, which was shaded by the big maple in which Grandpa had built a tree fort for Ricky.

As my parents and I drove along Main Street, toward the Big Houshe, I noticed wash pales on the porches of a few houses. And a few sidewalks that were swept clean. And some marigolds and petunias planted in a few window boxes. There were only a few, but it only took a few to constitute a population boom in Corcoran.

From the decor in the windows and the laundry on the clothes lines, it appeared that the new residents were an atypical type. Not the bent-over, hobbling old people who had been ejected from condemned apartments in Millerton, a city of about 100,000 located nine miles down the highway from Corcoran. Nor the sullen, leather-clad men with loud cars who had heard in some biker bar that cheap housing was to be had in a place called Corcoran. Grandpa's new residents, it appeared, were women — women who were clean, energetic and concerned about appearance.

"Looks like he's found a few new tenants," my father said, probably thinking, mistakenly, that Grandpa actually rented the houses out.

"Yes, well, they won't be here long," Mom answered, barely glancing out her window. "Nobody ever is. How anyone in their right mind could call this a town, I'll never know." And on that point, I couldn't argue with her. Corcoran was mostly just a clump of abandoned houses. It was like one of those little graveyards of America's past that dot the mid-western countryside. Or like a clump of garbage floating in the wake of a big ship: refuse cast over the side of the U.S.S. America.

The only business still operating in Corcoran was a small diner, located right on the highway, with a couple of gas pumps outside. The residential section of town, as Grandpa called it, sat about a quarter mile back from the highway, along Main Street and the three narrow roads that branched off of it. But those roads were like dead branches jutting out of a decaying tree trunk. Mostly, the branches were bare, but occasionally there was a dilapidated house, still hanging on like a dead leaf or a brittle twig. At the edge of town, beyond Grandpa's house, sitting up on a hill overlooking Lake Kilkenny, was a cemetery. From what Grandpa told me, it had been two decades since the cemetery's population overtook that of the town.

But Grandpa was a contrarian; or, if you listened to his children, a lunatic. Whenever he accumulated enough money from the crops that his surrounding farmland produced, he added to his Corcoran real estate holdings by paying off the tax liens on yet another long-abandoned lot or rundown house. "I got the old Collins house for a real bargain today," he'd say, coming out of the county courthouse after one of his purchases. Not that he ever did anything with all his property — he was just intent on preserving the place for that inevitable moment when its resurrection would come.

"Remember the past," Grandpa always told me, "and it won't turn against you." Which, from the sight of Corcoran, seemed like advice that had long since contradicted itself.

✧

Grandpa wasn't home when we arrived at the Big Houshe. "He probably went out deliberately," Mom said, with a familiar sneer. "Just like always — never there for his family, and after we drove all this way."

But she was wrong. It wasn't Grandpa who avoided her. And it certainly wasn't like Grandpa to miss out on visitors. In my mind, his absence was due more to the fact that we were an hour and a half early than to any desire to snub his daughter.

Mom waited all of ten minutes before suggesting that they get back on the road. "We want to get home before dark," she said to me. "Do you mind if we leave you all alone?"

"Let's see, I've been spending every summer here for the past nine years; yeah, I think I can manage," I answered.

"You're getting more like your grandfather every year," she snapped.

"You want me to say hello to him for you?" I asked. Even though I wouldn't see her for the entire summer, I still felt like irritating her. It was possible, I often thought, that I was a bit retarded myself, at least emotionally.

Dad said, "Have a good summer," and then told me he would forward any mail that came for me from the University of Minnesota. I had applied only a month earlier, and my father seemed petrified that his son would have no college to attend in the fall. Or maybe he was afraid that I would end up like Grandpa.

When Mom hugged me goodbye, she did it all with her arms, leaning over just enough to pat me on the back. It was like the kind of lean one makes to peer over the edge of a tall building — just enough to snag a quick peek, but with no risk of losing your footing. Our goodbye's were always like that — my mother so anxious to put Corcoran in her rearview mirror. Even though she grew up in the Big Houshe, she never displayed any inclination toward reminiscence. She never even walked through the house, just to see what props from her past still remained. And as she climbed back into the car, I detected that familiar uncertainty of hers — the uncertainty of what to say as a summer farewell. Her sense of social pleasantry demanded something like "Have a good time" or "Enjoy your summer," but her own memories would not let her admit that anyone could enjoy Corcoran — that is, anyone other than a retard.

✧

After my parents drove off, I walked over to Myron's. Separating his house from Grandpa's was a large, unkempt apple orchard. It had left so many rotting apples on the ground that a person had to have thick-soled shoes just to walk through it.

Normally, Myron was in the barn that stood behind his house and served as a repair garage. He used to work as an auto mechanic, before the accident in which a car fell off a jack and onto his leg. After he was released from the hospital and told that his injuries would prevent him from going back to work, Grandpa recruited him for Corcoran. Myron was one of Grandpa's few success stories — he had lived in Corcoran for almost twenty years now, keeping in marginal working order all of Grandpa's old trucks and tractors. Grandpa ran them into the ground, and Myron resurrected them: that was the arrangement.

Myron's house was surrounded by a forest of machinery parts. Most people would have called it a junk yard, but he called it his supply depot. Ricky used to love playing hide'n seek in Myron's yard.

But the barn was strangely silent as I walked by. There was no wrench-pounding or engine-revving, and no cuss words streaming out of Myron's mouth.

"Anybody home?" I called into the kitchen from the back door. "Myron? It's Glen. Anybody home?"

"What's that?" came Myron's crackly voice.

"It's Glen," I said, opening the screen door.

"What's that?" he called out again.

"It's Glen," I shouted.

"Oh Glen, you're here. Come on in, I need your advice."

It sounded as if his voice was coming from the first floor bedroom. "Myron?" I said, leaning my head into his doorway.

"Tell me, which tie do you like better?" he asked, throwing three or four onto the bed.

"What's the occasion?"

"Dinner tonight. Over at Julia's house. They're even having a cocktail hour. What are you going to wear?"

"Who's Julia?"

"Julia — down the block and across the street. Lives between Sharon and Lillie. I know, I had a hard time too at first, getting them all straight. So what's the guest of honor wearing? I don't want to be too dressed up."

"Myron, what are you talking about? What guest of honor?"

"You, you're the guest of honor. The dinner is a welcome for you and....Oh, hey, I'm awfully sorry about Ricky. We'll all miss him, especially Ardelle. I would have come to the funeral if I..."

"I know, I know. The flowers you all sent were real nice."

"Ricky mailed me a card at Christmas — he wanted to make sure I still had my telescope and that we'd watch the moon landing again this summer."

Ricky was like that. He never thought events happened in isolation. To him, life was a constant, repetitive ritual. Last summer, the summer of 1969, we watched on television as Neil Armstrong put his foot down on the moon's surface. ("Brosher Glen, ish he going to fight aliensh now?" Ricky had asked.) And with his ritualistic mindset, Ricky had been looking forward to this summer, when once again Neil Armstrong would make the first landing on the moon.

"It's going to be strange not having him here this summer," Myron said. He was not totally unlike Ricky in his desire for ritual. "But then, this summer is going to be different in a whole lot of ways I think."

"Who's this Julia you're talking about?"

"Don't you know? Hasn't your grandfather told you?"

"I just arrived, and he's not around."

"Haven't you talked to him lately?"

"Sure, but..." And then I just let my words hang — I didn't want to bring up Ricky's name again.

"That Eamon! I don't even think he knows how to call long distance. His generation, they think one call will bankrupt them."

"Myron, he knows how to call: he calls me all the time. We just haven't talked about this...Julia person."

"Oh yeah, well, now you mustn't take that personally," he said, looking worried that I might feel slighted by this exclusion from the communication link. "Your grandfather has been a very busy man, what with getting the houses livable and planting all the crops. He's planted all his fields this year, do you know that? Why, that hasn't happened in....Well sure, he's out in the fields right now, probably with Sharon. Yeah, she's the farmer alright."

"Who's Sharon?"

"She came when Julia came, and Lillie too. They all came together. Their husbands are at the war. Well, except for Sharon. I mean, hers was, but he got killed. A few months ago. They're putting on dinner tonight for everyone. So what do you think about a tie? Which one should I wear?"

I had never seen Myron wear anything but an old pair of stained, baggy work jeans and one of his many flannel shirts. The most preparation he had ever made for a dinner was to wash his hands and take off his cap. But now he was standing in his bedroom, wearing the pants from a suit that looked at least thirty years old, and holding wrinkled ties up in front of the mirror.

"Myron, it's only three in the afternoon. What time is this dinner tonight?"

"But I got to iron my shirt, and maybe wash some socks — and if anything needs mending, Ardelle said she'd sew it for me. You need any ironing done, or sewing?"

"No, I think I'm okay."

"You're the guest of honor, you know."

But I didn't feel much honored, or even excited. I was

skeptical. To me, Corcoran had always been a haven — a good place to be retarded. So I was naturally resistent to intruders.

"Myron, are you home?" came a female voice from the back door.

"Glen, that's Julia," whispered Myron, suddenly in a fluster. "Go to the door, will you? I don't want her to see this mess."

I expected to see someone who resembled my image of the typical farm wife. But what I saw was a woman in her twenties, maybe even early twenties, wearing shorts and a cotton shirt tied at her waist, revealing a thin line of bare midriff.

"I'm looking for Myron," the woman said, as I stood in the doorway with a surprised silence. "I'm Julia. I live down the street."

But it was even more surprising to hear those words: "I live down the street." No one had ever lived down the street before.

"Uh, he's a bit tied up right now."

"Oh, well I was going to ask him if he had a few minutes to help me — I need to move a table. Would he...? You wouldn't by chance be Glen?"

"Yes — Glen Kinsella."

"I thought so. I've seen pictures of you in Eamon's living room. When did you arrive?"

"Just a few minutes ago."

"You're coming tonight, aren't you? We're making a special dinner. Your grandfather's been very excited for your arrival..."

I had been coming to Corcoran for nine years, and

she was making it seem as if this was a one-time event, as if I were the guest here.

"...Say, I hate to impose, especially since you just arrived, but could you help me move a table?" she asked. "We need to have it for tonight."

Julia's pony-tail of auburn hair bounced as we walked along the gutted gravel street. But I didn't want to stare at her, so I sort of hung my head, gazing down at the ground. And I noticed the way her calves tapered down to the thin ankles that in turn disappeared into the small, white tennis shoes. I had never seen ankles and legs like that before, so smoothly mature and curvy — old enough to be alluring, but young enough to be free of imperfection.

"So, you manage your grandfather's farms during the summer?" she asked.

"Oh, I don't know if that's...," I started to clarify, though I did like the sound of the word "manage."

"Well, whatever you call it, I think it's a pretty amazing thing for you to do. You don't see many other boys your age doing such things."

But the "boys-your-age" comment hit me like a splash of cold water.

We walked up a dirt path to the old Sullivan house, which was what we still called it, even though the last Sullivan had moved out more than twenty years ago. Inside, a workbench had been set up in what used to be the dining room. On it were cans of varnish and stain, along with tools and paintbrushes. Spread out through the rest of the house were pieces of furniture in various states of repair, or disrepair, depending on one's perspective. Julia went immediately to a freshly-stained table standing in the center of the living room.

"Isn't it beautiful?" she exclaimed. "It's an antique. Your grandfather says it's probably a hundred years old."

"Yeah, well, there's plenty of antiques around here."

She laughed, and I suddenly felt older.

"Eamon should open an antique shop," she said. "He and Myron can do wonders fixing up this old furniture."

"My grandpa never sells. He keeps everything that's been left behind, just in case someone new moves in and needs it. But as you can see, there haven't been many takers."

And again, she laughed. An easy and comfortable laugh. One that came with a perfectly matching smile; not forced or insincere. She had a beauty that was varnished with the gloss of kindness. I could tell she was someone who would not have been afraid to talk to Ricky. That was how I often judged people — by how I thought they would react to retards.

"So tell me," she said. "Doesn't it get a little too quiet around here for a young man who's, what, seventeen?"

"Eighteen." And I'd already graduated to "young man."

"Not much of a social life though, is there? Or do you go into the city at night?"

"I keep pretty busy," I said, trying to maintain the impression that indeed I did manage Grandpa's sprawling farms. "We've got a lot of land, so we have to work into the evening, sometimes until the sun goes down."

She nodded as she cleared off the rags and brushes laying on her table. She also looked preoccupied and distracted, as if maybe my last answer had been a little too mature, a little too boring.

"Of course, on the weekends I usually go into Millerton — it's a college town, so there's always a lot going on," I said, trying to sound like a man who preferred his fun in the sophisticated company of the college crowd.

"I know, I used to work at the university," Julia answered, with absolutely no change in her tone.

"This place is about as dead as it gets," I added, trying out a different tack. "Unless you keep plenty busy, you'll die of boredom." Cynicism and dissatisfaction, from what I had seen in the movies, were the attitudes of Julia's age group.

"Well, I enjoy the peace and quiet. I think, if we tip the table on its side, we can get it through the door." And from there, our conversation focused on our task at hand.

"Careful of that doorway."

"Have you got it?"

"Try lifting it the other way."

Once we exited the old Sullivan house, Julia was at the lead-end of the table. She had to backpeddle and look over her shoulder as we proceeded down the street. So I had a chance to stare without being noticed.

Some people only looked good in certain poses or activities. Then, when taken out of those poses or activities, they appeared disheveled, blemished, or just completely out of control. But Julia wasn't like that. She looked even more graceful and confident as she was lugging her end of an old oak table.

While carrying the table down the street, to the old Collins house (or to what would from now on be known as Julia's house), and with our attentions focused on keeping the legs from scraping the ground, I asked: "So, did Myron mention something about your husband being in the war?" But as soon as I had spoken the words, I felt like an idiot — like someone who thought "the war" was some kind of foreign exchange program.

"Actually, he's in the army. He was drafted. We got married just before he left. I'm hoping to meet him in Honolulu when he goes on R & R, maybe in August."

She spoke more casually than I would have expected. I thought she would be more anxious, more fearful. But maybe he had a safe assignment. Maybe he didn't see combat.

"He was glad when I told him I'd moved here," she added. "He doesn't worry so much about me now."

"If he's in Vietnam, shouldn't you be the one worrying?" I meant it as a flippant, witty little remark; but when I saw the way her eyes tensed up, I was sorry I had said it. "So what brought you to Corcoran?" I quickly asked, veering away from the subject of war.

"We — Lillie, Sharon and I — met almost a year ago, when Lillie started organizing a Vietnam wives group. It was a support group kind of thing, something we could do to try to help out — at the hospital, writing letters, stuff like that. Anyway, we all came to a funeral here at the cemetery in Corcoran...oh, three or four months ago. It was for...well, I guess for someone who couldn't really be buried anywhere else..."

Grandpa did anything he could to bring people to Corcoran, even if it meant selling them cheap burial sites in a cemetery that had obviously been planned with a more populated Corcoran in mind. He specialized in desperation funerals — or, as Julia had said, people who "couldn't be buried anywhere else."

"...That was when we met your grandfather — he was real nice. Then Lillie met him again a couple of months ago. She was at the monument works, helping someone pick out a gravestone; and your grandfather was there getting one for his grandson — your brother, right?"

I nodded, remembering that Grandpa had said he put up a stone for Ricky in the cemetery. "He loved it here," Grandpa told me over the phone, "and he ought to be remembered here."

"Anyway, I don't know how the conversation got there," Julia continued, "but somehow Eamon gave Lillie the idea that there were places here to live for anyone who needed them..." — I knew exactly how the conversation got there, I felt like telling Julia; with Grandpa, the conversation always got there — "...And I didn't have a job. And neither did Sharon. And so we went for it. What'd we have to lose?"

"Yeah, that's Corcoran's only selling point: a place to go when you have nothing more to lose."

But Julia ignored my jab. "Lillie, she had a job; but she also has dreams of starting a kind of Vietnam wives' commune. So far, though, she's only got Sharon and me."

"Who's Lillie?"

"She's a nurse at the V.A. Hospital in Millerton. Her husband's got a desk job in Saigon, but I guess just about anywhere over there is a risky place," she said, sounding as if she was trying to convince herself that the world was fair, that her husband was as well off as someone who had a desk job in Saigon.

"And who is Sharon?"

"Her husband was killed in April. He was the son of

Martin Schlomberg, the owner of Schlomberg Manufacturing. You familiar with it?"

"Sure, the big factory in town. His son went to Vietnam?"

"Didn't even get drafted. Enlisted, all on his own. And that's not something you see very often, especially for a rich guy."

"So...why is a daughter-in-law of one of the wealthiest men in Millerton living here, in Corcoran?"

"I don't think she gets along with him, or maybe it's he with her. Sharon isn't exactly from the same social status as the Schlomberg's; and they weren't happy about the marriage. He fired Sharon right after his son shipped out to Vietnam — she used to work at the factory."

"But she must have money. I mean, she could probably live..."

"Schlomberg sent his lawyers to make a deal with her," Julia interjected. "But she refused them, said she didn't want anything, except for a large donation to a veteran's support fund. Needless to say, Sharon has become somewhat of a hero to the VFW and American Legion crowd. In fact, she's kind of taken over the wives club from Lillie."

"But she still ended up here?"

"Hey, she likes it here. And your grandfather's already taught her how to drive the tractor. I think she likes farming. You know, your grandfather isn't at all as I expected..." — Okay, I thought, now I was going to get the real story — "...When Lillie first told me about him, living out here in this...kind of abandoned town, I figured he'd be an ornery, rigid, close-minded man, but he's just the opposite. He has so many big plans, and he's so eager to be a part of ours."

Even after she quit speaking, I still expected her to add a proviso. But when she didn't, I realized how premature one would have been. We had only just met. And she was living, free of charge I was sure, in one of Grandpa's houses. Of course she wouldn't have told me the truth about her impressions of him. How could she possibly tell me that he was hopelessly out-of-touch with the world?

As we walked back to pick up the chairs, after maneuvering the table into Julia's dining room, I felt as if I was strolling down the street of some unfamiliar town. I had never stopped to imagine what Corcoran would be like with people who were different from the ones who had always been here. But new life seemed to have brought a transformation. The pot-holed, curbless street now seemed like an avenue of activity. The tall elms now provided a shade under which reclining women might be found, reading a book or laughing about some story. The sagging porches of the weathered houses were now ready to host conversations.

I envisioned coming home from working in the fields and waving to Julia as she sat on her front porch. I envisioned walking into Ardelle's diner and having Julia say something about how hard I was working. I thought about how she might ask me to help her with some fix-up projects, and how she might bring me a beer and sit with me as the summer sun set. After all, I told myself, Julia saw me as the grandson of the man who had given her sanctuary; to her, I wasn't just the retard's brother.

✧

Lillie drove up to her house, the old Mackey house, as we were carrying the chairs over to Julia's. When Julia called out to her, introducing me, the white-uniformed Lillie marched over and shook my hand in a firm and earnest way.

"It's so good to have you here," she said, glaring into my eyes. "You've been needed."

There was a smile on her lips, but it was dwarfed by the serious, almost scowling look in her eyes. It wasn't that she was unattractive - it was that she seemed too serious to even concern herself with as mundane a matter as appearances.

"I'm very sorry about your brother," she said, in an even graver voice. "Your grandfather told us all about him."

"Yes, we were all very sorry...," Julia added, her nervous voice trailing off into an inaudible mumbling. She was obviously not as comfortable with death as was nurse Lillie.

"You just graduated from high school?" Lillie asked.

"Yes."

"You're eighteen?"

"Yes."

"What's your draft number?"

In the way she asked it, I felt I should know the answer, just as I knew my telephone number. But I had no idea, except that it was one that had brought a sigh of relief from my mother. "It's 218," I answered, making up a number.

"That's good," Lillie replied. "You're safe for now."

I had never felt imperiled, but I did not tell this to

the tall, short-haired Lillie, who had a way of conducting a conversation as if it were a medical exam.

Myron

Myron did not really belong in Corcoran. He did not belong in a desolate and deserted town. Myron Banks was a gregarious sort. But he had no ambition. He stayed in Corcoran for the same reason that he had come to Corcoran — it was easier than finding a new job and worrying about mortgage or rent payments.

He loved to see Ricky and me arrive each June. "Thank God, someone new to talk to," he'd say. And on summer evenings, we often wandered down to the lake and sat out on the one rickety dock Myron was too lazy to ever bring in before winter. As he tried to teach Ricky how to skip stones across the water's surface, Myron would tell me all about the fish he had caught in this lake. (He was, I concluded, too lazy to fish anywhere else.)

But the evenings I liked best with Myron were those we spent in his woodworking shop. Unlike his house, Myron's shop was neatly organized and always swept clean. Most of his time was spent just tinkering with his workbench area — labeling jars of nails and sorting out different sized screws and rearranging all his wrenches. But every now and then, Myron would actually work on something, like an old piece of furniture. His radio would be tuned to the ballgame, and his refrigerator would always be stocked with beer. I had my first beer with Myron: it didn't bother him that I was underage. "A little experience before the day of reckoning doesn't hurt anyone," he had said.

Out in his workshop, while we sanded and sawed, the evening would disappear into night. As the darkness outside seemed to wipe away the rest of the world, a small swarm of mosquitoes would surround the bare, hanging light bulb. And with the radio providing a constant, crackling narration of the game, our conversation would become an offshoot to whatever repair project we were working on. I liked conversations that weren't about feelings or being young or what I was going to do with my future or what it was like living with a retarded brother.

✧

The only trespasser into those evening workshop sessions was the cranky scolding of Harold Nelson. Harold was the one resident of Corcoran who didn't live in a house owned by my grandfather. He was also the only resident who thought too many people lived in Corcoran. And he resented the changes Grandpa was always trying to make. He thought Corcoran should do just as he was doing — hunker down and wait for that last exhale of breath.

I always thought of Harold as being like one of those trees with the stripe painted across its trunk, marking it to be cut down come winter. In Corcoran, Harold was our striped tree, marked and waiting for removal.

Harold's parents had moved to Corcoran in 1939. They wanted a cheap place to retire; and there wasn't anyplace that had cheaper homes. When his mother died in 1958, five years after her husband had died,

Harold moved into the house — apparently, he had trouble holding onto a job. He often said he had moved to Corcoran to preserve "the family home," but the real reason was probably that there was no mortgage on it.

Harold Nelson saw himself as the minority opposition to Grandpa's despotic rule of Corcoran. He was constantly calling the county sheriff to complain about the traffic congestion at The Fieldstone or the cars that parked in front of his house during Sunday mass. Harold had even written to the Governor, asking that the state appoint a regulatory commission to oversee the unruly and lawless Corcoran. Without fail, whenever Myron and I had the radio on during our evening sessions in the workshop, Harold would shout from across the street to "turn down that racket" and that he was "calling the authorities."

"Why don't you offer to buy his house?" I once asked Grandpa, after Harold had complained about Ricky's bouncing of a ball against the side of his garage. "Maybe he's just looking for a way to get out of here."

"I only buy houses that have been abandoned," Grandpa answered. "The last thing I want is for Harold to leave."

"Why? Isn't he a pain in the ass?"

"But he's Corcoran's pain in the ass. And I can't afford to be fussy about who lives here. I've lost too many to be fussy."

Grandpa tended to think of people in terms of quantity, not quality. If they were still breathing and if they lived in Corcoran, then Grandpa wanted them. Grandpa even invited Harold to the party at Julia's house, but of course Harold declined. He was still enraged at all the commotion being caused by this “mad influx” of questionable tenants.

Lights in the Windows

Grandpa pulled his pick-up truck into the driveway as I was unpacking my bag in the bedroom that had long since been designated as mine. He was washing his hands in the kitchen sink when I came downstairs.

"You're here already," he exclaimed. "I didn't see your parents' car."

"They left. We got here early."

"Oh rats, I wish I'd been here. I wanted to show them that south 40 acres that no one thought we'd ever get plowed. Did your mother wait long?"

"No...I mean, yeah, for awhile, but they needed to get back. She didn't know how long you'd be."

"Did she have a look around? Did she see what I've done with the front porch?"

"She thinks the place looks great."

"I wish she could've met the new residents. Have you seen anyone?" he asked, with an excited upturn in his voice.

"Wait'll you meet Sharon," he said, after I told him that I'd met Julia and Lillie. "She's a brave woman, the kind of person who's just right for Corcoran."

"Isn't she related to the Schlomberg's?"

"That's what makes her so special. And she's bucking her father-in-law — he wants to take this land away from me, you know. He and some developer want to build an outlet mall, or whatever it is they call it."

Grandpa treated anyone who made a purchase offer on his land like a thief sneaking through a basement window.

"Now, whatever you do," he said, as he started up to his bedroom to change for dinner, "don't go putting down this place. These women like it here. Don't go repeating the kinds of things your mother says."

"Grandpa, do you really think the women are going to stick around? I mean, once their husbands come home?"

"Glen, they've got plans for bringing other people here. Sure, some of them may leave, but others will stay. So we got a lot of work to do this summer — in our free time we'll have to start fixing up the houses. I mean, look at Sharon — she's staying, and her husband's come home."

"Wasn't he killed?"

"Yes, and so she's not waiting for him anymore, see? She recognizes the opportunity here — they all do. They have a chance to build the kind of home they want, and to make an honorable living."

In Grandpa's world, there were very few ways to make an honorable living. He wasn't someone to whom his kids could have gone for career advice. Maybe that was another reason they didn't like him.

✧

"Aren't you going to wear a suit and tie?" Grandpa asked, after he had come back downstairs to polish his shoes.

He was sitting at the table, wearing socks, boxer shorts, a white shirt, and a tie much like the ones I had seen at Myron's. He would not put on his pants or coat until just before he left the house, so as not to wrinkle them unnecessarily — it was the same routine he followed every Sunday before church.

"I don't have a suit. I never bring one, you know that."

"Doesn't your generation wear anything but blue jeans?"

"Grandpa, don't you ever watch television? Remember last summer, when there was that concert at Woodstock?"

"Good god, those people were naked."

"Exactly, we don't go for formal attire."

"Good god, you can't go through life like that. But at least you don't wear your hair all long and straggly like those hippie people."

"It's just that I hate to comb it," I said; although that was only part of it. Actually, I had no reason to go to the trouble of wearing it long. The thing about having a retarded brother — you don't go to much effort to be cool.

"But couldn't you wear one of my ties tonight? I think the women would appreciate it," Grandpa said.

"Gramps, they're closer to my age than to yours, and I don't think they'll be offended by my not wearing a tie. Besides, I'd feel ridiculous in one of yours. When's the last time you bought a new one?"

"Your grandmother gave me this for our thirtieth wedding anniversary," he said, fingering his tie as he spoke.

"And that was when?"

"Well, let's see...we were married in 1916. So it would have been '46. Gees, it doesn't seem that long ago. It just doesn't seem..." And as Grandpa drifted off into one of his memory trances, our conversation about ties ended — until Myron came over.

"Glen, you're not wearing a tie?" he asked.

"Young people don't wear stuff like that," Grandpa said. "They like to go to concerts naked."

"We're not going to a concert, are we?" Myron asked, looking confused, as if he hadn't understood the invitation for tonight.

"We're going to dinner, at Julia's — you know, the old Collins house."

"Well, I'm calling it Julia's house from now on. I never knew the Collins."

"That's right, you were never around for the good old days of Corcoran."

"Well, I'm here now."

"And this is just how it once was — coming in from a day's work, cleaning up, getting dressed like civilized people, and then having a big cook-out with everyone in town."

"Well, it ain't hard to have dinner with everyone in town now," Myron quipped. "You can fit 'em all into one room."

"You just wait — you're finally going to see how it used to be in the old days," Grandpa snorted. He often talked to Myron just as he talked to me — like someone of a much younger generation. After all, as Grandpa was fond of reminding him, Myron had only lived in Corcoran for about twenty years — he was still a newcomer, ignorant of the ways and traditions of the past.

"My father always told me," Grandpa said to Myron, "that I should never abandon this land, that patience was the only real fertilizer. And see? — he was right."

"I don't know how many times I've heard what your father used to say to you. Hell, if he'd known how many times you were gonna repeat that stuff, he'd never have said anything. Now don't you go boring those young girls with them stories of yours."

"They like 'em. They're not as ornery as you."

"And they're a helluva lot better looking than you."

When Grandpa went up to his room to get a handkerchief for the front pocket of his suit, Myron asked me for a quick reassurance. "How do I look? Is the tie okay?"

"Hey, looking like you do, I wouldn't be surprised if you never make it home tonight."

"Get outta here — an old man like myself," he scoffed, but with eyes that didn't want to completely deny hope.

"Well, you're younger than Grandpa," I said.

"That is true," he answered.

✧

On the way over to Julia's house, Myron stopped by his garden and picked some daisies.

"Good idea," Grandpa remarked. "You pick the white, I'll get the yellow."

"Not so fast, Eamon. This is my garden. You want to take over some flowers, you get 'em from your own garden."

"My roses aren't even blooming yet."

"Then I guess you're outta luck."

The two men argued until I walked over and picked a handful of daisies for Grandpa. I knew Myron would never yell at me.

"Don't you want any?" Myron asked me.

"No, I wouldn't want to detract from you two Casanova's."

"Keep your eyes open Glen, and you'll learn a thing or two this summer about how to treat women," Grandpa boasted, as he winked at Myron.

We must have arrived early, because the three women were seated in front of the television. The evening news was on. And the pictures were of Vietnam.

I moved to the back of the room and stood up against the wall, while Grandpa and Myron sat down on the sofa, both still holding their daisies. The news reporter was talking about a North Vietnamese offensive in a place called the Mae Cong Delta. An army colonel being interviewed said that the Viet Cong had come from bases in Cambodia. I wasn't sure where any of these places were; nor did I know much about the military details of the war, except that it was going badly and that everyone seemed obsessed with getting out of it.

As I scanned the faces of the women, I tried to think of what I might say once the news ended. But watching Julia bite her lower lip and squint her eyes, I knew I would never be able to say the right thing; and I didn't want to start off the summer by making a fool of myself.

Lillie had changed into blue jeans and a red T-shirt. And from her now starkly plain face, I could tell that she had actually been wearing make-up earlier.

Sharon wore her hair tied up in a scarf. ("I'm sorry, I didn't get a chance to wash it today," she said, when we first walked in.) She was not as youthful or peppy-looking as Julia, but nor did she carry the weight of worry that Lillie did; and though her face bore the lines of experience, her smile possessed an almost innocent genuineness. Her eyes seemed constantly on the verge of doing something — smiling, winking, crying, laughing — and yet they were calm, unshakable, even distant. Maybe it was the dark eyelashes and eyebrows, or maybe it was the high cheekbones that seemed to push her eyes away, off to the shadows of her face, but her eyes seemed somehow aloof from her body. I could see why the son of the wealthiest man in Millerton would marry her.

As they watched the news, it was Sharon to whom Lillie and Julia directed their questions. It was Sharon who seemed to know best the wartime topography of Vietnam. She appeared to be the oldest, maybe in her late twenties. Or maybe it was just that she was the more experienced — in both life and death.

Even though the television was blaring ("Can you turn it up a little?...a little more yet," Grandpa, hard of hearing, had said as soon as he sat down), I felt as if I was sealed away in my own private world, standing there at the back of the room. I felt like an invisible intruder, able to stare without being noticed. And yet it wasn't the women about whom I was thinking. It was their husbands...well, sort of. I wondered if having someone praying everyday for your safety made it easier to be brave.

Being a coward was the worst. It was like a reactor chamber for the fusion of regrets. It felt worse than grief. It was worse than being a criminal, or a Viet Cong, or even a retard.

The house erupted in conversation and movement

as soon as the news ended. Flowers were put in vases, drinks were served, stoves were checked, the day's events narrated. The transformation was as complete as it was rapid. It was as if those moments of somberness in front of the television had never existed.

Grandpa began talking, as he usually did whenever he got excited, about some new plan for some old building, and then about the history of that old building. And I was ready for the usual reaction — for the women to begin fidgeting, and then looking around the room, and then making an excuse to go into the kitchen — but it never came. They all, even Julia, looked interested and asked questions. Grandpa had never been asked questions before.

The rest of the guests appeared soon after — all three of them. Ardelle Williams, who ran The Fieldstone Cafe. And Valerie and Lorraine Rusk, daughter and mother who lived in the old Cosgrove house. They were newcomers to Corcoran. They had moved here five years ago; and before that, they had owned a bridal shop in Millerton.

And that was it for the residents of Corcoran. Except for Harold Nelson.

At dinner, Julia gave a brief toast, welcoming me and joking about how much work they had saved up for me. And then she digressed right into an explanation of her most recent renovation project.

I liked watching Julia. I liked seeing her facial expressions when she talked. And I liked the way she quickly turned the focus away from me, as if realizing that compared to fighting a war thousands of miles away, showing up for the summer in Corcoran wasn't all that worthy of recognition.

✧

It was a new experience walking home that night. Shouts of "Goodbye" and "Thanks for dinner" and "See you tomorrow" gave Corcoran something it had never had before. In the houses I thought would never again be occupied, there were now lights in the windows.

The Retard's Brother

There were times when I hated Ricky. But a person couldn't really hate a retard. So I tried hating everyone else. But mostly, deep down, I hated myself.

The turning point came when I went into the seventh grade at Lincoln Junior High, after six safe years at the Catholic school. Ricky was all excited about the change. Before transferring into the special education program three years ago, Ricky had gone to the Catholic school — he spent five years repeating kindergarten; and during those five years, we walked to school together everyday. The thing about Ricky — he had an amazing memory about certain things, and couldn't wait to walk to school with me again. I dreaded it, but I knew I had no choice. Even if I refused to walk with him, he would just follow me anyway. Ricky was retarded, but he could trail you like a bloodhound. So when September came, I took to leaving early for school, to dropping Ricky off in Room 305 before the hallways started filling up, before the retard and his brother could be seen by anyone.

What I could never figure out was why they put Room 305 right in the middle of the school, in probably the most hard-to-reach location. What I could never figure out was why they didn't put it right by an outside door.

Room 305 was the special education classroom at

Lincoln Junior High School. At least that's what the school administrators called it. The students called it the retard room.

In the confines of Room 305, energy and vocalism replaced intelligence and good looks as the requisite leadership traits. Consequently, Ricky was the leader of the group. Everything he said and did was echoed by the other 305ers.

"Brosher Glen'sh here, Mishush Folcrum," he'd shout to his teacher, when I came for him at 3:30.

"Brosher Glen'sh here," then shouted whoever else was still in the room.

✧

About three weeks into my seventh-grade year, I was sitting in the cafeteria at lunch time, just on the outskirts of one of the more popular groups of kids, when suddenly a strange hush came over the room. And then I heard a frighteningly familiar voice.

"Shat looksh good. I want shome of shat."

Ricky had wandered past the boundaries of his world and into the normal world. He had drifted out of Mrs. Folcrum's line of special education students and was approaching a table of mortified-looking girls, heading straight for their food. As I later found out, the lunches for Room 305 hadn't been delivered, necessitating a rare visit of special-education students to the main cafeteria.

The girl whose plate Ricky was targeting started screaming. Her boyfriend, or someone who wanted to be her boyfriend, rushed forward and grabbed Ricky. Then the other special education students began yelling and jumping up and down. Somewhere along the line, someone threw a sandwich. And then some mashed potatoes, and then another sandwich.

The boys at my table were shouting at "the retards" and loading up on food ammunition. It was then that I saw Ricky notice me. The noise was so loud that no one else probably heard, but I could see him looking at me and calling out, "Brosher Glen."

It took two coaches and several teachers to finally surround the special-ed students and put a stop to the food-throwing. A few detention slips were handed out, and the kitchen workers soon appeared with their mops. But all the while I stayed in my seat. I never saw what happened to Ricky — I had my eyes buried in my tray.

I didn't pick up Ricky that day. I called and told Mom that I had an after-school project.

When I finally got home, the family was seated at the dinner table. Ricky was telling all about the excitement at school. When he saw me, he ran to me and hugged me.

"Are ya okay?" he said. "Did ya get hurt?"

"Brosher Glen wash shere," Ricky then announced to the rest of the family. "Washn't it a big fight?" he said to me. "But we beat 'em, didn't we?"

In his wildly exaggerated narration of the cafeteria incident, Ricky incorporated his favorite theme — aliens. He was convinced that Martians were behind the lunchroom attack, that they were out to get the leader of the opposition against them. Mom tried to say something to me, but I brushed her off. I could tell she believed Ricky's version of events — about how I had bravely defended my brother. I could tell she felt guilty for burdening her one normal son with a mentally retarded brother, but I never told her the truth.

I hated the normal kids for what they had done. But mostly, I hated myself for being a coward.

✧

Not that I had ever been above making fun of Ricky myself. Sometimes, just to entertain the neighbor kids, I put a sheet over myself, shined a flashlight through it, and pretended to be a Martian. It never failed to send Ricky into a panic, and to produce lots of laughs from my audience. Or at the Catholic school, during those times when young boys would compete for who can be the cruelest, I'd convince Ricky that one of the girls was hiding a Martian transporter under her dress. The nuns were always alarmed whenever a boy, even Ricky, touched a girl.

Or sometimes I'd just yell at him for no reason at all — no reason other than that he was always tagging along and begging me to play. One thing I learned from Ricky — people who love you bring out the meanest in you.

Evening Projects

I always thought Grandpa liked working in the fields, but he didn't put up any objection to Sharon's insistence that she and I finish the cultivating on our own. In fact, Grandpa adjusted to the new arrangement a lot easier than I did.

Every day of my first week at Corcoran, Sharon was already at the machinery shed when I arrived. She had both tractors filled with gas, and one of them coughing up a congested idle. Since, in my experience, it took twenty minutes just to start the sickly old tractor, I knew she had been there awhile. And as soon as I arrived, she called out a quick "Good Morning," followed by a "Let's get going." There was no half-hour of coffee drinking, no paging through the morning paper, no talk of what we'd have for lunch; and I realized how I had become accustomed to a 78-year-old work pace.

Sharon wore the same basic outfit everyday: a baggy and frayed pair of jean cover-alls, with a white T-shirt underneath, and her hair haphazardly stuffed into a 'John Deere' baseball cap. From a distance, she looked like one of those ornery farmers who care only about the height of her corn and not a bit about her own appearance.

We took only one break before lunch. It was when Grandpa brought out some of Ardelle's cookies and a jug of iced tea. He was always quite talkative about what everyone else back in Corcoran was doing — he seemed to relish spending his day roving around town, checking on everyone, monitoring all the activity — and I did everything I could to encourage his continued chatter.

"What's Lorraine and Valerie doing?" I asked.

"They're at the church."

"And Myron?"

"I'm trying to get him to fix that corn-picker, but he's off trying to tell Julia what color to paint the living room in the old Hanrahan house."

"What color does he want?"

"The damn fool thinks he's an interior designer, but he's as color-blind as a bat."

"What else are they doing to the Hanrahan house?"

But no matter how many questions I asked, after about fifteen minutes Sharon stood up, brushed the dirt off her cover-alls, and said: "Well Eamon, we better get back to work — we didn't get quite as far as I wanted." She said that everyday — we never got as far as she wanted. And then Grandpa would smile and nod, as if everything was beyond his control, and ask us if we wanted anything special for lunch.

Sometimes I felt that being with Sharon was like being with a younger version of Grandpa — the hard-driving version that his own children seemed to resent. (Whenever I complained about chores around the house, Mom would tell me about her own life as a girl, being roused out of bed at 5 o'clock on a winter morning to milk the cows.) And just like Grandpa, Sharon seemed so intensely locked in to Corcoran — she never went to Millerton, except in connection with her work at the

V.A. or the American Legion. With her indifference to anything but Grandpa's farm and the war, it was as if, like a cloistered nun, she had all but renounced the outside world.

✧

In the past, I had enjoyed the solitude of working in the fields. But now, I had to force myself to endure it. Quitting time was what I looked forward to: driving the tractor back to the barn, going home to wash up, and then walking over to Julia's house for dinner.

Julia had decided that she would fix dinner for everyone, every night. She had turned the whole first floor of her house into a community dining room. Aside from a television set in the corner and an old sofa up against the wall, everything else was chairs and tables. The news started at 5:30, and dinner was served at 6:30. Followed, inevitably, by a card game.

It was after the card games were under way that Julia and I went to work on one of her renovation projects. On our second evening together, she asked me to help her lift an oak door up onto a couple of sawhorses in the backyard. That was how our evening pattern was established.

With the sounds of the card game filtering out from the house, and with the scent of Grandpa's pipe spicing the air (Grandpa's favorite after-dinner activity was to sit outside on Julia's porch and survey his reborn Corcoran), Julia and I worked — and talked.

She had a comfortable way of talking, like the slow and steady trickle of water from a hose lying in the grass. And there was a kind of sexy friendliness about her —

the kind that said as long as we're going to talk we might as well have fun. But maybe what I liked most was Julia's illusions about me.

"So, you must leave behind a trail of lonesome hearts when you come out here for the summer," she said.

"Does my aunt Sylvia count?" I replied, figuring the best way to confirm Julia's supposition was to shrug it off with a joke.

"When I was your age, the boys I knew never did what you do," she said. "They spent every night hanging out at some joint, or racing their cars up and down the main drag, or doing whatever else they could think of to show off. So, are you going to college next year?"

"Yeah, I guess."

"What are you going to major in?"

"Engineering I think."

"That makes sense. You seem to have a real talent for mechanics, and for fixing things."

I didn't, not at all. But Julia thought just because I could hammer a nail that I was Mr. Fix-it.

"Are you worried about your husband?" I once asked. She almost never talked about him, but I spent plenty of time wondering what kind of man it would take to face death and terror every day. And whenever I thought about him, I always felt so irreparably young, as if I would never grow into such a man.

"I suppose I should, but I try not to think about it. I just hope for the best. Lillie considers me a bit of an airhead."

"Why's that?"

"She couldn't imagine taking such a passive approach. She's a very proactive woman, but also a little fatalistic.

She took that job at the V.A. Hospital in Millerton after her husband was drafted. I think she believes that if she's doing all she can to alleviate the war's suffering, then maybe God will spare her husband from contributing to that suffering."

"Sounds like my mom's attitude."

"It gets a little draining always being around people who expect the worst, doesn't it?" she said, in a smiling voice full of camaraderie. What I loved about Julia was that she seemed as if she couldn't even imagine that life would be any different with a retard.

"Is it hard getting used to living here, in Corcoran?" I asked.

"No, not at all," she said. "In fact, I feel really free here — almost like I'm on vacation. The birds singing in the morning, my own huge garden, no traffic. But then, I'm not doing the hard work you're doing. Myron and I — we have a lot of fun during the day."

"You don't miss living in Millerton? Having a real job?"

"I was fired from my job at the university," she said, so casually and without any self-consciousness.

"How could that be?" I asked. I thought it was like jury duty — no one could get fired if they had to serve on a jury, or if their husband was fighting in Vietnam.

"I worked in the dean's office, as a secretary," she began. And to earn overtime pay, she stayed late and helped with the social receptions hosted by the dean. Afterward, when everything was cleaned up, she would go out for a drink with some of the faculty and administrators who regularly attended those receptions. Then, one night, she was invited to a party — "just a get-together of some university people," she was told. But when she arrived, most of the "university people" were female undergraduates. Professor Donlin, an instructor in the English Department, held out a strange-looking pipe to her even before she took off her coat. That was when she decided, after seeing what was happening to some of the other women's clothing, to keep all of hers and head for home. Not long afterward, she was fired from her job. "I think I made some people rather uncomfortable when they came into the office.

"So they fired you? Just like that?"

"Well, I don't know how much that had to do with it. The real reason I was given was that I had improperly used the office for political purposes. See, I had typed up a leaflet that Lillie used to advertise a protest of some anti-war demonstrators picketing the V.A.; and then of course I had attended the protest — so I guess that made me some kind of reactionary wacko."

"They can fire you for that?"

"They can if you're on the side I was on. The university is afraid of the students, and it doesn't want to appear pro-war. Last year, a group of students took over the administration building for three days, claiming that the university and its research grants were all part of the military-industrial complex conspiring to keep the U.S. in Vietnam."

"Wasn't there anything you could do to keep your job?"

"I wouldn't have wanted to stay anyway. And the funny thing is, no one wants that war to end more than I do. But it's just so ridiculous, to think that little flowers painted on Volkswagen vans is the way to stop war. Although, I can see the logic behind pot and LSD: if everybody were high, they sure wouldn't be able to shoot very straight. Flower-power, what the hell is that anyway?"

I laughed and nodded, but Julia kept staring at me. "No, I mean it," she said. "What is it?"

I shrugged, holding back the urge to tell her how retarded I thought the world was.

"It's like free love, I suppose," she continued, skipping over my shrug. "But anyone who has ever loved knows that there's nothing free about it."

This time, I nodded, trying to look as if I knew exactly what she meant.

"Sometimes I wonder what the Vietnamese people must think of us," Julia muttered, as if she just couldn't pull free. "We're sending our soldiers there to die, and yet back here we're listening to songs like 'Tiptoe Through the Tulips.'"

A few moments of silence passed before Julia flipped back to a more light-hearted mood. "Anyway, thank God I made it to Corcoran. At least I don't have to listen to protestors everyday."

"Yeah, well, most people who end up here don't do much thanking to God," I quipped.

"You like to make fun of your grandfather and his town, don't you?"

"But even to call it a town is such a gross exaggeration."

"You're different from most guys your age. I knew it when I first saw you, from the look of your hair and your clothes. And you think differently too. I mean, I'm glad. I can say things to you I probably wouldn't to most people."

It was exhilarating being with Julia.

Being with Julia was like sitting in the sun on the first warm day of spring — I didn't need anything else to be completely contented.

✧

What I had observed of both Ricky and Grandpa was that there are no mirrors in the world of fantasy and delusion: that fantasy and delusion are invisible to the one immersed in them.

By the end of my first week in Corcoran, Grandpa, who had no trouble recognizing someone else's fantasies, obviously felt compelled to try to inject some reality into mine.

"So, has Julia heard from her husband lately?" Grandpa started asking.

"What do you say we take some pictures of the town to send to Julia's and Lillie's husbands?" he suggested one evening, as he rummaged through drawers looking for his old camera.

But Grandpa was easy to ignore. And besides, Julia seemed to be always making such coaxing comments: "It's so good to have a man around," and "If you want to come shopping with me, I'd love the company." Or at least they were coaxing to me. But what wasn't so easy to ignore were the intrusions from outside.

One afternoon, on my way into Millerton to pick up a part for a broken-down plow, I stopped by Julia's house to see if she needed anything. As I was walking up what was left of the front sidewalk, I saw her sitting on the porch, engrossed in a letter she held protectively in her hands. I could tell immediately, from her absorbed eyes and the way they seemed to backtrack to reread every sentence, that the letter was from her husband. I stopped and stared for a moment, and then started backpeddling. But Julia saw me before I got to the street.

"Oh hi," she blankly called out. "Do you need anything?"

"Uh, no, nothing. I was just coming to see if you wanted anything from town."

"No, thanks," she answered, just as blankly and without any questions as to why I was going into Millerton. And then her head dropped back down to her letter.

She never mentioned that letter to me, not even when I alluded to it later that evening — she just withdrew into a silent cocoon. And the following day, she was her old self, maybe even more friendly, as if to make up for the previous day.

The next intrusion came later that week. We were all eating dinner when someone noticed a car cruising the street outside. Everyone turned and stared — traffic in Corcoran wasn't exactly a commonplace occurrence. As the dark green sedan pulled to a stop in front of her house, Julia suddenly jerked in her chair and let out a frightened gasp before her hands could cover her mouth. The white lettering on the car door read: "U.S. Armed Services." It was the same kind of car, as Julia was urgently pressing Sharon to admit, that had delivered the telegram announcing the army's regret over the death of Sharon's husband.

With Lillie and Sharon gripping Julia's arms and repeating "It may be nothing" and "Now don't jump to conclusions," I watched, stunned and helpless, as Julia's face became white and taut, and as the faces of Sharon and Lillie became increasingly worried. I didn't even notice Grandpa get up from his chair and walk quietly out the front door to the men who had by now stepped out of their car. And I was still sitting motionless, staring dumbfoundedly at Julia, when Grandpa came back into the house, this time walking less cautiously and more noisily.

"It's okay, everything's okay," he announced. "They're actually looking for you, Sharon. They want to talk to you about some mix-up with your spousal benefits."

And just as quickly as it had erupted, the crisis subsided. Sharon patted Julia's hand, before standing up and walking outside. And everyone seemed to shoot a glance of gratitude Grandpa's way. He had established himself as someone who could be relied upon in an emergency.

✧

It was after the army-car scare that I resolved to begin acting like someone who could be counted on, who could get the crop in and make the houses livable. I resolved to begin acting like the true heir to the place the women now called home.

Starting the next morning, I would set the alarm a half hour early. I would cast off the mentality of a summer laborer, always waiting for Sharon to lead the way. I would take shorter lunch breaks; and I would show up late for dinner, so that everyone could see how hard I was working.

I also began studying the war. I asked Ardelle to hold for me, out of the stack that was delivered to The Fieldstone each morning, a copy of *The Minneapolis Tribune*.

I started going to the Millerton public library every Thursday evening and Saturday afternoon to read the weekly news magazines. Julia thought I was going into Millerton to "sow a few wild oats," and I did nothing to dispel that belief. I would rather be known as a young man with wild oats to sow than an ignorant boy who was just now trying to figure out a war that had been raging for years.

Sometimes, on Saturdays, I would stay in Millerton even after the library closed. I'd sit on the lighted patio of a Dairy Queen and read *Time* magazine. Then I'd go to a movie, by myself, so that I'd arrive back in Corcoran at a late enough hour to reinforce the impression that I was sowing a few oats.

Ardelle

Grandpa met Ardelle Williams at the Four Seasons Retirement Home in Millerton in 1960. He was visiting Martin Nowicki, who had finally yielded to his children's wish that he give up his house in Corcoran, to try to convince Martin that it wasn't too late to "get out of this dump and come back home." But Martin enjoyed having someone else fix his meals. He liked the air conditioning. And he was thrilled with the clear reception of the television set in the community room. So no, he would not be coming back to Corcoran, he said.

As Grandpa started to leave, a woman who had been sitting at the next table followed him to the door and asked if he was serious about wanting people to move to Corcoran. Without ever seeing the place, Ardelle told Grandpa that she'd leave the Four Seasons as soon as he had a house for her to live in. But she'd come only if he'd give her a job — she was tired of bingo games and television-watching, she told Grandpa. (Ardelle was a spring chicken at the Four Seasons, Grandpa said to me during one of his many stories about Ardelle's conversion — she was only 61 years old.) And that was when The Fieldstone Cafe got its second life.

Other than the cemetery, Ardelle was Corcoran's sole drawing card. Her beef stew on Tuesday's brought a standing-room-only crowd to The Fieldstone. And her blueberry pie kept a steady stream of pick-up trucks pulling off the highway. With her cooking as the bait, gasoline sales were healthy enough to produce steady profits, which Grandpa in turn used to buy up more vacant land and dilapidated houses.

There were two smells with which I associated Corcoran, depending on how the wind was blowing. When it came from the north, the whole town smelled like Ardelle's soup, or her pies, or whatever else she was cooking or baking. And that was one thing Corcoran had in its favor — there weren't too many abandoned towns that smelled like the inside of a bakery. But during the summer, the wind rarely blew from the north. Mostly, it came from the south, blowing in across Lake Kilkenny. On those days, Corcoran had a kind of fishy smell — probably because no one ever picked up all the dead fish that had washed up on shore.

The Fieldstone Cafe provided the only intersection between a dead town and the living world — the one spot at which Corcoran linked up to the world that had left it behind. And it was a spot that seemed to attract people who had found themselves in a situation similar to that of Corcoran. Like Ambrose Pytleski. The summer he went through bankruptcy he showed up at The Fieldstone everyday for breakfast, before going off to court.

✧

Besides Myron's house, Ardelle's was the only one in Corcoran that wasn't known as the old so-and-so house. It was simply Ardelle's house. And in it, she had a whole room loaded with toys and army soldiers and comic books for Ricky.

Ardelle didn't have any children of her own, and her husband had died in a car accident years ago. So she looked on Ricky as her summer grandchild. While Grandpa and I spent the day in the fields, Ricky spent it with Ardelle. She hooked up a television in the diner and fed him whatever he wanted. And she refused to serve any farmer who wouldn't let Ricky climb up into the cab of their truck. Ardelle had little concern for the diner's bottom line; though in reality, no one was about to risk being banished from The Fieldstone.

She might have treated me as a grandson too, if I had spent more time with her, or if I had shown to her the slightest inclination to be so treated. But as it turned out, most of our conversations were about Ricky.

"Now, do you read to Ricky — like at night, before bed?" she asked, as she fixed me a late lunch.

"No, not really."

"Well why not? I think he likes it. I think he learns from it. He's not beyond learning, you know. You can't give up on him."

"No one's given up on him, Ardelle; but, I mean, he doesn't know how to read."

"That's because no one reads to him. No one's taught him."

"He's been to doctors. He goes to school. If Ricky could learn to read, they'd..."

"Kids learn at home — that's where they learn. Not from strangers," said the women who had never had any kids.

"You don't understand, Ardelle. Ricky doesn't sit still that long. What could I...?"

"He sits still for me," she boasted. "Here, I'll give you a list of books he likes. He'll listen to those."

I never did read to Ricky. And I never believed Ardelle. I never believed that Ricky sat still for her. I think she read to him right after she served him one of her humongous sundaes. Sure, for a sundae, Ricky would always sit still.

Sometimes, with Ardelle, I never really knew whether she was talking about Ricky or about Grandpa. "I just don't know where he comes up with that stuff," she'd say, in a laughing voice, after taking some desert over to the table at which Grandpa and Ricky were sitting. Or she'd say: "God only knows the color of the sky in his world." Or, "What would he ever do if he had to go out into the real world?" But inevitably, I'd discover that these comments were all aimed at Grandpa. Ardelle was always much more worshipful of Ricky. Not that she held any hostility toward Grandpa — in fact, it was just the opposite. Maybe one of the reasons Ardelle so loved having Ricky visit for the summer was that it gave her the opportunity, if only for a few months, to play grandparents with my grandfather. In a town of delusions, Ricky was Ardelle's delusion.

Picnics From Reality

When Lillie and Sharon put on their first Sunday picnic, I was deliberately forty-five minutes late, with the excuse that one of the trucks just had to have its oil changed. But it was the foolishness of vanity that made me think anyone was going to pay attention to me, especially given the guests that had been invited — patients from the VA Hospital, men who had been injured in Vietnam.

Everyone was sitting on blankets spread out on the grass of Porter's Point when I arrived — everyone but the man in the wheelchair. It was the only place on Lake Kilkenny with a flat shoreline and broad sandy beach. Everywhere else, the steep lake bank dropped off sharply into the water.

Except for Porter's Point, the lake's shoreline was heavily wooded with oak and birch trees. But Grandpa always kept Porter's Point neatly mowed. It was like a grassy arrowhead that jutted out into the lake. Every town should have a park, Grandpa said, and Porter's Point was Corcoran's park.

Even before Ardelle saw me and started waving, I had spotted the man in the wheelchair. He was parked just to the side of one of the blankets. With everyone else sitting on the ground, he seemed out of place, like an onlooker. I couldn't tell if anyone was talking to him.

He wore a baseball cap and had a long, straggly beard. A paper plate filled with food sat on his lap. But it wasn't the plate that grabbed my attention. It was his lap, or lack of lap. Both his legs had been amputated well above the knee; and my first thought was to wonder how he could keep himself sitting up with so little of a base.

The sight of him scared me, just as the sight of Ricky's retarded face seemed to scare other people. But the thing about being with retards is that you never need to worry that they might resent you.

And then Ardelle shouted to me.

"Over here, Glen. We're over here," she called, as if I couldn't see them.

All eyes turned toward me, except for those of the man sitting on the blanket next to Valerie.

Sharon was the one who made the introductions. She took my arm and presented me, first, to the man sitting next to Valerie. His name was Seth, and I knew immediately why he had been the only person who hadn't turned to look at me — he was blind.

"Pleased to meet you," he said. "I hear you're the one who keeps this place going. Here we are sprawled out in the grass and you're doing the work — much obliged."

Needless to say, I liked Seth from the start. I returned his smile, without even thinking that he could not see it. And as I smiled, I looked into his eyes. They were dark and wide, and seemed foreign to his face. They were like decorator beads sown onto a piece of clothing: having no use, and added almost as an afterthought.

I started to say something about the food, wanting somehow to stay here with this friendly and likeable man, but Sharon veered me over to Jake, the man in the wheelchair. He muttered a "Hi," and then lifted a sandwich up to his mouth as I started to reach out my hand to him. I couldn't see his eyes very well — they were squinted and downcast — but they seemed even more lifeless than Seth's. And even though Jake's hostility was apparent, I felt strangely relieved. I didn't have to worry about what I'd say to him, because he wasn't about to let me say anything anyway.

After the introductions were over, Julia called me over to a spot on the blanket next to her, where she had fixed a plate of food for me. And as I started to eat, the others resumed their conversation, as if it was a stream of water resuming its flow after a blockage lifted.

"I still don't understand why Father Joe didn't join us for this picnic," Lorraine said. "I know for a fact that the priests have their Sunday afternoons free."

"Maybe he had other plans," Ardelle replied, more out of courtesy than interest.

"He didn't say anything about plans, and I don't know what could be more important than ministering to his people. After all, we only get to see him twice a month."

"I saw him just last week, maybe Wednesday, at The Fieldstone," Myron remarked, in between sandwich bites.

"No, he couldn't have been there. He would've stopped by if he was in town. He didn't stop by did he, Valerie?"

"Uh, no...I don't...no, no he didn't," Valerie answered. Usually she was tight on the heels of everything her mother said, but this afternoon she seemed consumed with helping Seth with his lunch. Her whole body was turned toward him, ready to hand him a napkin or soda or bag of potato chips. And Seth, who had obviously spent some time in the overcrowded wards of veterans' hospitals, seemed to be enjoying the personal attention.

"You must be mistaken, Myron," Lorraine said.

"Hell, I'm not mistaken. But if you don't believe me, ask Ardelle. She saw him."

The more agitated Lorraine became about her Father Joe, the more everyone else seemed to be content to lie back on their blankets and enjoy the breeze off the lake, almost as if Lorraine's chatter reprieved them of any need to talk.

It was a couple of nights ago, during dinner, when Sharon announced that she had invited some guests to a Sunday picnic in Corcoran. They were patients at the VA Hospital, she said, and it would be good for them to get out into the real world. I remembered those exact words, "real world," because they were the last words I would have used to describe Corcoran.

"A lot of patients are afraid of venturing back into the real world," nurse Lillie had added. "They feel their injuries make them freaks, and they're afraid of seeing normal people. So if it's okay with you all, we'd like to invite a few of them here. Since we're such a small group, it might be easier for them to break the ice with us."

"So what kind of engines do those army trucks have in 'em?" Myron was asking Seth.

"I just drove them, I didn't fix them — so I couldn't tell you."

"Do they use much oil?"

"Again, I couldn't say," Seth replied, passing a can of soda back to the waiting hand of Valerie.

"Well, I'd sure like to tinker around in one of them big army engines. How many cylinders did they have?"

I saw Seth smile and shake his head. I knew the words he was about to utter. As in a prisoner-of-war interrogation: no matter what the question, the answer was always the same — name, rank and serial number.

I tried to imagine Seth and Jake in the midst of combat. But it was like trying to imagine my grandfather as a young man. I wondered how much Jake had screamed when his legs were blown off. Or maybe it was even worse. Maybe he had made a mistake and acted cowardly, in a way that had caused comrades to die. Maybe he was having to live with that too.

"So you used to work for a construction company?" Grandpa asked Jake.

"Back when I wasn't a gimp," came the sneering answer.

A fearful hush descended on the group. Jake was gonna blow. He was gonna lose it.

"What do you think? Could one of those Cape Cod-style resorts be built here?" Grandpa continued. My mother always said he was the most oblivious and insensitive man she had ever known.

"I keep telling you, this is not the place," Myron interjected, in his familiarly argumentative tone. "You got to put it up on the bank. Leave this place for the swimming beach."

"You're not talking about the cemetery land?" Grandpa exclaimed.

"Who is ever going to come to a resort that has a cemetery? Are you crazy?"

"I'll tell you what a resort should have — a church,"

Lorraine said. "People should take a vacation to God, not from him."

"Well, we got a church," Grandpa nodded.

"You'd have to take a bulldozer to this place to get anyone to vacation here," Myron said.

I didn't know if anyone else felt as I did — that it seemed cruel to talk about resorts when in our presence sat two men who would never run along a beach or watch a sunset.

"Bulldozer!" I heard Grandpa exclaim. "You want this place to look like a war zone?"

"War zone?" Jake exploded. "What the hell do you know about a war zone?"

"I'm sorry if I....," Grandpa started to say.

"Yeah, what you're really sorry about is mentioning a subject that you'd all rather avoid. You have us cripples out for a lousy picnic and then congratulate yourselves for being so damned noble. But not one of you has the guts to mention the war. Hell, the country doesn't even have the courage to call it a war. Conflict, Vietnam conflict — what the hell does that mean? You know what it means? Take a look at my legs, that's what it is. It's no goddamn conflict, it's a fucking war."

"Hey, Jake, come on, lighten up," Seth retorted. "These people are doing something nice for us. Let's enjoy our time away from that stinking hospital. They're not the ones who blew off your legs."

"Why not? Why aren't they the ones? They're part of the country that sent us over there. They let us die over there while spoiled little college kids get laid at concerts and blow dope and burn their draft cards..."

He wanted to continue, I could tell. But he seemed to

run out of words. His emotions were still supplying the power, but his mind couldn't provide the vocabulary to harness it.

"You're right to be angry about all the people who've abandoned you," Grandpa answered. "But you're wrong if you think that everyone did. I know something of what you must feel. When I was in France, in the trenches, in 1919..."

"Give me a break, old man," Jake shot back. "You're not going to give me that American Legion 'back-in-my-war' crap, are you? None of you old guys understand. Maybe you fought in a war, but when you came back you weren't spit on and called war criminals."

"Hey, if you're going to lay your anger on these people, then let's pack up right now," Seth scolded. "I mean it, let's just pack up and go home. Lillie, take us back to the hospital."

"No, it's okay, let him speak his mind," Grandpa said. "Jake's right. You men fought in a dirty war — the very least we can do is talk about it. You're right. Except for the protestors who don't want to be drafted, the rest of America is trying to ignore the war. And that's a sin."

Grandpa's admission seemed to dampen the energy of Jake's anger; and a few moments of eerie silence came over the group, until Jake could recover his fire.

"Okay, tell me old man," he said, with a renewed combativeness. "What's this war mean? You're voting for the politicians and paying the taxes that's buying the bombs, can you tell me what it's all for? Anyone? Can any of you tell me?"

Of course no one was going to speak. No one other than Grandpa.

"I'm afraid what it means to those fighting it may have little to do with why the war is being fought in the first place. When I went to Europe in 1919, I didn't know anything about the Kaiser or the Hapsburg empire or the French and British alliances. I fought not because of who was in the opposite trenches, but because of who was in mine, next to me. I don't know why wars get fought, but when they do it seems that our only choice is to either stand with our country or reject it, either be loyal to our comrades or betray them. In a way, it's a test of loyalty to something larger than yourself."

"Shit, you sound like a fucking recruiting poster, old man," Jake scoffed.

"I don't think you should doubt what you did, and why you did it, just because there are a lot of people protesting the war," Sharon piped in. It was a welcome interruption, because she spoke as if she were sure of her position, and yet wouldn't go too far in espousing it. "My husband went to Vietnam. He died there, and I can only imagine the horror he saw. But I'm proud of him. Maybe this isn't the best war, maybe it isn't the clearest or the easiest. But it's the one at hand. And I think it takes even more courage to fight in a muddy war, because there's no certainty to fall back on."

I wondered if Julia would join the testimonial, but she remained silent. All during Jake's tirade, she had occupied herself with the picnic basket, folding napkins and arranging bottles. Not once had she looked up at the man in the wheelchair.

"That's all great and good of you to talk about going to war," Jake said. "But I'm talking about coming back from war. I'm talking about coming back to a country that despises me. And to a girlfriend who's disgusted by the sight of me."

I saw Lillie move toward Jake, as if about to tell him the standard line — that no one, especially someone who loved him, would be disgusted. But before she could say anything, Grandpa intervened.

"I'm not going to tell you that there aren't people who feel that way. And I don't know your girlfriend, so I can't speak for her. But you got to keep going, and you got to find something that keeps you going."

"Easy for you to say, old man. I got no home. I got no family. And what kind of job can I ever get, with half a body?"

"I'll give you a home," Grandpa replied. "And I'll find a job for you. You can start a new life here, in Corcoran. I want you. I want both of you," he said, looking back and forth between Jake and Seth. "You got to have a place, and I'd be grateful if you chose this place — we all would."

Valerie was the first to echo Grandpa's sentiments, followed quickly by a chorus of "absolutely's" and "most definitely's."

✧

I doubted that Jake or Seth really believed my grandfather, but I knew he was being sincere. He wanted them more than they'd ever know.

Jake, in my opinion, was just the type of person who should live in Corcoran: the type who had nowhere else. Suzanne Corr — she was a different story.

Valerie

Valerie and Lorraine Rusk, daughter and mother, had arrived in Corcoran only four years ago, though it was difficult to tell whether it had been good news or bad that had brought them.

Lorraine had owned a discount bridal shop in Millerton, which she sold when the doctors gave her less than a year to live — a rare blood disease being the diagnosis. But somewhere along the way, in the course of selling the business, Lorraine had let her health insurance lapse.

As it turned out, Lorraine was not a dying woman. She was later told that what she had was a kidney disorder; and that with the right treatment it could be cured, which in fact it was, but only after depleting her bank account. So now Lorraine was poor, and with a daughter who had no viable employment prospects. She was the perfect candidate for Corcoran — someone for whom not even death had gone right.

Valerie was thirty-seven years old. She had a weight problem and was developing a bald spot in back of her right temple. But she hadn't given up on love. She drove in with Ardelle once a week to visit the Millerton Public Library, where she pulled out of the recycling bin every bridal and love-advice magazine she could find. She even looked on me as a potential resource.

"Glen, could I talk to you about something?" she asked one day in Ardelle's diner. I was up at the counter picking up a sandwich, and Valerie was sitting at a table, with the newspaper laid out in front of her.

"Sure," I said.

"Um, would you like to sit down for a moment?"

I made the mistake of glancing up at the clock, which then led to a five minute back-and-forth dialogue of: "Oh, you haven't got time," and "Sure I do," and "No, I don't want to hold you up," and "Really, I've got time, I'm on my lunch break." Finally, Ardelle gave me a push, along with a stare that said, "just go and sit down with the poor girl."

"I was just wondering what you thought of this problem, I mean, from a man's perspective, I mean, since you're a man and all," she began saying, after I had sat down. All the while, her head kept dropping down to the newspaper.

"Yes?"

"Well, here, in 'Dear Abbey,' a woman writes and asks what she should do to get her husband interested in her again. She says he doesn't pay attention to her anymore, that he just comes home from work and flops in front of the television, and that they never...you know, go out anymore. So, from a man's perspective, what should she do? I mean, why does that happen with men?"

Poor Valerie, she didn't even know enough to give up. Here was a woman who would never get a date asking someone who had...well, never really had many dates. It was something for which I had always blamed Ricky; but in truth, Ricky was just an excuse.

When she wasn't reading 'Dear Abby,' Valerie was most likely mopping the floors or washing windows at the Church of the Sagging Roof. That's what Myron called it — the church that had been built by Grandpa's father. Its real name was the Church of the Sacred Heart. It had originally been built at the center of Corcoran, but as the town's buildings had been rather asymmetrically torn down, the church now stood at the western edge.

Despite its sagging roof, the church was the best kept building in Corcoran. Luckily for Grandpa, Lorraine and Valerie were devoted Catholics. The mother, and her tag-along daughter, were intent on scrubbing their way into heaven. And they may have been the reason that a priest still came out from Millerton every other Sunday to say mass...although maybe it had more to do with the envelope I often saw Grandpa hand to the priest.

After mass, Lorraine and Valerie huddled around the priest like groupies around a rock singer. They invariably invited him to their house for Sunday lunch, and he invariably declined. Yet on the way out of town, his car frequently made a quick and covert stop at The Fieldstone.

✧

"This church is the symbol of God's compact with Corcoran," Grandpa once said, in dismissing a suggestion that the old church be torn down. But he was also giving full rein to his sense of the dramatic: "God's compact with Corcoran" — just like God's compact with the Israelites during the time of Moses.

"If God had wanted Corcoran to die," Grandpa theorized, "then he wouldn't have saved this church during the tornado of '52." But those who disagreed with Grandpa's premise said that Corcoran had long ago died and that the tornado of '52 was just nature's way of mopping up.

The Cemetery Visitor

There were no curbs or public sidewalks in Corcoran. And it was accepted practice, since the streets were so narrow, to park up on the grass. The lawns were long and spacious, and no one had ever minded the outermost six feet of grass being used as a parking space. That is, no one except for Harold Nelson, who lived next door to Julia.

When I drove up to Julia's house for dinner one evening, about a week after our picnic with Jake and Seth, I had to pull over and park on Harold's lawn. There were already three cars parked in front of Julia's house. Lately, Lillie had been driving straight to Julia's from the V.A.; and sometimes Sharon parked there too, if she had just come from some errand in Millerton. Nor was it uncommon for us to have dinner guests. Since the picnic, Lillie and Sharon had invited V.A. patients to dinner on three different occasions. The women were unwavering in their conviction that Corcoran was a therapeutic retreat for recuperating veterans. So when I saw the unfamiliar car parked in front of Julia's, I just assumed it was another such guest.

"Hey, you can't park there," an ornery voice barked from Harold's screened-in porch. "What do you think this is, a parking lot? Do I go pulling my car onto your grandfather's lawn?"

"He'd love it if you did, Mr. Nelson. My grandfather loves visitors," I answered.

"I'm calling the county sheriff right now. They're going to break up this commune you all have going here. Everyday there's new weirdos coming in. You'd think this place was Grand Central Station."

"Why don't you come over and join us for dinner?"

"I'm not gonna fall for that. Hey, what about your truck? I'm calling the sheriff if you don't move it," he shouted, as I walked toward Julia's house.

"Tell him to watch out for all the congestion. I wouldn't want him to get stuck in traffic here."

"Goddamn it, this place is going to hell. If my parents were alive to see this they'd...." And as I walked around to the back of Julia's house, Harold's whining decrescendoed to a mummer, and then disappeared altogether.

Lately, I had established a routine. Before going inside, I would wash up in Julia's backyard, at the outside pump which brought up water from the underground well. And then I would walk into a house filled with people sitting in front of the television with drinks in their hands. Grandpa and Myron with shirt and tie. Julia with her hair pulled back in a ponytail. Ardelle with her feet up on a footstool. Valerie and Lorraine fussing over the setting of the table. Sharon and Lillie watching the news. All of them relaxing; all of them waiting for me, the provider.

The thing about having a retarded brother — whether you know it or not, you learn how to fantasize.

As I started to work the clanky pump, I knew Julia would come to the back door any moment now. If I was late enough, she'd have started everyone eating, and then would serve me specially. But tonight I wasn't that late. Dinner would still be waiting, but Julia would claim that it had been ruined, that the chicken would be tough and the vegetables soggy.

"Do I have to get you a watch, or maybe a huge alarm clock to prop up on your tractor?" she called out, as I was splashing water on my face. "I'm going to have a riot on my hands if you don't get in here soon."

"Sorry," I muttered through the rinsing water, knowing that some superficial sign of apology was expected of me.

"You put in another long day, huh? I hope you're hungry."

"I'm always hungry — that's why I put in such long days, just to enjoy your dinners all the more," I said, trying to sound as if I was kidding.

"Have you put in too long a day to help me with a broken window after dinner? I've got blueberry pie for desert."

"Ala mode?"

"Oh no, I don't have any ice cream. Is that how you like your pie?"

"Well, in that case, I don't know if I'll have time for the window."

"Okay, so I'll have to come up with something else to bribe you with. You think that's possible?"

"I suppose anything is possible."

"Wash up well," she said, as she pushed open the screen door. "We have a guest. Here's a clean shirt for you."

When I turned around, she tossed me a white, short-sleeved shirt.

"What's this?" I asked.

"It's Frank's. I think the size is about right."

Frank was her husband.

After catching the shirt, I just stood there and stared.

"I told you, we've got company," she said. "Now hustle up, we're waiting."

I took mine off and then pulled Frank's shirt on. It felt cold and bristly, and huge — as if it would overwhelm me, the way wearing women's shoes makes little girls stumble and fall.

When I walked into the dining room, I saw that tonight's guest was not from the V.A. Hospital. She was introduced as Suzanne Corr. "And she's going to spend the summer here," Grandpa added.

"Now hold on," the dark-haired girl said, smiling cautiously as she spoke. "I said I'd think about it."

"I met her this afternoon up in the cemetery," Grandpa said. "I gave her the tour."

But Suzanne Corr didn't look like the kind of person who would go for one of Grandpa's cemetery tours.

"She could stay in the old Carson house," Myron suggested, looking over at Julia. "How are you coming with it?"

"Not exactly fit for habitation, not yet anyway."

"Suzanne, you could stay with me," Ardelle said. "I've got a whole second floor that's just going to waste. You'd have lots of room and plenty of privacy. There's even an outdoor porch up there."

All summer, there had been a quiet sadness in Ardelle's eyes, a loneliness for what she had possessed during previous summers. But now, a trace of her old vitality had returned.

"I got room too," Myron said.

"She can't live with you," Ardelle scoffed. "That place hasn't had a proper cleaning in years."

"Hey, I clean it all the time. Just because I don't make a big show of it like you do, taking out all the rugs and shaking them in the front yard where everybody can see, doesn't mean I don't clean."

"What everyone is trying to say is that there's lots of places for you to stay," Sharon said. "We all have room. It's up to you."

The only people not bidding for the newcomer were Valerie and Lorraine. They were filled up. Besides, they were suspicious of newcomers. They didn't want anyone trying to horn in on their church gig.

"You're all very generous, but I just came to..."

"Her grandfather's in the cemetery, and Suzanne came to see him," Grandpa interrupted. He always spoke of the cemetery inmates as if they were still living.

"You're interrupting the girl, Eamon; let her speak," Myron scolded. "You got to really push to be heard around here sometimes," he said to Suzanne.

"Have you got a job for the summer?" Ardelle asked.

"No...not yet," Suzanne answered, in a slow drawl, as if wondering whether she was giving the correct answer.

"We'll get you a job, no problem," Myron said.

"There's a ton of jobs you could do," Grandpa added. "You could even work up in the cemetery and be with your grandfather. I've been meaning for years to do some landscaping work up there."

"You could certainly work with me," Ardelle said. "The fellas would just love you. Tell her, Eamon, tell her she shouldn't worry about any of that."

"We got more jobs around here than there are fish in that lake," Myron quipped.

"That's very kind of you all, but I really...I just came for a...and I don't want you to have to make up work for me."

"Don't you think that for a moment, honey," Ardelle said. "No such thing as a made-up job around here. And if you're really ambitious, you could help out with the farm work. Isn't it just about bean-walking time, Glen?"

"That's a lousy job," Myron grunted. "She shouldn't do that."

"What's bean-walking?" Suzanne asked.

"It's where you walk the soybean fields and pull out the weeds," Ardelle said.

"We chop 'em with a hoe, we don't pull 'em," Grandpa clarified.

"That'll be a big job, won't it?" Sharon said, looking at me.

"Damn right."

"Glen, your language," Lorraine snapped.

"Well it is a big job. And it's hard work, especially if you're not used to it. And it probably takes a whole summer before you learn all the tricks to it."

I just didn't see the reason for all the fuss being made over this newcomer, and I felt like throwing a sour note into their chorus of admiration. So I didn't mention that we had never before had enough help to finish the bean-walking, that every year the beans grew too high before we could walk all the fields. Grandpa had never even been able to recruit the migrant farm workers that drifted north to Minnesota for the summers. He offered them houses, food, the most lenient working hours, but he could never guarantee them cash, not until the crop was harvested. And if there was one thing the migrant workers weren't interested in, it was IOU's.

"Hell, bean-walking's not that hard," Grandpa remarked. "Why, back in the old days..."

"Suzanne, if you're worried about paying your way, don't," said Sharon, who had already become comfortable cutting off my grandfather's "back-in-the-good-old-days" reminisces. "We've got plenty of work, but don't let us talk you into anything."

"At least sleep on it," Ardelle pleaded. "Stay at my house tonight. Tomorrow you can look around the place."

"I think I've already seen it, haven't I?" Suzanne asked, in a tone I figured had to be sarcastic.

Julia was starting to serve dinner, and I sat down at the only table with an open spot — the table with Lorraine and Valerie. The table with a second empty chair, where Julia would sit.

"Now are you glad I gave you a clean shirt?" she whispered, when she sat down next to me. She was smiling, but I couldn't tell if it was in a teasing or expectant way — or if she was hoping that I'd just scoff at the suggestion.

The more I watched Suzanne converse so effortlessly, so confident of being well-liked, the more I resented the way she had taken over — the way everyone was fawning all over her and setting themselves up to be spurned, like desperate fools. She was just like those perky girls who sat at the popular table in the cafeteria, so certain that everyone wanted to sit next to them. There were the clothes — she'd probably never even been in a discount store. And the hair — so perfectly imperfect in the way it casually dropped to her shoulders. And the chin — as if she'd been tutored to hold it so high and erect and aloof.

Suzanne reminded me of Patty Thompson — the stuck-up girl who had screamed and threw a fit in the cafeteria that day when Ricky reached for her tray. Suzanne, I figured, was a retard-hater. If Ricky were here now, she'd be petrified of him; and she'd be trying desperately to avoid his big, retarded eyes.

✧

Whenever we walked through the hallways at school, the passing students would swing wide around us, as if mental retardation was contagious. And when we strolled past the practice fields, the football players would stop and stare, as if waiting for Ricky to do a trick.

People instinctively retreated from Ricky whenever they saw his big, friendly, retarded eyes approaching them. They were afraid of him; they were afraid he might embarrass them and force them to talk retarded with him. Ricky had a way of making anyone look weird.

Sometimes, when my mean streak showed itself, I'd use Ricky as a weapon against the people I didn't like. If we passed by a group of guys gathered around a hot car and trying to look cool, I'd tell Ricky that the car was the military's newest alien-tracker and that the undercover agents standing around it would probably want to meet with him. And then I'd watch as Ricky would run over to them, all excited and with arms flailing away. I'd watch as the guys became red-faced and self-conscious, nervously looking around to see if anyone had noticed them with the retard.

The thing about retards — they're completely immune from embarrassment.

✧

"So, tell us about your grandfather," I heard Sharon say to Suzanne.

"I don't know that much about him. He died when my dad was just a baby; and then my grandmother moved away and married again. But I've always known that he's buried here."

"That's quite a thing for someone your age to come all this way just to visit the grave of a man you never knew," Ardelle said.

"Where is it you live again?" Myron asked.

"Seattle.

"We've had someone from Seattle come visit the cemetery before, I think. Or was it Sacramento?" Mryon said, looking around to Grandpa and Ardelle for help. "One of those 'S' cities anyway."

"Are you thinking of that couple from San Diego — the ones doing that book?" Ardelle asked.

"Good god," Grandpa thundered. "You're not talking about those fools taking pictures for some goddammned coffee table book on cemeteries?"

"Eamon, your language," Lorraine scolded.

"My apologies, Lorraine, but I kicked their butts outta here when I found out what they were doing. Mocking the past, that's what it is. Can you imagine someone putting a coffee cup down on your grandfather's headstone?" he said to Suzanne.

"So when did your grandfather die?" Myron asked.

"1921. It was 1921, wasn't it, Mr. O'Shea?" she said,

with a sudden flush in her face. I could tell she wasn't certain of the year, that earlier today was the first time she had learned of the date, and that she was afraid of being one of those people who were indifferent to the past. Suzanne Corr probably lived in a house that was filled with coffee table books.

"Actually, it was 1924, but the headstone is worn at the 4, so it looks like a 1. We could get that fixed, if you want?"

"Well, I...I don't know. I don't have any..."

"That's okay, we can discuss that later," Grandpa interrupted. "I don't want to load you up all at once."

"How long did your grandfather live here?" Sharon asked.

"According to Mr. O'Shea..."

"Call me Eamon, everyone else does," Grandpa interrupted again.

"Not me," Myron proclaimed. "I call him deluded, and sometimes deranged. Or just dreamer."

"Don't mind either one of them," Ardelle said, reaching over and patting Suzanne's arm. "Now you tell us about your grandfather."

"I guess he was only here for a couple of years," she started to say, glancing over at Grandpa for verification. "According to Mr...er...Eamon, he worked for the railroad. He and my grandmother were expecting their first child, my father."

"They lived above the general store," Grandpa said. "There weren't any empty houses back then."

"Is it still standing? The general store?" Suzanne asked.

"It burned down in, I think, 1951 — no, 1949."

"I thought you said that row of buildings burned down during the war?" Myron said.

"Those were across the street. Donnelly's general store burned down after...well, I take that back, it could have been '46 or '47. I'd have to check my journals."

"What did he do for the railroad — Suzanne's grandfather?" Lillie asked Grandpa, side-tracking an obviously ignorant Suzanne.

"He was station manager. He came when the Chicago & Northwestern Railroad opened a grain-loading depot here. And he wasn't the typical corporate type — looking to put in his time and then move on to a bigger station. Your grandfather bought forty acres on the other side of the lake," he said to Suzanne. "He was an ambitious man, and wanted the farmers to trust him — so he farmed those forty acres at night. When your grandmother left, she left everything. Didn't sell the land, just quit paying the taxes. My father acquired it when he paid the delinquent taxes years later. Maybe you want to work that land this summer? — your grandfather would like that."

"I'd love to see those forty acres," Suzanne replied.

"So how did your grandfather die?" Myron asked. "He was a young man, right?"

Suzanne again looked to Grandpa. She had probably learned the story only hours earlier, and she probably felt awkward in repeating it in front of the man who had just told it to her.

"He died in one of the grain bins that were used to load up the train," Grandpa said, seizing Suzanne's cue. "He was working alone at the time. It was at night, during harvest, and he had to work all night to get the train loaded. The general opinion was that he slipped, hit his head, became unconscious, fell into the grain and died from suffocation. It was a shock to everyone — him being so young and all. The day after the funeral, his wife and baby boarded the passenger train and left for good. And up until today, no one's ever visited Henry Corr's gravestone."

Watching Grandpa tell his story, I was pretty sure I knew what he was thinking. But Suzanne was not the Corcoran type. It was so obvious.

"So you came to Corcoran just to see your grandfather's grave?" Sharon was asking at the next table.

"I just graduated from high school and I thought I'd take a trip or something. I've always been curious about my family's history, so I decided to drive out here."

"That's a nice lookin' vehicle you got," Myron said. "Is it new?"

"My father gave it to me as a graduation present," she casually replied, as if a new car was no big deal.

"Wow!" Myron exclaimed. "Looks like one of them new Pontiac sports models."

"What's your father do?" Ardelle asked.

"He's a lawyer."

I sensed an immediate deflation of mood around the room. Even Grandpa looked disappointed. That was it. She would return to her land of new cars and lawyer's incomes. There was no use in holding onto any hope.

As if an intriguing toy had just been taken out of the store window and all the gaping children had dispersed with dejected faces, the diners in Julia's house retreated their attentions from Suzanne and back to the food in front of them. Conversation settled into the usual: "Please pass the pepper," and "Julia, whatever did you do with this salad?" and "I could use some of that butter."

I wanted to think that Julia was just as relieved as I was that Suzanne would not be staying, but she was probably too nice to feel that way. Or too secure. Suzanne couldn't hold a candle to Julia.

What I hated about people like Suzanne was that no one ever stood up to them. No one ever made them feel like a retard.

✧

Right after Ricky died, I felt besieged with mean-spirited urges. Following my high school band concert, a reception was held in the cafeteria. I saw a woman, a friend of my mother's who had always been very uncomfortable with Ricky. She had always been careful never to get caught in the direct line of one of his hugs. She was always reminding my mother of the miracles those "special institutions" were capable of. Anyway, I went up to her and said, in voice as loud as Ricky's: "Itsh sho nishe to shee you; come shit wish me."

✧

"So, what do you think of our mustard crop this year? You think it looks good?" I asked Suzanne.

"Yes. Everything is so green here."

"Honey, mustard plants are weeds," Ardelle said. "Glen is pulling your leg."

"Oh." And she laughed. And everyone else laughed.

"Seriously, do you get a chance to travel much?" I asked. "I mean, other than road trips?"

"I've been to New York quite a bit. My mother goes twice a year just to see the shows."

"Hey, we love shows here. The Millerton summer theater is putting on 'Sound of Music' this year. Ever seen it?"

"Sure. But it was the movie I saw."

"Don't you like live theater?"

"No, it's not that at all. I just...I go to the theater all the time."

"Pretty expensive though, isn't it? To go all the time?"

"I didn't mean all the time. But movies are definitely cheaper."

"Yeah, I love going to the movies. I sneak in my own popcorn. Ever do that?"

"Um, no, I guess not."

"Is it expensive in Seattle? Concession stand popcorn?"

"I'm not really sure."

"Oh, someone else pays for it, huh?"

"Well, I just..."

I could feel her on the verge of cracking.

"Suzanne, you want more potatoes?" Ardelle asked, with a forced smile.

"Yes, have more salad," Sharon added.

"How about another of them dinner rolls?" Myron said. Suddenly, everyone was shoving food at Suzanne.

"So, is it going to be difficult to get a summer job when you get back to Seattle?" I asked, as soon as there was a pause in the offerings.

"I don't think so." The eyes weren't as confident as before. They were falling increasingly to her plate.

"What kind of jobs have you had in the past?"

"Well, I really haven't had like a full-time job before."

"What kind of part-time jobs can you get in Seattle?"

"I usually take a class during the summer."

"So you've got all summer to travel then, huh? Must be nice. Oh, I'll bet you're a shopper. And you heard about the good country antique shops we've got around here?"

"No, I didn't come to shop. I came to see where my..."

"Oh, right. Your little family history project."

"Look, I just needed to go somewhere, and so I came here. Why? Is it a problem?"

And just like that, the crowd came roaring back.

"Hey, Glen, lighten up."

"No, of course it's no problem."

"He didn't mean a thing."

"He's just kidding around."

And just like that, the dashed hopes were resurrected.

"So why did you need to go somewhere?" Ardelle asked.

"I...oh, it's a long story. I don't want to bore you."

"Did you run away from home?" Valerie ventured.

"From home? No," Suzanne said, letting out a nervous laugh.

"From something else?" Lillie asked.

"Well, I don't know that I really have a home, or which home is mine. My parents are in the midst of getting a divorce. And I guess I'm their battleground. But it's not that either one of them particularly wants me, it's more like they just don't want the other one to have me. Know what I mean?"

Lillie nodded her head in the way she must have done hundreds of times before, listening to patients go on about their troubles.

"My dad has a twenty-six year-old girlfriend, my mom has gone to California to find herself, and my sister lives in some sort of commune in San Francisco. I guess I just didn't feel at home with any of them."

"Finding yourself — what's that all about anyway?" Myron blurted out, seemingly missing the point of everything that had been said.

"Father Joe says you can find yourself only in your own soul. I think people should go to church more," Lorraine said.

"Well, your mother would certainly find God here," Myron quipped, "'cause there's nothing else to distract her."

"Yes," Grandpa added, in a revved-up voice. "They ought to come here, your parents. They ought to come and visit your grandfather. That would help them find themselves."

"Do you need to contact anyone? To tell them where you are?" Ardelle asked.

Suzanne shook her head, timidly, as if she might be regretting her revelations. Yet she couldn't help but add, "the less they know or think about me, the better."

What followed was a hearty round of empathy — assurances that of course her parents cared; reminders that everything has a way of working out; and urgings to look on the bright side. But it wasn't really empathy that everyone was feeling, it was reinvigoration. There was still a chance for Suzanne and Corcoran, a place whose residency requirements commanded a troubled life. But in my opinion, unless you had a husband in the jungles of Vietnam, or a brother who was retarded, you had no business being in Corcoran.

"Well, we're all castaway's here — Julia, Lillie and me, anyway," Sharon said with a smirk. "It may not be the most exciting place, but there's a spot at the table for you."

"What do you mean, not exciting?" Grandpa exclaimed.

"You could really do a lot of good at the V.A.," Lillie said.

"And I'm gonna build a diving raft down at the beach," Myron added, with the same promise he'd been making for years.

Even Valerie joined the chorus. "I'm in a pen-pal club. We write to soldiers. I could get you in if you wanted."

"With a little help, I might be able to open up The Fieldstone on weekend nights," Ardelle speculated.

I felt sorry for Ardelle. Grandpa had told me how much she had always wanted a daughter, and I could see in her eyes a certain motherly enthusiasm. Grandpa was accustomed to disappointment, but Ardelle rarely got her hopes up for anything.

Julia had made strawberry shortcake for desert. Given the renewed excitement at the dinner table, and the quickened pace at which people ate, she had to serve it sooner than usual.

And then, just as everyone started getting up from the table, Valerie announced: "Hey don't forget, it's CARE package tonight."

Cigarettes, Candy Bars and Dreams

On CARE package night, we all sat out on Julia's porch and assembled packages to send to soldiers in Vietnam. Sharon had obtained funding from the American Legion to pay for the cookies and candy and cigarettes we crammed into the shoe-size boxes. The supplies were stored in Julia's basement; and every Wednesday evening, right after dinner, we all went out to the porch where we were assigned our role in the assembly line. Last week I had tootsie rolls; the week before it was gum.

Valerie was the most eager of the assemblers. She was always the first one out on the porch, where she positioned herself in the chair at the far end — the last stop in the assembly line. She didn't think we knew that she snuck into each box a little hand-printed card that read: "We're praying for you and are grateful for your bravery. Valerie Rusk, Corcoran, Minnesota, 507-235-9038."

To my knowledge, she had never received a reply from any of the recipients. Perhaps that was why she was constantly urging us to upgrade the contents of the packages.

"Couldn't we send them some mosquito repellant?" she once asked. "The bugs must be horrible in those jungles."

"Or how about a clean shirt, for when they go into town?" she suggested another time, as if they were cowboys who went into town every Saturday night.

After Valerie, the next most energetic assembler was Myron. But he was energetic at anything in which the women were involved.

"You know, Myron," Grandpa told him one evening as the three of us walked home, "no matter what you do, you're still an old man. And you're making a fool out of yourself."

"Oh, and you aren't? Holding on to this town like it was some forgotten gold mine. Dreaming about resorts and curbed streets."

"You're living here, aren't you? And the women moved here. That's something. That's more than just a pipedream."

"I'm a lot younger than you are."

"Yeah, young enough to act like a fool."

"Fool? Who buys old houses that are falling down? Who sings songs by himself in a cemetery?"

"Who's been building a diving raft for ten years?"

And on and on they went. Every four or five days they erupted into a volley of bickering, almost as if it was necessary to maintain some kind of friendship equilibrium between them. But there were never any stabs of revenge or barrages of resentment. There was just the grumbling of old men who knew that the world was leaving them behind.

✧

On the night of Suzanne's arrival, there was one less person in our assembly line. Ardelle had taken a tired

Suzanne home, "for a hot bath and cup of tea before bed."

As we filled the boxes, Grandpa sat on the porch steps and smoked his pipe. The night breeze blew all the lake smells straight into Julia's porch, making you feel as if the waves were about to splash against your face. Somewhere, a blue jay was arguing with a blackbird. The clatter of claws sounded as squirrels ran up their trees. Out of the muffled hum of the highway traffic came the chirping of crickets. And at the end of our assembly line, Valerie slipped her dreams into boxes bound for a war America was losing.

The 305 Curse

Suzanne probably had the kind of graduation my mother had envisioned for me. A nice, dignified party, with an endearing graduate, and lots of photos with smiling friends and congratulatory teachers.

"Oh, I almost forgot," my mother had said to me, during our first telephone conversation after she had dropped me off in Corcoran. "I just got the photos back from your graduation. They're...good. You want me to send you a second set of prints?"

I had noticed right away that pause between "they're" and "good." She was probably going to say something else, maybe "great" or "with all your friends," but then stopped herself.

✧

When I was handed my diploma, I had one of the loudest cheering sections of any of the graduates. But my cheering section was the room 305 crowd.

There was at least one 305 graduate each year. They weren't given a regular high school diploma, just a certificate that used the words "pride" and "special person." Mrs. Folcrum, their teacher, made sure all her students were on hand to witness the single event all year in which one of their own merged into the larger, normal world of

Roosevelt High. And it was this uninhibited group that gave the day's most vibrant applause to "Brosher Glen."

"Hey, it's Brosher Glen."

"Hey, Brosher Glen."

"Look, Mrs. Folcrum, it's Brosher Glen."

"It's Brosher Glen — and he's all dressed up."

If Ricky were there, he'd have been uncontrollable. He'd have wanted to sit with me. He'd have wanted his own cap and gown. Ricky loved dress-up. He probably would have imagined himself a scientist battling an alien invasion. If Ricky were alive, I'd probably have wished he were dead.

When commencement ended, I met my parents in the courtyard. They were standing near the flag pole, not talking to each other, just waiting, as were all the parents, for the obligatory hug of congratulations and viewing of the diploma. As I walked up to them, I saw my mother begin fumbling for her camera.

"Hold it, stop right there," she called out, when I was still twenty feet away. "I want to get a picture of you with the school in the background."

"Okay, smile. Come on, Glen, smile."

It took Mom forever to snap the photo. It always took her forever.

"Oops, I need to take another. I think I got someone else in the photo," she said, lifting the camera back up to her eye. "Smile, Glen."

The crowd around us had parted, watching and waiting for the photo to be shot. Inside the no-man's circle I stood, feeling a self-consciousness to which I thought I had long ago become immune. Then Mom ordered my father to join me, and I could see the reluctance all over his face. All of us, except for Ricky, hated it when my mother was behind the camera.

"Don't be macho now, put your arms around each other."

"Just take the picture, Katherine," my father said.

"Let me get a second one, just in case this one doesn't turn out," she said. My mother was always making contingency plans.

"Here, I'll get you with Glen," my father barked, rushing toward the safety of the camera. He grabbed it so quickly from my mother that he almost ripped off the carrying strap that was wrapped around her wrist.

Dad snapped the photo even before Mom stopped brushing the hair out of her face. Then he put the lens cover on and walked over to us, as if to finally let the crowd spill into no-man's land. That was when I missed Ricky the most. If he was here now, there wouldn't be any strained silences. The thing about having a retarded brother is that there's never a lull.

I had my back to them, so I didn't see the 305ers approaching through the post-commencement crowd. But my mother saw them, and I could tell by the startled (and maybe embarrassed) look in her eyes that something was about to happen.

They were still under the supervision of Mrs. Folcrum, who was trying to lead them to the small orange bus that would take them home. But on such an exciting day as this, with so many people in those funny gown costumes and wearing those flat hats with tassels, the 305ers just had too much energy to stay quietly in line. And when they saw me, they must have seen their chance to join the party.

They had broken into a run. The boy whose desk had been next to Ricky's was leading the charge. Maybe he couldn't slow down in time, or maybe he had just forgotten to allow enough space in which to stop; but for whatever reason, he ran right into me, almost knocking me over. Then the others thought we were playing a game of pile-on, so I had the whole group banging into me.

Even though I was doing everything I could just to stay on my feet, I saw the crowd around us part once again, but this time in a circle much wider than the one that had formed when Mom was taking her pictures. I didn't care though. For a moment, I felt as if nothing had changed, as if Ricky was still with us.

When I turned to my mother, I saw her crying. At first, I thought they were tears of sadness. But as I watched her start to backpedal, I saw the look of fear in her eyes. Fear that her only living son would never escape the curse. Fear that her family would never achieve what for her had been the most elusive of dreams: that of being a normal, everyday, average family. My mother did not have grandiose dreams, just unrealistic ones.

In a way, my graduation party felt as if it was my parents' coming-out party. They had looked so forward to it. A perfectly normal party for a perfectly normal graduate. But I wasn't the most friendly or appreciative graduate. I didn't want my parents to think that normalcy would be that easy to achieve.

Suspicion

I figured Suzanne would stay a day, or maybe two. But when it came to the fourth day, I began thinking she might actually stick around. And why shouldn't she? Everyone doted on her as if she were a messenger from Readers' Digest sweepstakes. Ardelle had already closed The Fieldstone twice just to take Suzanne shopping in Millerton; and when it was open, Suzanne was a bigger attraction than Ardelle's pies. Even Julia had taken to her. Suzanne was helping her fix up the old Dillon place; and Julia had begun to call Suzanne whenever she needed help moving something.

Sharon asked Suzanne to help us with the bean-walking, and it took practically half the day to teach her the difference between beans and weeds. Then for lunch, Ardelle sent out a heaping picnic basket with Julia, Myron and Grandpa. It was like our Sunday picnics. If I hadn't stood up to go back to work, we probably would have wasted the whole rest of the day.

"You sure don't seem too friendly toward Suzanne," Myron said, one night in his workshop. It was the first time this summer that we had gone to his shop after dinner. Julia had asked Suzanne to help her hang wallpaper — she wanted to give me an evening off, she told me.

"I just don't get it. Why's everyone so worked up over

her? They're making a bigger deal out of her than they are over Julia and Sharon and Lillie — and they're the ones who will save this place...if it can even be saved."

"Maybe we treat her different because she doesn't have to be here. Because she's here by choice," Myron answered, without looking up from the chair he was gluing. "Maybe we get excited over her for the same reason we look forward to your visit every summer, because we all crave a little injection of youth."

His last sentence stunned me. I had never heard anyone say that before, aside from those exchanges of pleasantries that always took place either on the day I arrived or the day I departed.

"You know, Glen, I think she could use a friend — her own age, someone who...you know..."

"You're crazy, Myron. She doesn't need friends. Believe me, I've known lots of people just like her." And I could have gone on: spoiled and arrogant, and accustomed to everything working out for them.

"Maybe you should get to know her before you decide that you do know her."

"Are you trying to give me advice, Myron?"

"I'm trying. Should I just give up?" he said, laughing.

"I've never known you to give me advice before."

"I've never known you to need it."

"You've got to be kidding me."

"No, I'm not. You've always been very mature and responsible, maybe even too much so. Maybe you need to loosen up a little and have some fun. I know the past summers haven't been the most exciting for you, but this one could be different."

"Believe me, Myron, I need more advice than most people. But regarding Suzanne — believe me, she comes from a different world. She knows how hopeless and backward this whole place is. She's probably constantly laughing at us, underneath that plastic smile of hers."

I didn't think I had said anything that would surprise Myron. But the injured look on his face was unmistakable. He and I had always joked about Grandpa, but maybe he never really believed that it was all hopeless and backward. Or that people would have any reason at all to laugh.

I always thought Myron saw through Grandpa, but maybe I'd been wrong.

I tried to think of some joke to make, of something to say that would wipe away my previous words. But the moment passed, and Myron went back to work on the chair he was fixing.

✧

We never discussed the war at dinner. We talked about it during the day, and we watched the news of it on television, but we never discussed the war at dinner. Until Suzanne brought it up one evening. She said something innocuous enough — asking Julia how she felt about her husband being in Vietnam, as if he was away on some fishing trip with his buddies and had left Julia behind, a fishing-widow — but it still triggered an almost unthinking reaction. As if her question were a sandwich thrown in a school cafeteria.

"We're proud of him, we're all proud of him here," I interjected.

"I didn't mean to imply that you weren't," she said, in a voice of retreat.

"But you're against the war, aren't you?" I said. I didn't know for sure, but it seemed a safe bet.

"Well...that issue could take all night to debate," she answered, maintaining that unflustered look of hers.

"So you're afraid to discuss it?"

"I'm not afraid. I just don't think it's courteous to monopolize the conversation. If you want to debate, we can do it after dinner. And those who don't want to listen won't have to."

"That's right, we have enough talk of the war. Let's enjoy the dinner," Ardelle said.

But I continued. "You think we're committing a war crime by being over there? You think we ought to pull out?"

"I just don't think America should be interfering, that's all," she snapped.

"That's an interesting way of putting it — interfering. So helping the South Vietnamese maintain their freedom is just 'interfering'? Living up to our promise to defend them is just 'interfering'?"

"You really think we're there because of some noble generosity? You don't think we have our own agenda?"

"I see. And if we have any self-interest in the matter at all, then we're just 'interfering'? Is that it? If a doctor treats a sick patient, then the fact that he might get paid makes his actions suspect, is that it? If someone is being given free room and board, then the fact that she is doing a little work means only that she is trying to squeeze out more for herself, is that it?"

"Alright, Glen, that's enough," Grandpa barked.

"Glen, I think you should apologize, right now," Ardelle added; and then, turning to Suzanne, said: "Pay no mind to him, honey, I've never seen him act so rudely before."

"Well, I'm not going to apologize," I said, pushing my chair away from the table and throwing my napkin onto my plate. "At least I'm honest — I don't make up some theory of interference just because I'm too cowardly to fight. You anti-war demonstrators are such chicken-shit's," I said, as I stood up and walked out the door. Although, technically, I had no idea as to whether Suzanne was actually an anti-war demonstrator.

I went into Millerton that night. Though I had announced that I wasn't afraid to fight, I was a little afraid of facing anyone after that display at dinner. But at least Julia, and Sharon and Lillie, now knew they could rely on me, and that I'd be brave for them.

✧

Myron was the first person I saw the next day. I had slept late, and Grandpa had already taken the truck to pick up some fertilizer.

"And I thought Johnny Carson was entertaining," he said, when he saw me walk into his barn. "Maybe I'll start selling tickets to our dinners. And to think that people look on this little ghost town as boring. She's got herself under your skin, hasn't she?"

"What are you talking about?"

"You know damn well what I'm talking about."

"Myron, you're so wrong. I don't know what happens to people when they get older — they must think every guy and girl is just a romance waiting to happen. Believe me, Myron, you're wrong."

"Am I? And who did you think I was talking about?"

I tried to appear disgusted, but Myron probably only saw the embarrassment.

"Hey, Glen, don't take it so seriously. In fact, enjoy it — that's what youth is all about. It's been a long time since there's been any of that here in Corcoran. So have a little patience with us old nosey koots, okay?"

I was glad to be working alone that day. I even skipped lunch; maybe I was a little afraid of going to The Fieldstone. But I kept telling myself that I was the one who occupied the privileged status here, that Suzanne was the one who should be afraid.

After quitting work early and walking into the house through the back door, I stood guzzling a bottle of milk in front of the open-doored refrigerator when I heard voices out on the porch.

"....I guess in some way it was the death that kept me here in Corcoran," I overheard Grandpa saying, as I peeked around the corner of the doorway that led toward the front porch. Through the screen door, it was easy to hear his loud voice as it spoke to Suzanne. "I guess it seemed too much a betrayal to leave. I know most everyone buried up there in that cemetery."

"But no one knew my grandfather very well, did they?"

"Oh, yes, of course. It doesn't take long in a small town. You see, he represented the great promise of Corcoran — the railroad. Nearly the whole town gathered at the depot the day he died. It was a shock. We had become so accustomed to sickly people dying that somehow I guess we were shocked when someone as strong as your grandfather died."

"What do you mean, sickly people?"

"TB. Tuberculosis. There must have been more than a dozen people who died from it. My mother had it. She battled it for a whole year."

"How old were you when she died?"

"Oh, she didn't die from TB. She was one of the few who survived. I was eight years old when she took to her bed. And I sat with her every afternoon. A woman from down the street came for the mornings."

"That must have been very difficult for you."

"Actually, I remember it quite fondly. My mother was a good storyteller. She began with her earliest memories, and every day she continued where she left off. That's a helluva lot of stories; I don't think I could ever come up with that many."

I silently disagreed. But I had never before heard that about Grandpa's mother.

"Remind me to show you the jar of soil my mother carried with her from Ireland," Grandpa continued. "She always wanted to remember why they had to leave, so she kept a jar of Irish soil under her bed. And she wanted to remember why she had come to Corcoran: to have enough land so that no one in her family would ever again have to leave. But, I guess, the land just wasn't enough," he said, with a sigh of regret.

"So your mother? — she recovered alright?"

"Funny thing, it was my father who died first. Healthy as a horse he was until that winter of 1908, when he came down with pneumonia. Died two days later. I was the youngest and still at home, so I became the man of the house. I had to quit school to take over the farm work. My brother always said that was why I loved farming, because I never had to put up with my father."

I heard Grandpa chuckle as he said this, but the chuckle had a ring of truth in it.

"So you didn't have much of a youth?"

"I think I had a great youth. I had freedom and authority, before anyone else my age. When I was in my teens, I was doing everything the men were doing. I helped build the church. I went to hear Teddy Roosevelt speak in Millerton when he made a stopover on his way to a hunting vacation in the Dakotas. I even got elected to the town council. I suppose I loved Corcoran because I never felt imprisoned here, and I never had to rebel in order to find my bearings."

"That's not the way it is with most people."

"And it certainly wasn't the way it was with my brother Matt. He and my father had a terrible row the day he left....Oh, your glass is empty, let me get you another lemonade..."

"No, I'll get it," Suzanne answered. I could hear her standing up. "Can I get you one?" she asked.

I quickly scurried across the kitchen and slipped out the back door, even though I had never heard the story about the fight between Grandpa's brother and his father. Actually, I had never really heard any of it.

I cut across Myron's yard, glancing back over my shoulder to make sure I was staying out of the line of vision of the porch. But once I was safely out of sight, I realized I had nowhere to go. And the truck was back at Grandpa's. So I walked over to the church.

In summers past, I had been a rather frequent visitor. It had been my escape, my safe-house. A place I'd go when I needed to get away from Ricky. He never thought of looking for me in the church. To him, it was a place you went only for Sunday mass. So I could sit there for hours, never having to keep an alert ear for an intruding Ricky.

It wasn't that I considered myself very religious, but I had always felt a certain comfort when talking to God. As if there was nothing that a god who had made Ricky couldn't understand.

✧

At St. Patrick's Catholic school, Ricky occupied a special place in the nuns' attentions. They saw him as a justification for faith, as a sign that God could give a soul even without a mind to appreciate it. But their vision of Ricky seemed to irritate my mother, who tended to see Ricky as God's cruel warning that he could just as well have done that to the rest of us. And as for the rest of the world: well, it seemed as if it was becoming used to living without a soul.

✧

The quiet spaciousness of the church and the subtle wood smell of the pews induced a kind of imaginative freedom within me. In the Church of the Sagging Roof, I could suspend reality. It was where I went to escape Ricky, and yet it was where I became most like Ricky — where I let myself become submerged in fantasy. As if God was all about casting off the ropes of logic and probabilities. ("A belief in God enables one's imagination to expand beyond themselves and their present," Grandpa often said, during his Sunday breakfast lectures. "Only God can give people the power to rise above the empty quest for self-gratification.")

Just last summer, the summer of 1969, I had spent hours sitting in the church, imagining myself doing something heroic and historic, as Neil Armstrong had done when he landed on the moon. I imagined myself being famous, being interviewed on television. I imagined the reaction of my former high school classmates. 'Wasn't he the kid who had the retarded brother?' they'd say to each other.

"I was wondering if I was going to see you in here again," Lorraine's husky voice boomed from behind me. "I haven't seen you in here all summer," she said when I turned around. "I thought you'd forgotten the place."

Lorraine had a tattered red bandanna wrapped around her hair. She was carrying a pail of cleaning supplies. (I'd forgotten that escaping from Ricky had its price.) She also had a habit of saying things that were so ludicrous. The church was the equivalent of a block and a half from my grandfather's house. How could I possibly have forgotten it?

"You used to come in here so often, Glen," she said. "I've been meaning to talk to you, but I didn't want to intrude."

"It's been a busy summer, Lorraine."

"That's no excuse. Think how busy God is."

It was people like Lorraine, I thought, that so often gave God a bad name.

"I'll remember that. Well, I guess I need to get back...," I started to say as I stood up.

"You sit back down there now," she scolded, pushing her hand against my rising shoulder. "I've got work to do in the sacristy. God wouldn't forgive me if I interrupted a visit from one of his not-so-frequent visitors."

As soon as Lorraine disappeared into the sacristy, I stood up and tip-toed down the aisle toward the door. On the way, I passed by the water fountain that Ricky always dipped his fingers into. And I suddenly remembered what I had so often prayed about in his church... and I suddenly felt a big hole in my stomach...and I suddenly knew why I hadn't been back here this summer.

I wasn't twenty feet outside the church when I saw Julia come out of her house, skipping down the front steps.

"Hey Glen," she shouted. "Are you doing anything? Do you want to go into town with me?"

"Do you mind driving?" she asked, after I had walked over to her. "I'm running a little late and I still haven't finished my list."

She didn't wait for my answer, she just threw me the keys and walked over to the passenger side of the car. As I climbed in, I expected her to be nervous and rushed — it was already five o'clock. But her energy was more of a giddily excited type.

"Three letters came today," she announced, when I asked her the reason for her mood. "His platoon was out on a mission — that's why he wasn't able to send them earlier."

According to Lillie and Sharon, bad news often came after a long absence of letters. The army, they said, wanted to make sure before it sent out "missing in action" telegrams.

"I'm thinking of barbecuing tonight," she said, as she jotted down items on her sheet of paper. "How about handling the grill for me?"

But on the drive into Millerton, as she started talking

about her husband, Julia steadily became more glum and morose. Her face was almost plastered against the passenger-side window — and I knew there was nothing outside worthy of that intense a stare. Then I heard the sniffles, and the quick gasps through which she tried to suck in her tears. But when she turned away from the window, her tears had hardened into a look of bitterness.

"I don't know if I could take it, I really don't," she said, speaking more to the floor of the car than to me. "I see all those mangled men that Lillie takes care of, all the arms and legs and faces that have been blown off. I just don't know if I could take that with Frank. So many of the ones who come back do so as half-men. I don't know if I could take it if Frank ended up like that Jake."

"I don't think you should torture yourself, Julia. Most likely, you'll never have to face that."

"Oh yeah, he might not come back with half a body, just a dead one. But all the parts will still be together, all wrapped up in one of those body bags."

"That's not what I meant. Odds are that...," I started to say, in preface to quoting the casualty figures that I had learned during my nights in the library.

"I don't think I'm that strong," she interrupted. "Not as strong as Frank or Lillie or Sharon. Sometimes I even wonder if Frank and I should have gotten married when we did, so young and all..." And then she stopped, as if a door had slammed shut on her thoughts. She stared down at the glove compartment for a minute or two; and when she popped her head up again, her mood was suddenly more perky. She said, laughing: "But what's that your grandfather says? — that every minute you spend doubting your past is one less minute you have to appreciate it?"

And I too had to laugh. To think that Grandpa was actually being quoted.

"Look at those protestors," she said, as we passed a group of anti-war demonstrators on the campus of the state university in Millerton. "Do you know what Frank would have given for a chance to go to college? I hate 'em, Glen, sometimes even more than I hate this lousy war."

I knew she was angry, but all I could feel was vindication. I had done the right thing at dinner last night, I told myself. There was no reason for me to feel ashamed — in fact, Julia had said what she had just said precisely because of what I had told Suzanne yesterday in her dining room.

Slumming

It was a late Friday afternoon, down at the lake. I had finished work early and gone for a swim. It had been a suffocatingly hot day, with humidity that soaked my clothes and made them stick to my skin. The dry dust from the fields had coated my neck and arms and face. Throughout the day, sitting atop that simmering old tractor, all I could think about was diving into the cool lake. It seemed like the only way I could cleanse myself of the heat and sweat and dust.

I was pulling myself up onto the dock when I heard a rustle in the grass. Startled, I spun around and saw Suzanne.

"I'm sorry, I didn't mean to startle you," she said.

"You didn't startle me."

"You looked like you were startled."

"Well, I wasn't, so there's nothing to apologize for."

"Maybe not for this, but I feel as if I should apologize for something."

She had come to the edge of the dock. Her hair was pulled back into a ponytail, and she was wearing a long-sleeved shirt.

"What do you mean, apologize?"

"I mean that I must be doing something to bother you. If you just tell me, maybe I can make it less painful for you."

"Painful?" I answered, with a mocking laugh. "I'm not pained. Nothing you've done has caused me any pain," I said, emphasizing the word pain.

She took a deep breath. "Okay, maybe that was the wrong word; but since I've been here, we haven't spoken at all, other than to argue. And for as small as this place is, I guess that seems to me a little strange, as if...maybe I've done something to bother you."

"Wow, you've been here a few days and already you have such power over me, is that it?"

Her face lost its casual demeanor and became draped with a curtain of glinty steeliness.

"So much for the friendly hospitality of small towns I keep hearing about."

"Well, this place doesn't even qualify as a small town, just for your information. It's a cemetery, with a few people around to mow the grass." I was going to oppose Suzanne, even if it meant ridiculing Corcoran.

"Oh how clever. What's with you anyway? Everybody else seems to like you, and from what I can tell you're pleasant enough around them. So what's your problem with me? And don't give me any crap about not having a problem. If you want to play a game, go pull up a chair at your grandfather's checkers board."

"Of course, that's what's been bothering me this summer. My mother hasn't been here to lecture me. How lucky for me that you've come to take her place."

"Forget it; I was just trying to be friendly," she snapped, shaking her head and starting to walk away. But she stopped a couple of steps later and turned back toward me. "What's the matter, are you afraid I'll get in the way of your little adolescent crush on Julia?"

"What the hell are you...?"

"What the hell am I talking about? Good god, your little boy obsession with her is so obvious. Everybody can see it. You're making such a fool of yourself."

"And what a mooch you're making of yourself. But then, you seem to be a real expert at that."

"I've known some uppity brats, but you really take the prize. I'll bet that's why you spend your summers here — because nowhere else will people tolerate all your pretensions of superiority."

"Pretensions!" I countered. "Talk about pretensions! I don't know why you're here, but don't think you can fool me as you have everyone else. I know your kind."

"My kind? And just what kind am I? Come on, spit it out. Or are you afraid?"

"You're the kind who wouldn't be caught dead with the likes of Grandpa or Myron or Ardelle if you were back at home," I shot back. "It's called slumming. Who knows, maybe your few days here will make for a humorous little essay — 'What I Did Last Summer.'" Though what I really felt like saying was that she was the kind of person who would snicker encouragingly when someone else made retard jokes.

"And here I thought I never left much of an impression with people," she said, her voice slightly shaken. She was staring off across the lake, not even looking at me, as though she was actually thinking about what I'd said. And the longer she stood in silence, the more regretful I felt. The more I wished I hadn't said most of what I'd said. Yet I couldn't just retract it. Nor could I apologize. So I just stood on the dock, looking off beyond the lake bank.

But it was ludicrous of me to even think of feeling

sorry for Suzanne. To feel sorry for her would be like Ricky feeling sorry for me because I got a "C" on a test. And yet I was sorry, because she looked as though she was taking seriously what I had said. Then I remembered her comment about Julia and me.

"I'm sorry I gave you that impression," she finally said, in a resigned voice. "I certainly didn't mean to, and... well, I don't know how I conveyed it, but I'm sorry."

"Look, I didn't..."

"No, you don't have to explain," she said, dismissively waving her hand. "But you're definitely wrong about how I feel toward the people here. Right now, this place seems like the only home I've got. To me, it's not, as you put it, a cemetery with people around to mow the grass. Maybe you can't understand my feelings because you've always had this place. I don't know. I don't know how you really feel."

Then she turned and started walking away. A couple of steps later, she stopped once again and added, in a flatter and more removed voice: "I want to stay, but if I'm causing any problems or discomfort or anything, just let me know and I'll be gone. Oh, and I'm sorry about the comment about, you know, Julia."

"Forget it, I didn't pay any attention to it."

"No, I'm sorry, really."

"Forget it. It's nothing."

✧

I was, in a way, scared of the men who attended our little picnics by the lake. And yet, I found myself slightly envious of them. I imagined how simple and invigorating it must be to have a real flesh-and-blood enemy to be afraid of. Perhaps that was the secret to courage: to have one fear that would wipe away every other one.

Lillie and Sharon had to borrow a special van from the VA Hospital to bring the four men who came for the picnic that was to be Suzanne's first. Two of the men were in wheelchairs, and a van equipped with a mechanical lift was needed to transport them — they were both very large men. Seth had also come back, along with a man whose face was completely covered with a cloth bandage.

Suzanne, it turned out, was not near as aloof and put-off as I had expected her to be. I figured the crippled and maimed vets would make her uncomfortable, but they didn't. She displayed no hesitancy in sitting down next to the men and talking to them, and occasionally helping them with their plates of food. In fact, she spent a great deal of her time with the most challenging of them — the one whose burn scars could be seen extending out from the edges of the bandage that covered his face.

Sharon told us that he had been back in the states for nearly seven months; and several weeks ago, he had been transferred to the psychiatric unit. He wore the bandage not because of any medical necessity, but because of his shame at how he looked. (He had been badly burned during a napalm explosion.) And yet somehow, he had let Lillie convince him to attend this picnic.

According to the bits of conversation I overheard, Suzanne had coaxed him into talking about fishing. She had never done it herself, she told the man, but she was fascinated by it. Apparently, he had grown up near a lake in upstate New York.

With Suzanne occupying the man with the burns,

Lillie and Sharon turned their attentions to one of the wheelchaired men, while Valerie hung close to Seth. Grandpa and Myron talked farming with the man whose biceps looked as if they had spent years baling hay and lifting bags of fertilizer. Julia orchestrated the food, and Lorraine suggested to anyone who looked as if they might listen that next time the men should come earlier, in time for mass. All the niches were filled. So I just laid back in the grass and let the sun warm my face.

The buzz of all the conversations around me almost lullabied me to sleep, until the sound of loud music and raucous voices came shooting over from across the lake. Two cars, each pulling a speedboat on a trailer, were positioning themselves to dump their boats into the lake. There looked to be about eight or nine people, all in their late teens or early twenties. It wasn't entirely uncommon for the more adventuresome to drive out and launch their boats into Lake Kilkenny, where the traffic was so much less than on the lakes in Millerton.

Tape decks were cranked up, coolers opened, and skis thrown out for the first skier. Then the boats started their high-speed circling of the lake. The whirring of the engines died down only when one of the skiers fell.

"Who the hell ever invented speedboats?" Myron replied. "Sailing, that's the only real way to travel the water."

"At least it's quiet. Doesn't scare the hell out of the fish," Grandpa said.

"Is that true? Does noise like that scare the fish?" Suzanne asked her conversational partner.

He shook his head shyly, as if not wanting to get drawn into any group-wide discussion.

"How much do boats like that cost anyway?" Ardelle asked.

"A lot," Myron said.

"Probably thousands of dollars," Grandpa added.

"Surely not more than a car," Lorraine exclaimed.

"Actually, they can run more than ten thousand dollars," the bandaged man meekly said.

"All that money going just to occupy idleness," Grandpa said, sounding as if he was about to climb on his soapbox.

"Where do they get all their money? Isn't the factory having troubles?"

The Millerton newspaper had carried dozens of stories about looming job cuts and increased foreign competition. As one editorialist put it, the pie was shrinking and the scramble was on to grab a piece. (There was nothing noble or pretty about living with reduced expectations, or so said Grandpa.)

"Don't they know there's a war going on?" Myron grumbled — a remark that made me sneak looks at our guests.

"Guns and butter," Sharon said. "That's what they call it — guns and butter. Fighting a war without cutting back on anything at home."

"Well, if any of 'em get to Vietnam, they'll find out soon enough what happens to their butter when they get a gun shoved in their hands," said the man to whom Grandpa and Myron had been speaking.

"Chances are they'll never go," Sharon and Lillie's man said. "I never knew anyone over there who could afford boats like those."

"I knew a guy who came from money," the burned

man said. "He was our lieutenant. He spent his evenings reading books. And he was always getting packages — clothes, tape players, books, fancy foods, things like that. He didn't do much with the platoon — he let the sergeant take care of most everything. Someone even said he was working on his resume. It didn't matter though. He was at the front of the column when he got hit. Blew a hole in his gut a foot wide. He lived for, oh, five or six minutes I suppose. Screamed like everyone else though, when the time came. Didn't matter what his resume said."

"You psych-ward guys always have the nicest stories," Seth replied.

"I'm sorry you had to go through all that," Suzanne said, touching the man's arm.

"Yeah, well that's all we get, pity."

"I didn't say I pitied you. I said I was sorry you had to suffer through a war."

"At least over there I had a face that didn't make people vomit."

"You still have a face. You could try showing it, you know."

"You have a thing for grotesque scars?"

"No, of course not. But nor do I have a penchant for handle-bar moustaches or hair that's combed over bald spots. But I like eyes. I like looking into the eyes of people who interest me. And I like yours."

Suzanne had broken the circle. She had stepped into the void.

"Wouldn't it feel good to throw away those hot, sweaty bandages?" she said. "Now that you're home, don't let us fill you with fear."

Then Suzanne leaned over and kissed him on the

neck, on the scars that weren't covered by the bandages. And I saw his adam's apple take a deep gulp.

I glanced over at the other men. They were sitting absolutely still, almost like statues. Almost as if Suzanne were speaking directly to them.

The two boats sped by, now racing each other. The shouting voices of the beer-drinkers sounded in a different world — a different world from this moment on the grassy shore, where a young woman had kissed a man whose face had been lost in some jungle in Vietnam. But gradually, eyes turned toward the boats to watch them speed away to the other side of the lake. And the two worlds joined.

"This is sure a nice spot you got here," one of the men said to Grandpa.

"It's peaceful," Seth added.

"You boys ought to move here," Grandpa replied. "Before the place gets turned into malls or cul de sacs, or whatever they're called."

Interlachen

"Eamon, I've been thinking, about ways we can bring a little life to Corcoran," Ardelle remarked, one day during lunch at The Fieldstone. It was a remark that grabbed my attention — normally, she took no part in Grandpa's delusions. "Why not revive the ballroom? Suzanne tells me that kids now days are going to concerts and dances in droves. It's still one of the biggest ballrooms in the county. We could do a little to fix it up and then bring in some bands."

It was not like Ardelle to be so enthusiastic about a new venture: she hadn't even changed her menu in all the time I had been coming to Corcoran. But as I later discovered, Ardelle had been showing Suzanne her scrapbook from her Broadway days. And Suzanne had played on the piano several songs she had written.

During the 1930s, Ardelle had been a dancer on Broadway. She had a scrapbook she kept in the diner, and didn't hesitate to push it on anyone who hadn't already seen it ten times. She had also kept all her Broadway costumes — hoping, she told me, that she'd have a daughter to pass them on to. Ardelle once tried to interest Valerie in her memories, but Valerie was not at all like Ardelle.

In my mind, when Ardelle made her suggestion to Grandpa, she didn't really care about Interlachen or

Corcoran prosperity. She was only interested in what she had always been interested in. And all that had to be done was get a band together and fix up a ballroom that hadn't been used in more than a decade.

To Ardelle, Will Kramer was a miracle sent from God.

✧

Corcoran had never been a microcosm of America. It had never even been typically American. The cycles of its history had gone exactly opposite to those of the nation.

When America was mired in the Great Depression, Corcoran reached its peak. Though soup lines formed all across the country, there was no food shortage in Corcoran, where gardens outnumbered the sidewalks. But then, when America prospered in the '50s and '60s, Corcoran withered away. It wasn't economic depression that killed Corcoran, it was economic prosperity. A town that by comparison to the rest of the country didn't look so bad during the Great Depression lost all its appeal when the good times returned.

According to Grandpa, Corcoran had some pretty zesty Saturday nights, especially during Prohibition. Being such a small town, and without any police force, Corcoran attracted a large, alcohol-deprived clientele who enjoyed the product of old man Sullivan's still. On Saturday nights, they'd stop first at Sullivan's to pick up a pint or two, and then go over to the Interlachen Ballroom, find a table for themselves and their brown-bagged Prohibition alcohol, listen to the orchestra, and maybe find someone with whom to dance. Afterward, everyone would wander over to The Fieldstone Cafe for a bite to eat.

Interlachen Ballroom was the largest ballroom in a four-county area. It had been built in 1921, and quite by accident.

The town council had decided to erect a small meeting hall. It ordered the lumber from a warehouse in Milwaukee, but somewhere along the line the order must have been confused with some other one. Because when the lumber arrived by train, there was enough for a dozen meeting halls. For months, the lumber sat in a huge pile next to the train depot. But before it could be hauled away, the warehouse went bankrupt. So, in a town where waste was looked upon as the worst sin ("Waste not, want not," I once heard an elderly neighbor of Grandpa's say, as she picked up pieces of string and wire and put them in a drawer marked 'Things which have no use'), a vote was taken and the decision made to build a ballroom. And they kept building until the lumber ran out.

Interlachen became a prime attraction for the orchestras and big bands that toured the Midwest in the 1920s and 1930s. Because of its size, and because ticket prices were the only source of revenue back then, Interlachen attracted the creme of the crop. John Philip Sousa performed there on the Fourth of July in 1923, and again in 1925, as did Benny Goodman and Glen Miller in the late 1930s.

The ballroom was still standing in 1970. It hadn't been used for years; but aside from a leaky roof and dozens of broken windows, it was more or less intact. It stood as a dark, ghostly, sprawling reminder of Corcoran's better times. Kids from Millerton used to drive out late at night and break into the building to drink and smoke. But eventually, Interlachen lost even that clientele.

Ballads of Hope

Before Will Kramer arrived in Corcoran, I had not known much about Sharon's husband. Nor had I been very curious.

Of course, everyone knew that Craig Schlomberg was the son of Martin Schlomberg, the owner of Schlomberg Manufacturing — Millerton's largest employer. And everyone seemed to know that he had enlisted. That was what everyone said about Craig Schlomberg: the son of the richest man in town, and he had enlisted. A fine example of patriotic duty, the old men and women from the American Legion said. His funeral, I heard, was a majestic ceremony of military ritual. He was a fallen hero. And all the honor that would have gone to him now went to his widow.

This was really all I knew about Craig Schlomberg. It was not until after Will Kramer arrived that I became more curious. During one of my trips to the library, I dug up some back issues of the newspaper from the period following Craig's death.

The February 11, 1970 issue of *The Millerton Observer* carried the news under the headline, "Craig Schlomberg Killed in War." The article reported that Lt. Schlomberg had taken his platoon out on a nighttime reconnaissance mission. Rumors of a Viet Cong offensive had put all the troops in the sector on alert; and it was Lt. Schlomberg's mission to search out and locate the enemy. As the article quoted an army spokesman, it was "a high risk, but vitally necessary mission."

The radio operator was just finishing relaying their position back to headquarters when the transmission suddenly broke off. Lt. Schlomberg had found the enemy; or more accurately, the enemy had found him. Faced with "overwhelming enemy superiority," Schlomberg's entire unit was wiped out within minutes. The next day, a massive air strike hit the sector and the offensive was thwarted. Lt. Schlomberg was awarded, posthumously, the bronze star.

The first mention of Will Kramer appeared in the issue of *The Millerton Observer* that came out a day after Craig's funeral. In this issue, it was reported that Lt. Schlomberg's entire unit had not in fact been wiped out, because one member of the platoon had not gone out on that night's mission — instead, he was lying on a bed in an army field hospital, with a bullet wound in his foot. There was suspicion that the wound was self-inflicted — a desperate attempt to escape combat.

The day after his platoon was decimated, Will Kramer was put under house arrest by the military police. "Cowardice in the face of the enemy" was the charge. He was dishonorably discharged a month later, apparently because of some agreement reached between him and the army. He would not contest the charges; and in return, the army would not send him to prison.

It had taken Will Kramer several months to make his way to Corcoran, and to Craig Schlomberg's widow.

I first saw him that afternoon when Sharon, Grandpa

and I came in from the fields together. We had been walking the beans and had come home earlier than usual, about four o'clock. When we drove up to Sharon's house, we all saw the strange man sitting on her front steps.

Normally, Grandpa would have made a great fuss over a visitor, but I think even he could sense that this man had come for a very specific reason — he had the look of someone on a mission. I think Grandpa could also see that the mission involved something about the war and Sharon's husband. We had all become quite familiar with the look of Vietnam vets.

I was taking a shower when Grandpa, sitting on the front porch, spotted the man walking toward the highway. By the time I was finished, Will Kramer was drinking a beer with Grandpa and being given the hard sell on Corcoran. When I walked onto the porch, Grandpa introduced me, quickly adding that Will was a carpenter.

"We sure could use a carpenter around here. There's more than a few houses that need some immediate attention," Grandpa said, probably for the third or fourth time to Will.

"Do people live in those houses?" Will asked.

"Of course not. That's why we need to get 'em in shape. You can't expect people to live in pig sties."

"You have people waiting to move in here?" Again, the tone was of disbelief.

"You gotta have the chicken before the egg. With just a little bit of work, we can make this place hum again. Did you know that in the last few months we've practically doubled our population?"

Maybe Will Kramer wasn't a vet, I thought. He didn't show the usual signs. There was no army camouflage jacket, and no long, rebellious-looking beard. Nor did his eyes seem to fit the either-or category I had come to expect from vets: either consumed with a harsh anger, or filled with a grateful relief of having survived the war. He was tall, with an unassuming posture. His grip of the beer can was strong and definite, but his demeanor appeared shy. He wore jeans that were frayed at the bottom, and boots that looked old and hot.

When I asked him how he knew Sharon, assuming as I did that his sitting on her front steps implied some degree of acquaintance, he replied that he had only just met her, but that he had known her husband in Vietnam. That was all he said, that he had known Sharon's husband and that he had come to pay a visit to his widow.

"And I have some business in Millerton," he added.

"Is that where you're living now?" Grandpa asked.

"I just got here. I haven't found a place yet."

"Where's your car?" I asked, glancing out over the street.

"Haven't got one. I've been hitching."

"Then stay here," Grandpa said. "We've got plenty of places. You can bunk up with us, or next door with Myron, or you can even have your own house, though most of the empty ones are still in the fix-up stage."

"That's very generous of you, but I think I'll just head into Millerton."

"Nonsense. You pay no rent here. We furnish your meals, and Julia's a great cook. And you can use my truck whenever you want."

"Well, that's very kind, but I..."

"Tell you what, at least stay here until you find a place in Millerton. Housing is very tight there, and expensive.

You'd be best served to do a little looking around before settling in anywhere."

I could tell from Will's debating eyes that he was tempted by Grandpa's offer. I could tell he was tired.

"Look, you must be hungry and worn out from your journey," Grandpa persisted. "We'll take you over for some dinner and then you can hit the hay and get a good night's sleep. How about it? Have you had anything to eat?"

"I was thinking of stopping into that diner I saw on the highway."

"That's The Fieldstone, but it closes at three. We'll take you over to Julia's for dinner. She fixes dinner for all of us. Sharon'll be there."

I hadn't thought until then that it was unlike Sharon not to insist that he stay for dinner, especially his being a vet — especially having known her husband.

"Oh, well, no, I can't. Really. No." Will's voice was definite. His eyes were determined and his head was more erect. If he had been tempted by Grandpa's earlier offers, he certainly wasn't by this one.

"Now don't you be worried about being a burden. Julia makes lots of food, and we love visitors. It'll be no trouble."

"It's not that. It's...I just...No, I don't think..."

"Stop your worrying. We'll take you over, and you can come back as soon as you're finished eating."

"You don't understand. I just don't think Sharon would appreciate my presence. I don't know how to explain, and I don't think I can, but dinner — I just can't go."

"Okay, okay," Grandpa replied, in a rare retreat. "Tell you what, I'll send Glen over to Julia's and he can bring back some food. I'd feed you here myself, except my cupboards are bare. Been gettin' a little spoiled I guess," Grandpa said, flashing a smile. "I'll take you upstairs and show you the bathroom. When you finish cleaning up, Glen will be back with the food. Go on, Glen," Grandpa ordered.

Seeing no sign of objection from Will, I stood up and walked over to Julia's. I didn't give much credence to Will's apprehensions about Sharon. It was just natural that his sudden appearance would cause a great shock to her, perhaps dredge up some sad memories, and maybe even cause an outpouring of tears. But she would be fine tomorrow, I thought, and maybe even by dinner. Will Kramer seemed like a nice guy. He was just being overly sensitive.

Julia was sitting on the couch when I walked in the door. Her arm was around Sharon, whose face was red and slightly swollen — but I didn't detect any tears.

"What's wrong?" I asked.

"Nothing, nothing at all," Sharon said, sitting up straight and pressing her lips together.

"Listen, Glen, maybe we should skip dinner tonight. Can you spread the word?" Julia said, as she walked over toward me.

"No, absolutely not," Sharon called out. "You're not canceling dinner. Not this late. Not when everyone's relying on it. Look, I'm just going to go back to my house." Then she stood up, adjusted her shirt, and started walking toward the door.

"I'll come with you," Julia said.

"I'm okay," Sharon replied, shaking her head. "In fact, maybe I should be alone for awhile. Come over after dinner, okay?"

"Are you sure?"

"Yes. I'll see you. Bye Glen."

Julia watched from the door as Sharon descended the front steps. Then she turned and walked bruskly to the kitchen.

"Awful early for dinner, aren't you Glen?" she called out, as she opened the refrigerator.

"Actually, I was wondering if I could get a plate of food, to take back home."

"You're not eating with us tonight?"

"Well, it's not for me. It's..."

"Is your grandfather feeling okay?" she asked, in a voice pitched with alarm. She was staring at me from around the corner of the kitchen door.

"Oh yeah, it's not for him either. But he asked me to see if I could get some food for a guy who stopped by..."

"It's not for that man, is it? Tell me it's not." Julia was now standing in the middle of the doorway, her hands on her hips.

"You mean the guy who came to see Sharon? Will Kramer?"

"Is your grandfather taking him in? No, don't tell me, I don't even want to know."

She disappeared into the kitchen in a huff of anger, but then reappeared a couple of seconds later. "Do you have any idea who he is and what he's doing here? He's going to make trouble for Sharon, I tell you. And God knows, after what she's been through, she doesn't deserve this now. Why can't people just let things be?" she scowled, as if she were lecturing the world rather than talking to me.

I had never seen Julia so worked up. When she disappeared again into the kitchen, I heard a couple of pans drop, followed by a long string of cussing.

"They're just upset," Grandpa said, after I told him the reasons for my empty hands.

"Yes Grandpa, of course they're upset. That's the point."

"They'll be over it by tomorrow. It's just the shock of the moment. Everything will be fine. But maybe you're right, maybe we should keep from stoking the fires anymore tonight. We'll go into town to eat. Will can come with us. It'll be fine tomorrow."

Grandpa was like that. He always thought things would be fine. He was kind of retarded in that way.

But there was something else, I could see it in his face. He had only one thought on his mind: one more house would be occupied. Corcoran would be one person closer to its revival. And a carpenter besides. Just think of what could be accomplished.

✧

Grandpa's dreams easily overpowered Will Kramer's reluctance. Will stayed with us that first night, and then moved into the old Finnegan house. Grandpa tried to persuade him to take the Kaisling house, which of all the empty houses was in the best shape, but Will insisted on the Finnegan house, which conversely was in the worst condition. I figured it was Will's way of punishing himself — he was a man who looked as if he wanted to punish himself. But also, the Finnegan house was the one farthest away from Sharon's.

At first, Will's presence caused a rift between the women (Sharon, Julia and Lillie) and everyone else.

They saw Grandpa's embrace of Will as a direct affront to Sharon. But Grandpa just brushed off the developing tension: "That's what living together is all about; everyone'll get over it, we just have to give 'em time."

When Julia stopped hosting dinners at her house, Ardelle went back to her old hours at The Fieldstone. And all of us naturally gravitated there. Grandpa said it was because we had grown accustomed to eating together, but I thought it was just because we had grown accustomed to good cooking.

For her part, Ardelle seemed to have an ulterior motive. She used those dinners at The Fieldstone to recruit for her new project — the renovation of Interlachen. Will was already engrossed in the job (Ardelle had somehow pried him away from Grandpa), as was Myron, who was repairing all the broken tables and benches. (Myron had become unusually irritable — he didn't like all the work that was being thrust upon him.) Ardelle had even convinced Lorraine and Valerie to help out. The bait had been Ardelle's promise to lend Will's carpentry talents to the church.

Given all my sudden free time in the evening, I also hopped on board, even though Interlachen had become almost as much Suzanne's project as Ardelle's. But I had cooled in my hostility toward Suzanne. I wasn't used to being confrontational, and maybe I had been wrong about her — and besides, Will Kramer now seemed the much greater threat.

"He's not doing any of this for anyone but himself and his guilt," Julia had said, when I questioned her about why Sharon was so opposed to Will's presence in Corcoran.

"Doing what?" I asked.

"Just...everything," she snapped. "Sharon shouldn't have to keep reliving her husband's death."

"But how? What's Will doing?"

"Oh...he claims he made a promise to Sharon's husband. Something about a monument to be put on some land his father either owns or used to own in Millerton. But his father doesn't want it, and Sharon doesn't want to get dragged into some big fight. And who knows if her husband even made that request. Personally, I think Will Kramer is a creepy guy."

I shared Julia's opinion. Even more so since Will Kramer was obviously a shameless coward. And the last thing I wanted was for cowardice to creep back into my life.

Anyway, with my sights set on Will, I sort of relaxed my suspicions of Suzanne, who really had been making a valiant effort in the bean-walking. On those hot, dirty days in the fields, where the thick stalks continually scraped your legs if you wore anything but long jeans, Suzanne never complained; and she wore not only long pants, but long-sleeved work shirts as well. Nor did she talk much while she trudged her way down the rows of beans — she was struggling too hard to keep up. I never told her that I didn't even try to get all the weeds, just the big ones.

Suzanne wore her hair pulled back into a tight ponytail when she worked. But by the end of the first row of beans, several long strands would come loose, probably from all the bending over. They fell over her eyes, as if trying to tell her that she really didn't belong in bean fields. And she was forever trying to blow the loose hair away from her hot face; across the rows, I could hear the whistling sound of her frustrated blows. Then, whenever we took a break, she would pull out her ponytail and redo it, capturing the hair that had worked loose.

One evening at The Fieldstone, after Suzanne had left early to go over to the ballroom, I asked Ardelle if she really thought Interlachen could be ready in time. "I mean, before Suzanne leaves for college," I said. (Ardelle's plan was not only for Interlachen to reopen, but for Suzanne to perform in it.)

"She's not going," Ardelle answered, barely paying me any attention as she began washing the dishes.

"What do you mean?"

"I mean she's not going."

"Why?"

"No money."

"But aren't her parents...?"

"They're too busy fighting. And besides, I don't think there's much there. Whatever came in went out just as fast, apparently. But I don't think Suzanne wants that as public knowledge, get my drift?"

Still, even if Suzanne wouldn't be going off to college in a couple of months, I doubted that Interlachen could ever be revived. Ardelle was suffering from a case of Corcoran delusions if she thought it could be. But as far as her delusions about Suzanne's musical talents — well, I was wrong on that point.

With the summer a particularly hot one and everyone keeping their windows open, we could all hear Suzanne as she played the out-of-tune piano Ardelle kept in her dining room. It was mostly ballads that she sang. They resonated perfectly with the surroundings across which they traveled.

Ballads about longing and loss and dashed dreams. Ballads that collectively became the anthem of Corcoran.

Suzanne played late at night, after the evening's renovation work had been finished and the ten o'clock news had ended. The soft chords of her music were like the desert to a long meal. They made everyone push back from the table of the day's work, take a deep breath of contentment, and cross their legs in relaxation. I never specifically asked anyone, but it seemed to me that we all started going to bed earlier — that we all wanted to be our most comfortable, and alone, for Suzanne's nightly concerts. Maybe it was just my imagination, but it seemed as if bedroom lights were going on and living room lights were turning off earlier. At least, that's how it was with Grandpa and me.

I just assumed that her nighttime audience was unknown to Suzanne, that we were all undetected eavesdroppers. Until she added something new to her repertoire. Now, in between her own compositions, Suzanne inserted occasional songs from the 1940s. They were ones I'd heard before on Ardelle's phonograph: she called them "war songs." Anyway, the next day, after Suzanne first played those "war songs," she was bombarded with audience feedback.

"What was that one you sang about the wife thinking about her husband who had enlisted?" Lillie quizzed Suzanne.

"'That Soldier of Mine,'" Ardelle interjected.

"Could you play it again tonight? — I loved it."

"And how about 'It's Been a Long, Long Time'? Will you do that again?" Julia requested.

"How did you ever come to know those songs?" Myron asked.

"They're mine, I've got the sheet music," Ardelle again interjected. "I figured Julia and Lillie and Sharon could use some real war songs, instead of all that modern stuff about Nixon and Ho Chi Min. Those are more like protest chants than songs."

"Hey, could you play 'Danny Boy'?" Myron asked. "I've been listening to Eamon butcher that song for years — just once I'd like to hear what it's supposed to sound like."

And so began Suzanne's request line. But it was Ardelle who took credit for this musical success, and it was Ardelle who began to live more and more through Suzanne.

✧

Ardelle's Broadway scrapbook was now a permanent fixture in The Fieldstone. It was as if she had brought it out so as to prepare for the next chapter in it — the Suzanne chapter. When a new customer came in, it was the scrapbook he was shown, not the menu. Suddenly, and to the chagrin of her patrons, Ardelle was more interested in talking than in cooking. But almost all her stories were prompted by Suzanne.

Suzanne was like that. She seemed to bring out everyone's stories. Like Grandpa's story about Franklin Roosevelt's visit to Corcoran.

"Wasn't it Al Smith?" I asked, remembering something about an Al Smith presidential campaign stop in 1928.

"That was in 1928," Grandpa scoffed. "But FDR also

had Corcoran on his itinerary in 1932 — he was going to give a farm speech at the Interlachen."

"But he didn't come?" Suzanne asked.

Grandpa nodded. Then he set down his fork and wiped his mouth with a napkin.

"Two weeks before his scheduled visit, there was a mill-worker strike in Millerton. It shut down all the grain mills, which left the railroad in a tough spot, since it had its trains parked at the mills and ready to be loaded. So the railroad approached the mill here in Corcoran, my mill, and asked if we could fill its train. It was a huge job for a dinky little operation like ours, but we decided to go for it," Grandpa boasted.

"How long did you have, to do the job?" Suzanne asked.

"We didn't even have the first car loaded before the strikers got wind of what had happened to the train. They showed up in droves. It was late, after dark. I had gone home to catch a few winks. We'd been working around the clock. There was a scuffle — some strikers started throwing things around. One of the lanterns they were carrying got thrown into a pile of grain dust, which is extremely flammable. Anyway, there was a fire. The elevator sustained a lot of damage — and we got a reputation as a strike-breaker. Not long after that, FDR canceled his visit."

"Is that when my mom's brother Matt died?" I asked, a circuit suddenly connecting in my mind.

That was how I described him — my mom's brother. I guess I didn't even think of him as Grandpa's son. It was my mom who always talked about Matt, and in possessive terms, as if it was she who loved him and tried to protect him from Grandpa.

I knew Matt had died in an accident, but the details had never been stated — other than that my mother blamed Grandpa. Or if the details had been discussed, I hadn't paid that close of attention. I never fully trusted Mom's interpretation of events; everything she ever said about Corcoran was so predictably hostile.

"Uh, no, that wasn't it," Grandpa muttered.

"What happened to your uncle Matt?" Suzanne asked, looking innocently back and forth between me and Grandpa.

"That was a couple of years later," Grandpa reluctantly began, as if feeling that he had no choice. "He died in a car accident. Went off the road, where the lake comes up almost to it, and drowned. Hasn't your mother told you about it?"

"She just said accident," I answered. Actually, she had said much more, though most of it being about how she faulted Grandpa for being so domineering and controlling and unforgiving.

"Well, she was being kind then, because she thinks I was responsible. All my children do. You see, earlier that day, the day he died, Matt had taken the plow into a patch of virgin land that I'd been setting aside. It was a stupid idea, I know, but I wanted to preserve a little piece of Corcoran the way it was. Dumb — like saving the first dollar you make. But when I saw what he'd done, I got pretty upset..."

Grandpa paused. Maybe he thought he didn't have to finish the story.

"You wanted to preserve something. There's nothing wrong with that," Suzanne said.

"You don't understand. I'd pushed Matt before. This

time...well, I pushed him too far. We had a big fight, and he stormed off. The car was going too fast to hold the road there at the curve."

I wondered if my mother had ever heard it from Grandpa's mouth. I wondered if she had ever really stared into his eyes, or listened to the regret in his voice. I wondered if he had ever tried to talk to her. I wondered so much that I didn't say anything all the while Grandpa gazed down at the table.

"So don't you see? If trying to preserve Corcoran cost my son's life, how can I possibly abandon it now?" Grandpa mused, as if answering a refrain of arguments that repeated endlessly in his memory. "The funny thing about it, I was a lot meaner during the good times. It's the hard times that have mellowed me."

Blinkers

A couple of days later, Suzanne and I were all alone in the field. Grandpa had gone into Millerton to meet with a developer who was trying to get the county to force Grandpa to sell. They said it was in the public interest — jobs and development and all that.

Lately, especially since Will Kramer's arrival, there had been a lot of trips into Millerton. Will was going everyday, borrowing Grandpa's pickup truck, and even one of Grandpa's ties. (Will hadn't brought much of a wardrobe with him.) And Sharon was also going in more often. Just this morning, I had seen her get into her car, dressed as if she was going to some kind of business meeting — not in the kind of clothes she wore to the V.A.

And so it was just Suzanne and me, and sixty acres of beans and weeds ahead of us.

"I never would have imagined that places like this existed," Suzanne said, when we took our first break under a big oak tree.

"What do you mean?"

"I mean this little pocket of life, tucked away where it's practically invisible, where the number of residents is less than the number of students in my French class."

"They're called blinkers — if you blink as you're driving along the highway, you miss them."

"Blinkers — I've never heard that term. Did you make it up?"

"Not really."

As she stared out across the field, she blew away a long strand of hair that had fallen over her eyes. "Maybe it's a blinker, but I've seen things here I've never seen before," she said.

"Right, like crazy people living in falling-down houses." I wasn't sure I wanted to take Suzanne seriously.

"No, I mean it. Back in Seattle, I never saw the war as I do here. You want to hear something silly? Since I've been here, I've gone into the public library in Millerton, just to read up on the war. Isn't that silly? I had all the chances in the world to read about it in Seattle, and yet it's here that I finally do it."

She looked at me as if she really expected an answer. "I guess it all depends on when your interest is sparked," I said.

"And I guess you midwestern boys are more mature than your counterparts on the west coast."

"How so? What are you talking about?"

"Like the war — you know an awful lot about it. And like the picnics — you're so...at ease with those men. And they can be kind of scary. All the injuries and mutilations, and all the volatile emotions. But you can handle it."

She was picking at some grass as she spoke, and her head was pointed down, away from me. I felt almost guilty, as if it were me who should be saying those things to her.

"So how many summers have you spent here?" she asked.

"I don't know — maybe seven or eight, or nine."

"What do you like best about Corcoran?"

"Getting away from home. My grandfather's easier to live with than my mother."

Suzanne looked at me as if she thought I was just being flippant. "Yeah, I guess I could say the same about Ardelle," she said. "But...well, you know what I like? I like the closeness of everything. The way the fields come right up to the houses. The way I can look out my window and see where I'll be working that day. The way all Ardelle's customers never have to look at the menu. Even the cemetery — I like how close it is. I always thought it would be spooky living by a cemetery, but it's not."

"But remember, you're seeing Corcoran during unusual circumstances," I said.

"And can you just imagine the circumstances under which Will is seeing it?"

"You mean, other than trying to assuage his guilt, at Sharon's expense?"

"Imagine what it took for him to come here, what he must be going through. And I think the women are being kind of cruel to him. I mean, they do so much for vets they don't even know. Shouldn't they be a little kinder to Will?"

"Being kind is a lot different than forgiving."

"You really think he has to be forgiven? And what difference would it have made? If he had gone on that mission, he'd just be dead too. It wouldn't have saved anyone. And you don't think it takes guts to come here and face everyone?"

"Let's not argue about it."

"Okay, but I'll tell you something: seeing Will Kramer

makes me realize how small my own problems are. Seeing someone like Will Kramer makes me forget about my own petty anxieties."

Funny, I thought, but it was just the opposite for me.

Suzanne glanced over at the rows of beans; and when she looked back at me, her slightly raised eyebrows carried a questioning look. Is it time to be getting back to work, or are we going to talk more? the look asked.

I wanted to pick the latter. I wanted to head down to the lake and stretch out on the cool grass and feel the breeze blow over my face. Mornings were the best time of day during the summer. The sun wasn't yet hot, the bugs weren't out, and there was still the faintest fragrance of dew on the grass.

I wanted to lie back and close my eyes and let Suzanne talk. I wanted her to say something that told me the slate was wiped clean with us. But I was deluding myself. We couldn't have talked so comfortably if we made such a deliberate attempt at it. I had learned that with Myron, and then Julia — it was the distraction of work that took the self-conscious edge off of talks like these.

"I love your grandfather — we won't argue about that, right?" she said, out of the blue. "I've never known anyone like him. And his dreams. My father's only real dream is to retire early, and buy a beach house."

"Don't be comparing rational dreams to delusions," I replied, stopping myself before mentioning Ardelle's Interlachen fantasy.

"I thought we weren't going to argue."

"I was just clarifying."

"You poke fun at him, but you're very protective of

your grandfather, aren't you? That's why you've been so... guarded around me: you're afraid I'm taking advantage."

She flashed me a quick, glancing smile. It seemed like a testing-the-waters kind of smile. But I didn't know how to respond. I didn't think I could do it in the one or two sentence way that she had done.

"What do you think about Valerie's big move?" Suzanne asked, not letting the silence between us stretch on.

"What move is that?"

"Asking Seth to dinner, tomorrow night. She's all excited."

"Well, I guess she should be — she's waited a long time."

"Though not as long as Myron."

"Myron? My god, who has he asked?"

"No, not that. I mean his G.E.D. — he's taking a correspondence course."

"You're kidding. Why?"

"I think the real reason is because you've just graduated, and he doesn't want to feel behind."

"That doesn't sound like the Myron I know. But why didn't he tell me?"

"Maybe because you've got so much to do; because he doesn't want to bother you. Everyone seems to look on you as the man in charge."

"Grandpa's the only one who's ever been in charge around here."

"That's not how he sees it. He thinks you'll fix everything that he's messed up."

The nice thing about deluded people, I had learned, was that they sometimes saw you through the lens of heroic delusions.

"No one could ever take Grandpa's place," I said.

"Yeah, he does have a way of making people believe."

And yet again, we fell into a silence.

"Ardelle talks a lot about your brother," Suzanne said, picking up a twig from off the ground. "She misses him."

I braced myself for her to be condescending, to tell me what a patient brother I'd been. I waited for her to be presumptive, to make some comment about how tough it must have been. I waited for her to be nosy, to ask how I could have spent so much time with a retarded brother. I waited, but Suzanne didn't say anything.

"Well, I suppose we should get back to work," was what she finally did say. And with that, she grabbed her hoe and stood up.

But as I watched her begin chopping at the weeds, I felt like telling her that I wasn't as they all saw me. I felt like talking about Ricky.

Blooms of Light

From the grassy bank of Lake Kilkenny, we could see the Fourth of July fireworks being set off at the county fairgrounds, two miles away. Every year we had our own July Fourth celebration there on the lake's edge. Myron built a big bonfire; Ardelle brought marshmallows; and Grandpa arrived with a bag of sparklers, and occasionally a few firecrackers and bottle rockets. Then we sat down on blankets and watched the fireworks display. Afterward, Grandpa lit the sparklers and we all twirled them around in contrived playfulness — except for Ricky. There was nothing contrived about his excitement. He was, I thought, the only reason for our Fourth of July ritual. So I was surprised when this year, on the day before the Fourth, Grandpa asked me to drive to South Dakota to pick up some fireworks.

"There's more of us this year, so get a lot," he said, handing me a roll of folded bills. "And get a few extra boxes of sparklers — everybody seems to enjoy those."

I wanted to tell him that Ricky was the only one, that the rest of us had only provided the props for Ricky's annual dance-of-the-sparklers. But I could see in Grandpa's eyes that he had never considered himself just a prop. Nor, it turned out, had anyone else.

Myron, not about to have his bonfire overshadowed

by Grandpa's fireworks, had me hitch up a wagon to the tractor and then directed me to a spot in the woods on the other side of the lake where he had seen a large scattering of fallen branches. "Take the chain saw with you," he said. "Give me a full wagon, I want an extra big fire this year."

To Myron, the size of a bonfire was determined not merely by the height of its flames, but by how much it seemed to dwarf the people sitting around it. As Grandpa once said, "Someday that fool is going to deliberately burn down this town just to have a big bonfire."

Ardelle was also making special plans. She was going to serve shishkabob this year, in addition to the marshmallows. Ricky had never liked shishkabob.

Grandpa was so excited about this year's Fourth that he invited all his children and their families. But not surprisingly, they all declined. Mom had already told me that she and Dad and my sister were going to spend the Fourth at the Country Club.

✧

What always amazed me was how much my parents liked the Country Club, even though it didn't seem to like us. It wasn't where we belonged, and yet my mother was always volunteering to serve on some committee or work at some social event. She volunteered there more than she did at the Catholic school, which to me was the only place that truly accepted the Kinsella family, genetic flaws and all. It almost seemed as if my mother was embarrassed of all the attention Ricky received at the school, as if she didn't want to be known as the retard's mother. So instead, she concentrated all her social energies on being a normal member of a club that would never see her as normal.

Once, during public affairs night at the Country Club, the lecture was on the need for population control. Even though the discussion centered on birth control, there was a constantly implicit message about the increasing numbers of dysfunctional people burdening society — people who, in Darwin's scheme, weren't supposed to survive; people like Ricky. Mom sat attentively through the lecture, and never once voiced any criticism of it afterward. But to me, it was a sign that our family was not meant for the enlightened society of modern times. And that was something else I liked about Grandpa — that he never made any effort to fit in, that he was culturally retarded.

But what I couldn't understand about Grandpa was why he kept butting his head against the wall of his children. It was as if Mom was right: Grandpa was so insensitive that he couldn't take a hint, even if it kicked him in the ass.

✧

I didn't know how it happened exactly, but the rift between Grandpa and the women got patched up. Even though it had only lasted three or four days, it was a great relief when Corcoran ceased being a town divided.

Maybe it was outside events that had made Sharon less angry at Grandpa and less hostile toward Will. Maybe she had come to feel a little sorry for them. Or maybe, in comparison to their mutual antagonist, Will suddenly didn't look so bad to her.

Martin Schlomberg had Will arrested on the second day that he appeared at the front door of the Schlomberg house, refusing to leave until someone came out to talk to him. The incident was reported in *The Millerton Observer*, in a sidebar to an article in which Martin Schlomberg denied rumors that the Schlomberg aeronautics factory would be laying off workers after the election.

Martin Schlomberg was running for Congress. And the newspaper article focused on the proposed economic development projects that he said would revitalize Millerton. The biggest of those projects involved the Lakeview Development project. The lake referred to was Lake Kilkenny, and the property to be developed was Grandpa's. I had seen a diagram of the project in the newspaper. On one end of the lake, where Myron had sent me to collect the wood for our bonfire, was to be a specialty shopping mall — one that featured only designer shops. Along the highway, there was to be a second mall, an outlet mall, for those shoppers who couldn't afford designer prices and who didn't demand lakeside scenery while they shopped. And along the east side of the lake was planned a housing development — something called "Country Estates."

Grandpa ridiculed the development; he called it nothing but a distraction. "The problem with that Schlomberg fellow is that he's never had to struggle through tough times," Grandpa said.

'Tough times' was a recurring theme with my grandfather. It was what America was all about, he said. But I thought it was only what Corcoran was all about.

"Tough times are here, and nobody wants to recognize what needs to be done to start over," he said.

To my grandfather, America was also about starting over.

And for all the obvious reasons, Sharon likewise had very little affection for her father-in-law. But in addition, Martin Schlomberg was running as an anti-war candidate; and he had recently led a protest at one of Sharon's war-wives community events. There were also times when Sharon indicated that she believed the rumors about Martin Schlomberg to be true.

✧

We all stared hypnotically into the western sky once the fairgrounds' fireworks display started. Somewhere around the fourth or fifth explosion, I forgot that I was sitting there out of habit, out of deference to the traditions of summers past. I quit sneaking side-long glances at the others to see what they were doing and how they were reacting. I didn't try to see if Will was cringing every time a boom was heard. Instead, I did what I'd done for years before, when Ricky used to sit by me and rock up and down on his knees with each new rocket explosion. I followed the rising stems of light until they reached their peak and went suddenly dark, erupting a moment later into a bloom of shooting rays of light. Hypnotized by the methodic bursts of meteoric bouquets, I instinctively let out my sighs of wonder. To the chorus of "ooh's" and "aah's" coming from the banks of Lake Kilkenny, I added my own notes of amazement.

Even after the last rocket exploded, we all continued to sit in expectant silence. Hoping that there would be one more. That our chorus of wonder could harmonize one more refrain. That we wouldn't, not just yet, have to split up into our own solo voices.

We used up all five dozen sparklers. We had never done that with Ricky. And Grandpa had me shoot off all the bottle rockets and Roman candles. We never had Roman candles before — it was too difficult to keep Ricky away from them.

When I went to bed that night, I listened for a song from Suzanne, hoping that something of what I had felt during the fireworks had remained. Or maybe I was just trying not to think about what had been missing, what I had felt as I walked past the empty bedroom between Grandpa's and mine.

Forgiveness

When dinners at Julia's resumed, and with Will now joining us, all conversation about the war pretty much stopped. And Valerie was the first to fill the void.

"Lillie, do the vets get any relationship counseling there at the V.A.?" she asked.

"What do you mean, Valerie?"

"Well, they've been away at war, and it's not like they've been focusing on their personal life. So do they get advice or counseling on how to reconnect with that part of their life?"

"There's a whole psychiatric counseling wing at the hospital."

"But just everyday sort of advice, I mean. Maybe they haven't got any major psychological problems, just that they don't know how to go about getting into relationships...or dating. Does the hospital have that?"

"Valerie, what are you talking about?" her mother asked.

"I'm just curious as all. I mean, fighting in a war isn't probably a good relationship-builder."

Will Kramer rarely spoke at all during dinner. His attention was always fixed firmly on the food. He possessed a voracious appetite. Invariably, he would decline when anyone asked if he wanted another helping; but after being pressed, he would relent and once again fill his plate.

Julia often peppered Will with questions as she waited on him. Not questions that called for long, expository answers, but just for one-word confirmations.

"So how long has it been since you've had home-cooking?"

"How do you like the walleye?"

"Do you take onions in your salad?"

"Did you like getting letters from home?"

"It's not too difficult adjusting to being back, is it?"

✧

Despite the resumption of Julia's dinners, I spent my evenings in the new routine I'd developed — working on Interlachen.

Suzanne and I were removing some old windows from the ballroom when she asked, "Why do you think Will wasn't thrown in prison? I would think cowardice during wartime is something the military would go ballistic over."

"You have a different theory about Will?"

"He was in Vietnam for three straight tours of duty, that's two more than he was required to do. I don't think that's the mark of a coward. And besides, he was decorated for valor."

"How do you know that? Did he lay that bullshit on you?"

"No, he didn't," she snapped; and then, in a more retreating voice, "My dad's ex-partner is a Congressman. I gave him a call."

Suzanne's family was chummy with a member of

Congress? She knew him well enough to ring him up and ask for a favor; and he actually granted it? Suzanne was that intrigued with Will Kramer to instigate an investigation?

Suzanne was staring at me, waiting for me to say something. "Why do you like him so much?" I asked.

"Why do you not?"

"Who said I didn't?"

"Right," she said, with a sarcastic smirk. "I think maybe you have a hard time forgiving."

But as I stared back at Suzanne, I wondered if she meant the opposite — that I wasn't very good at asking for forgiveness.

"Or is it that you've never done anything that needs forgiving?" she then said, with a teasing smile that took the edge off her previous comment. "That's it, isn't it? That's what all this clean Corcoran living has done for you."

"Yeah, right. And what makes you an expert on forgiveness?"

"Isn't there enough guilt and regret in life without adding unforgiveness to the mix?"

"And what do you know about guilt and regret?"

"What do you?"

I almost felt like telling her, but I knew she couldn't understand. Her voice was too confident, her curiosity too innocent — she obviously had little experience with such emotions. And how was it, I thought, that a retard's brother could open up to a Congressman's confidant?

"I thought we were talking about Will," I said.

"I know we disagree on our views of the war," she said, after we had gone back to work on the windows, and in a fresh voice. "But I have to admit that it does seem terribly unfair that war protestors are taking over buildings, and yet Will gets thrown in jail for just wanting to talk to someone."

"Although, I imagine it's awful to feel guilty about other people's deaths," she added, as we moved on to another window.

The Retarded Years

In 1965, Ricky and I went home for the Fourth of July. Our parents wanted the family to be all together for the holiday. So they came to Corcoran and picked us up.

We spent the day at the country club, where a barbecue and fireworks display were scheduled. That's what everyone called it, the country club, but it was really just a golf course with a renovated old barn as the clubhouse — the kind of big, open, one-room building often found at public parks.

Dad was with a group of men huddled around the barbecue grills and Mom was fussing over Clare, who was just a baby, when a machine-gun crackle of firecrackers suddenly turned everyone's head. Some boys had thrown a whole pack of lit firecrackers at Ricky's feet, and he was hopping around the blasts like the town fool in a western movie who is forced to dance when the outlaw bully shoots at his feet.

"Shomeshing's happening," Ricky was screaming as he danced. "Itsh an attack. Brosher Glen, itsh an attack of marshiansh."

The explosions were over in a matter of seconds, but Mom just kept yelling at Dad, in front of everyone.

"You've got to watch him, Robert. I can't do everything. You've got to watch him. He could have set off the whole fireworks supply and killed himself," Mom shouted. When she was mad, she never called Ricky by his name, only by "him" or "he."

"Kate, I doubt it was Ricky who did the lighting," my father answered, in a loud whisper that tried to quash the scene his wife was causing. "And besides, the fireworks supply is over in the..."

"There you go again, making excuses. You can't just go off and leave him to..."

Her voice trailed off as Dad grabbed hold of her arm and turned her away from the gawking crowd. My father didn't like to have family discussions in public, especially when they concerned Ricky. At least in his public appearance, he was still in denial about Ricky. Mom used to be that way too. When as little kids we used to call him "Ricky Retardo," after Ricky Ricardo on 'The Lucy Show,' Mom would lecture us about not using such words in public. But as the years went by, she became too frazzled to worry about her family's public image. As the years went by, Ricky wore her out, probably because she spent so much energy blaming herself.

I didn't hear the rest of my parents' argument that day at the Country Club. I was paying more attention to the boy who had tried to scare Ricky with the firecrackers. He was surrounded by a couple of friends, and they were all laughing like weasels. I wanted them to be exposed as the culprits. I wanted them punished. I wanted to stand up for my brother. But I never did.

✧

We didn't see the fireworks display that night. And on the drive home, an icy silence existed between my parents. I knew they'd fight later that night, after we were all in bed.

Maybe it was in my own bed where I learned to be a coward, or maybe that's just where I realized I was one. I hated my parents' fights. It wasn't that I thought they were coming after me; I just hated the screaming, and all the sharp words. I'd pull the blanket over my head and curl up into a ball, as if bracing myself for a barrage that never came. My father always said I was an overly sensitive child.

The fights almost always involved Ricky, in one way or another. Sometimes, when Dad was late coming home for work, Mom would park herself at the kitchen table with a tense jaw and simmering eyes, holding Clare, and letting her anger rise to a boil. When Dad finally came in, with expectant eyes and arms waiting for a hug or two, she'd immediately issue a command about Ricky. ("I sent Ricky to his room — he got into some paint cans in the basement — you need to talk to him;" or, "Ricky needs watching — I have to finish getting dinner ready;" or, "I can't do anything with that son of yours — why are you so late?") Often times, on such evenings, the arguments would start even before we sat down to dinner. Ricky was like a bad chore that my parents were continually passing off to each other. I rarely saw them together with him — I rarely saw them smile around him.

Friday nights were the worst. It was as if my parents still, out of habit, looked forward to the weekend and carried this latent expectation with them throughout the week. But when Friday evening came along and there was nothing awaiting them other than a son who never made progress from one week to another, their expectation quickly sunk into an irritable resentment.

✧

One night, when I was nine years old, when my older sister was out on a date and my younger sister still a baby, the yelling jolted me from my sleep. Dad had gone out to the country club after dinner. He used to like to play cards there.

"You don't care, you've never cared," my mother was shouting. "You just close your eyes and pretend that nothing's wrong. What kind of a father are you?"

"And you never let us forget, never. My god, Kate, do we have to give up our entire lives just because..."

"Just because of Ricky? You'd like to put him in an institution, wouldn't you?"

"It's not him that's ruining our lives, it's you. It's as if you won't let us even try to live a normal life. I went out tonight. What's the big deal?"

"You're drunk."

"I've had a few, so what."

"You come home drunk?"

"Where else would you have me go?"

"While you were getting drunk, Ricky swallowed a handful of pills..."

"Is he all right? What kind of pills were they? Did you call the doctor?" My father's voice had suddenly gone from belligerent to panicked.

"He's okay, now. But..."

"What kind of pills were they? I thought we'd hidden everything dangerous."

"Well, they were just vitamins this time, but the point is..."

"Vitamins? You're bitching to me about vitamins?" A

moment of relief in his voice had quickly given way to a renewed anger.

"The point is that it could have been worse. He could have swallowed something worse, like turpentine or drain cleaner or..."

"Vitamins?"

"The point is that he has to be watched constantly. I take care of him all day, and at night I need a break, but you go off drinking."

"I went out for the first time in over a month, and I wish you'd go out too, but you never let us get a babysitter. You're so damned sure that all hell is going to break loose any moment."

"And it will, you just don't understand. Those vitamins tonight were a sign, a danger sign."

"Hell, Kate, everything is a danger sign to you."

"He's your son, Bob. If you can't handle the responsibility, then leave, go on, get out."

"You won't even try to live a happy life, Kate. You're destroying everyone in this household. Yeah, I do think Ricky would be better off in a place that can handle him."

"How dare you! If you gave me any kind of real help, we could manage. But you're nothing but a drunk. Get out, get out..."

"Damn right I'm getting out..."

Then their voices moved out to the living room, and I didn't hear anything more until the front door slammed. But the next night, my father was back at the dinner table, trying to act very interested in Ricky's day.

Recruiting Missions

The couple of weeks following the Fourth of July were the most peaceful and relaxed of that summer in Corcoran; and they coincided with the quiet period in the growing cycle. The crops had all been planted. They had been fertilized, weeded and tilled. And now they were on their own.

The corn was chest-high, and the beans had spread out so much that the space between the rows had disappeared. This was the time of year, in a farmer's life, to begin shifting gears for the fall. To prepare the corn-pickers and harvesting machines. To make sure all the necessary maintenance parts were on hand. To change the oil and check the engine belts. To get ready for the non-stop harvesting that had to be timed perfectly for that small window between crop-maturity and snow.

At least, that's what I had always heard about this time — the time when everything humanly possible had been done, and the crops turned over to God and the weather. But I had never before experienced this transition. We had never been able to plant all the acres in time, nor had we ever tilled all the rows before they became impassable. And of course we had never been able to walk all the fields of beans and clear out all the strangulating weeds. Before, when God was handed the reins, the crops were already at the miracle-needing stage.

Accompanying this lull in the farm work, a quiet routine had settled into the life of Corcoran. The renovation of Interlachen had become the primary task to which almost everyone, in one way or another, had become involved.

Sharon had decided that the ballroom would make an excellent meeting and conference center for the various veterans' support groups she was organizing. And maybe it was these plans that helped further ease her hostility toward Will. He was, after all, a very good carpenter.

One day, while Julia was in Millerton, Grandpa accepted an overseas package delivery for her. When she arrived home, she was so excited that she tore open the box right in front of Grandpa. But as soon as she saw the contents, she started crying. The delicate wood carvings were all broken, some in several places. Grandpa tried to comfort her, and then he took the box to Will, who didn't show up for dinner that night — who didn't show up until he had fixed the whole set.

✧

At first, I had spurned Will out of principle and fear: the principle that cowardice should not be coddled; and the fear that his cowardice was contagious. But eventually, both the principle and fear gave way to a feeling of kinship. I wanted to see him conquer his guilt and regrets, and I wanted him to show me how to do it. Besides, there was something in his manner that made me want to drop the charade.

"So you spend every summer here, helping your grandfather?" he asked one day, when we were working together on the ballroom.

"Yeah" — I didn't feel like mentioning Ricky.

His hands moved steadily and confidently over the siding we were replacing, almost as if he could do this job in his sleep. And I wondered if he was as steady with a rifle or mortar or knife. Or if his hands had shaken, as I was sure mine would.

"That summer, before you went into the army," I said, "were you scared of going?"

"I hardly remember what I was thinking," he answered, without interrupting his work. "That was back in 1965. I didn't know much about the war, or about Vietnam. I suppose I thought I'd go over there, beat up on a few hapless jungle-fighters, have lots of wild times on furlough, and then come home."

"So what was it really like, once you got there?"

"Oh, I don't...," he started to say, with a frustrated and dismissive laugh, of the kind that told me he found my question either too complicated or too naive. But then his laugh suddenly stopped, and when he spoke again it was as if he was speaking to himself in some far-away place. "Alone, that's what it was like," he said. "That's the word I'd use — alone. I always felt alone. Even when our whole company was out on patrol, I still felt alone. That's what Vietnam did to you. It made you feel all alone, and that you were going to die all alone."

There was so much I wanted to ask him. The questions were all bunched up in my throat like children rushing for the door at recess. I tried to get them to line up in some orderly fashion, and to let the student who had performed best that day be the first one out. I wanted to be the wise teacher, to show all the other teachers how well I could manage my class; but in reality, I was just one of the pushing students, wanting to squeeze out the door before anyone else. I didn't want Will moving on to another subject of conversation; and I didn't even care if my questions were stupid or naive.

"How could you feel all alone?" I asked. "I mean, being surrounded by the whole U.S. Army? Everyone in the same boat?" In the army, I thought, it didn't matter if you had a retarded brother.

"It was the death that made you alone," Will answered, staring at the board he was nailing. "People didn't die all together. They died one at a time, in deaths that were showy and gruesome. It was Stalin who said a thousand deaths are a statistic, but one is a tragedy. And the Vietcong know that. They kill one at a time. That's why they use booby-traps so much. They defeat their enemy not through slaughter but through fear. You have no idea what it's like for a platoon to pass by a soldier who's set off one of those booby-traps. It's as though there's no way to protect yourself, as though death has already picked out its individual targets and is hanging over them, watching them, waiting for the moment when they're all alone."

He stopped talking for a moment as he reached for another board. I wanted him to continue, but all my questions had filed out the door. I was too consumed with wondering what it felt like when on patrol: wondering if death had already singled me out.

"The uncertainty, that's what drove men mad," Will continued, as he started nailing the new board. "The enemy didn't wear a uniform. It didn't carry a flag, and it didn't march in rank. One time, we came into a village — it seemed quiet and friendly enough — and we were passing through, in two columns. A young woman came out of a hut with a bouquet of flowers in her hands. She walked up to the lieutenant, as if she was welcoming us to her village. Then, after he had reached out his hands to take them, she flung herself against him. It was a split second until the grenade exploded, tearing out the bellies of both of them. That's what drove us crazy. The uncertainty of it all. And that's what people back home don't realize, especially when they hear about atrocities committed by American soldiers. You go insane when you have no idea where death is coming from, but yet can feel its cold tentacles."

"Yeah, we get a pretty one-sided view of things back here," I said, trying to sound knowledgeable.

"But the one thing you'll never get is maybe the worst story of all — the number of officers who get killed by their own men. That's the atrocity the army will never reveal. But that's the trouble with not knowing who or where the enemy is — you turn on yourselves."

"What was combat like? I mean, were you afraid beforehand? How many battles did it take before you quit being afraid?"

"Glen, everyone was afraid, everyone — and all the time," Will said, turning to look directly at me. "The issue wasn't banishing your fear, it was enduring your fear. And that was a big problem — there was just too much fear. It corrupts an army, fear does. Hell, the only brave people over there are the journalists. They're the only people who don't try to get out of assignments. They're the only ones rushing to get in on the fighting. The rest of us — we just wanted to go home."

"Will we win the war?" I asked.

He coughed out a frustrated laugh and looked back at the boards he had just nailed onto the side of the ballroom. Twice he started to say something (something sarcastic and mocking, from the sneering look on his face) before he simply said: "We'll probably never even finish it; and there isn't a soldier over there who doesn't know it. When you listen to the politicians' speeches, all you hear is how we're sending fewer men over there, how we're getting less involved. That's not the talk of victory. Nixon and his generals may still be fighting the war, but on the streets of America it's already been lost."

I asked him what he liked best about being home.

"Sleeping," he said.

"So were you and Sharon's husband good friends?" I then asked, after another long silence.

"Sort of, yeah," he said. "Actually, not really. I was his sergeant."

✧

Will Kramer's integration into Corcoran had given Grandpa another of his brainstorms. He wasn't going to wait for people to come to him; he wasn't going to just rely on those small-scale picnics — he was going to start being more proactive. He began making trips to the VA Hospital, hoping to recruit wayward, listless and lonely vets to come live in Corcoran. Maybe the rest of America was uncomfortable with Vietnam vets, but Corcoran was eager to embrace them, he told whomever would listen. For Grandpa, the war had become a golden recruiting opportunity.

About a week after the Fourth of July, Grandpa decided to hold an ice cream social in Corcoran, with all the patients of the VA Hospital as invited guests. And surprisingly, a full busload came out on that Sunday afternoon, which led me to believe that those hospitals must be every bit as bad as their reputation.

Ardelle served the pies and cookies, and Lorraine and Valerie scooped the ice cream. Will and I had moved the piano out onto the front lawn of the church, where the party was being held, and Suzanne serenaded the crowd with song. Lillie, Sharon and Julia were assigned as hostesses, making sure everyone was taken care of — but in truth, Grandpa just wanted to make sure the women were in full view. "Men will go anywhere there are women," he told me.

After everyone had been served ice cream and cookies and iced tea, Grandpa called the meeting to order and outlined all the benefits of residing in Corcoran. No-cost housing. Automatic jobs on the farm. The best dinners in the county. A scenic lake untouched by the corrupting hand of development. Free burial plots. And then, of course, there was the litany of promises and possibilities: new businesses that could be created; the grain mill that could be renovated; the excitement of Interlachen's reopening.

Before they all got on the bus for the return trip to the hospital, Grandpa put out a sign-up sheet for any interested potential residents. Only a couple of men scribbled their names, but Grandpa figured it was because no one wanted to appear too greedy. "I'll put up a sign in the hospital recreation room with my phone number," he told me after the vets had left. "You wait and see, I'll have plenty of takers."

That night, Grandpa took me up to cemetery hill. I

didn't want to go, but he insisted. It was the best vantage point from which to view Corcoran.

✧

Usually, when Grandpa went to the cemetery, it was during one of his bouts of melancholic nostalgia. Sometimes, Grandpa would begin the evening recollecting some memory; and the one recollection would lead to one more, and another, and then another. When the bottle of Bushmills was brought out, I knew Grandpa would end up in the cemetery that night. From my bed, I could hear Grandpa's out-of-tune fiddle (he had learned from his mother how to play it) screeching refrain after refrain of "Danny Boy." It was not uncommon for us to have to go up to the cemetery the next morning to pull Grandpa up from the ground and bring him home for breakfast.

So I was stunned to find him there with Suzanne that day the county tax assessor came to do an appraisal. From the front gate of the cemetery, I saw Grandpa sitting up against the big elm at the far end of the gravestones. But it wasn't until I actually walked up to him that I saw Suzanne lying in the grass, hidden behind the massive trunk of the old tree.

I could tell they were talking about something serious by the suddenly silent looks on their faces. And after I told Grandpa about the tax assessor, he hurriedly rose to his feet, which was not like him, especially when he was sitting in his beloved cemetery, and especially for someone like the county tax assessor.

"I didn't mean to interrupt anything," I said.

"Your grandfather was just telling me stories. I guess

time got away from us. It sure is peaceful up here." She made no attempt to move or stand up. In fact, she leaned further back on the arm that was braced against the grass.

"So which story was he telling you this time?"

"Oh, about some of his regrets over the years, like about the big fuss he made when his daughter Sylvia was getting married."

"My aunt Sylvia? What fuss was that?"

"Here, sit down, out of the sun," she said, sliding over a few inches. "You know, the story about how your aunt blames him for the break-up of her first marriage."

"I've never heard about any first marriage."

"Well, maybe I got the story wrong," she replied, in a diplomatic voice, as if she shouldn't know stories that I didn't know.

"Oh no... I've probably just forgotten about this one."

"According to your grandfather, Sylvia married a man who, again according to your grandfather, was filled with get-rich-quick schemes. Just after they were married, they came to him and asked if Sylvia could sell a piece a land that had been put into a trust for her. Apparently, the man needed some cash for a business deal. But your grandfather refused; he and Sylvia ended up getting into a big fight — she said he cared more about his farm than he did about her. Well, you can probably guess the result. Financial problems, fights, divorce. Eamon said the marriage didn't even last a year; although he still feels bad about what he did."

"No, I'd never heard that story," I said. "But that's pretty much been the story with Grandpa and his children, I guess — lots of fights and arguments."

"Why's that?"

"I think they all hated growing up here. I think they still resent Grandpa for pushing this place on them as much as he did. And I think they see him as a demanding, domineering perfectionist."

"Well, what do they say about the hog-poisoning incident?"

"The what?"

This time, Suzanne didn't hesitate before telling me the story. "When he was a teenager, his chore was to feed the hogs. But one day he was in a hurry, he wanted to go into town with some friends, and he accidentally fed some kind of poison to the hogs. All of them died. It practically wiped his family out, he said."

I stared at Suzanne, expecting her to say it was just a joke. I couldn't picture Grandpa ever making such a horrendous mistake. He had always been a bit bizarre and off-center, but I had never seen in him the capacity to err in such a way. A completely unrealistic dreamer, yes. But a dangerous incompetent, never.

I wondered if my mother knew this story. I wondered if she knew how close the O'Shea family had come to leaving Corcoran, before she was ever born.

Beginnings

Grandpa's father, John O'Shea, had come to Corcoran in the 1880s. He had seen a flier in a Boston pub that advertised free land for anyone who could make the trip to Minnesota. It was an advertisement John O'Shea could not pass up, Grandpa told me. Free land. As if such a thing really existed. Back in Ireland, where most of the land, and all of the good land, was owned by English landlords, an acre of dirt was to an Irishman what heaven was to a Christian. Not that the two were incompatible, Grandpa said.

It took him six months to work his way from Boston to the plains of Minnesota. His first sight of Corcoran, with its gentle hills sloping up from the winding lake, made him immediately homesick, although he would later discover that those gentle hills were not the best farmland, which is probably why it was still available.

For three years, John O'Shea worked for Thomas Corcoran and slept in his barn. In the evenings, he farmed the forty acres the government had given him; and in the winters, he worked on a railroad gang that cleared the tracks of impassable snow drifts. After another four years of building a house at the edge of the town Corcoran was becoming, John met Bridgett McNally. She was the daughter of one of the town's more genteel residents

— the owner of the general store. Yet despite being a member of Corcoran's upper class, Bridgett McNally agreed to marry the man whose house still didn't have any windows. And their youngest son turned out to be my grandfather, Eamon O'Shea.

According to Grandpa, Corcoran's zenith occurred in the 1930s. Not that Corcoran prospered wildly; just that, relatively speaking, it suffered much less than did the big cities. At least there was food and clothing: the gardens still produced their vegetables, the chickens still laid their eggs, the sheep still grew their wool.

In 1936, as evidenced by a photograph that hung in Grandpa's living room, Corcoran could boast of a bank, a grocery store, a lumber yard and hardware store, a grain elevator, a restaurant and a ballroom. The town only had a population of about 300, but farmers from all around came to buy their supplies, deposit their checks and have a piece of pie. Having bought out Thomas Corcoran twenty-five years earlier, the O'Shea family owned several of the businesses, as well as hundreds of acres of farmland surrounding Corcoran. They also lived in the biggest house in town. But that was before times turned against my grandfather.

✧

"Beginnings — it's the best word in the entire vocabulary; and tomorrow's another beginning." It was something my grandfather always said, especially after a disappointment. "There's no failures, only new beginnings," he'd say.

People considered Grandpa an optimist. But what they didn't realize was that, most of the time, he was just talking about his image of Corcoran.

Confrontation

Ever since Ardelle had brought over a cooler of beer to the ballroom after a long hot evening of working on the roof, Suzanne and I had adopted the drinking of a few beers on the grass outside as a nightly ritual. Sometimes Ardelle joined us, and sometimes Grandpa or Myron or even Will, but other times it was just the two of us. We would lean back in the tall grass, soaking in the night breeze, and let the cold beer slide down our thirsty throats.

"Your grandfather has a phone, right?" she asked, stretching her leg out to rest on a large, round fieldstone that was sitting in the grass.

"Yeah, of course. We also have electricity, in case you haven't noticed."

"Very funny. But, it's just that I never hear phones ringing around here, except at the diner."

"Doesn't Ardelle have one at her house?"

"Sure, but it never rings. I don't think it's rung once since I've been here. And what I meant was — I love never expecting the phone to ring."

"You get a lot of calls back in Seattle?"

"No. In fact, just the opposite."

"I don't believe that."

"Well believe it. You know, even though you grow up

in a place, and know lots of people there, it can still be a pretty lonely place."

"What do you mean?"

"Oh nothing," she said, shaking her head in a dismissive way. "So tell me, do you find your summers here to be a welcome break from all those adolescent romantic obsessions?"

There was a bite in the way she said "those adolescent romantic obsessions."

"I don't know," I shrugged.

"I should have known better — you're a guy. You get to make all the first moves."

"There's no law against girls making them."

"Hey, you want to hear a funny story about my one venture into that area?" she said, her voice turning light and playful.

"Sure."

"I was a sophomore. My friends kept telling me that this really cool senior had a thing for me. So when I broke up with the guy I was kind of seeing, I let my friends talk me into making the first move. I wrote him a poem — you know, trying to be coy but giving lots of hints — and then stuck it in his locker. The only problem was that I had the wrong locker. And for the rest of the year, I had this scary-looking biker guy cruising my house."

"Whatever happened to the cool senior?"

"Actually, he later asked me out — I think he got the word that I was interested. But he turned out creepy. Or maybe I was just too young. At any rate, it was a lot of adolescent romantic obsession for nothing."

She took a quick swig of beer, with motions that were jerky. "Aren't first kisses just about the most retarded?"

she said, looking as if she didn't even realize she had spoken that word.

"Have you been on some nightmare dates?" I asked.

She started telling me stories; and what I most enjoyed hearing about were all the mechanics — the ways she was asked out, the seating arrangements in the car, the exit strategies. But there didn't seem to be any from the past year and a half or so. The way she talked — it was as if dating was a stage she had just given up.

The thing about having a retarded brother is that you're naturally drawn toward people with low expectations.

"You're not a big talker, are you?" she said, after I had yet again passed on another opportunity to expound on my own experiences. "I guess in that respect you don't take after your grandfather," she added.

I occasionally got the impression that Suzanne thought my lack of loquaciousness was a sign of modesty, or even intelligence. She had a distorted view of me, and I was intent on keeping it that way. Primarily because I had begun fantasizing about becoming her boyfriend. There were just things she said.

"Do you think you'll ever be a farmer, maybe even live here in Corcoran?" she once asked. "You think I could ever turn out to be a real country girl?"

Yet I didn't feel all that rushed — because for now, Suzanne was doing all the work. Not of the romantic variety, but of the friendship kind. She was the one who stopped over to Grandpa's house when Grandpa and I were sitting out on the porch. She was the one who always asked after an evening of work on the ballroom whether I'd like to have a beer. And she was the one who always took the lead in our conversations.

✧

When Suzanne told me that she and Julia and Sharon and Will were going into Millerton for a movie, I jumped at the invitation. I thought it would be fun to be out with Suzanne, somewhere other than Corcoran.

It had been over a month that I had known Sharon. We were clearly not intimate friends; but we had been exposed to the Corcoran effect — the feeling of false familiarity that comes simply from seeing another person or passing by their house every day. And the only people with whom I had ever seen Sharon associate were the sober-looking crowd from the American Legion or the VA Hospital Auxiliary. Certainly no one like the long-haired woman in embroidered bellbottoms who approached us at The Glass Menagerie, a bar where we had gone for a drink before the movie.

"Sharon, is that you?" the woman called out as she walked up to our table. "Where have you been keeping yourself? No one's seen you. Hey, what's with the Squaresville threads?"

If I hadn't seen the look of embarrassed recognition on Sharon's face, I would never have believed that she knew this woman who was wearing glasses with small flowers painted around the edges of the lenses. Sharon, on the other hand, was dressed more like my mother — a sleeveless denim shirt tucked into a pair of khaki shorts, white tennis shoes, and her hair pulled back into a loose ponytail.

"Haven't you even been to Shiek's?" the woman asked, ignoring the rest of us. "People still ask about you. Oh god, you're not becoming a nun or something, are you?"

Sharon wasn't really looking at anyone — not the

woman, nor any of us. "Actually, we've got to get going. We'll be late for the movie," she said, glancing at her watch and taking a last gulp from her beer. "Good seeing you again, Cynthia. Maybe we'll....er, I'll see you around," she added, as she stood up and gestured for us to follow. The bills Sharon threw down on the table amounted to a hefty tip.

"There's a huge party out at Torge's later on — you know, the usual. Come on out. It's all cool." And then Cynthia's voice died off into the background noise of the bar.

We were twenty minutes early for the movie. As we sat in our seats, waiting for the lights to dim, I thought I heard Julia ask about Cynthia. But I couldn't hear any of Sharon's answers.

Afterward, walking out of the theater, we all agreed that "Where Eagles Dare" was one of the best wartime suspense movies. We were immersed in a discussion of clues and their credibility when we started crossing the street to cut through Memorial Park on our way to the car.

The park occupied a full block in the downtown section of the city. It was where summer concerts and music festivals were held. But on this night, it was where a large crowd was gathered around a man standing in the gazebo and speaking into a megaphone. Every three or four sentences, he'd lead the crowd in a chorus of "U.S. out of Vietnam."

"Sharon, let's go around," Julia called out to Sharon, who had broken away from our group and was heading in a determined pace straight for the middle of the demonstrators.

Julia had a tense and uncomfortable look on her face.

But Sharon could just be taking a shortcut to our car, I thought. It seemed odd, our confused faces all told each other, but we followed her just the same. She was the one who had driven.

As it turned out, it wasn't Sharon who drew the attention of the protestors. It was Will, and the army T-shirt he was wearing.

When we came within sight of the man standing on the gazebo, he abruptly stopped his speech and pointed to Will.

"Brothers and sisters, we have a war criminal right here, in our midst," he cried, turning everyone's head toward us. "That man, wearing the clothing of aggression, is the one who has come to build a war monument on Sisseton Heights..."

And in that moment, I realized why so many vets at the VA wore long hair and scraggly beards — they wanted to camouflage who they were and where they'd been.

"...But I say no to war," the speaker continued. "I say we create a peace monument. I say we dedicate Sisseton Heights, not as a place of hate and killing, but as a place of love."

I don't know if anyone was really listening to the speaker. They seemed too intent on shaking their fists at us and crowding around us with their shouts of protest.

"Maybe we can't stop the American killing in Vietnam, but we can certainly stop this man from erecting his monument of war and aggression," the speaker shouted.

"U.S. Out of Vietnam!"

The protestors closed in around us as they began shouting their own epithets.

"Baby killer!"

"Peace, not war!"

It was just Will, Julia, Suzanne and myself being surrounded. Sharon, who had been up ahead of us, had disappeared into the crowd.

"Murderer!" I saw a woman yell at Will. Her face was red with anger; veins were swelling up under her skin.

Somehow it seemed as if I wasn't really there, as if I had suddenly been transported into a television set, and into one of the protest scenes that I had so often seen broadcast. I felt as if I was just watching from a different angle, from an inside angle. The more the protestors moved in on us, the more distant my eyes felt. All that seemed to connect me to the actual events around me was feeling Suzanne grab hold of my arm.

"War-monger!"

"Hail to Ho Chi Minh!"

I couldn't even hear the speaker — that is, if he was even still speaking. The crowd was on its own, moving to its own command. I felt Suzanne's arm tighten around me as the crowd swelled toward us. I watched Will, who in turn had his arm around Julia. And the more I watched him, the more awake I became — and the more I looked to him for direction, for leadership in the fight that was sure to erupt.

Just then, the first protestor to break the plane of the small space that separated us from them lunged forward at Will, spitting in his face. "That's for all the napalm," she yelled.

I started to work my arm free of Suzanne, getting ready to follow Will into combat. Yet the only thing on my mind was Ricky. The singular thought of him was blinding me to everything else. I was ready to go. I was ready to fight back. I'd follow Will, I'd do what he did. I wouldn't be afraid.

But Will did nothing. In fact, he acted more cowardly than I ever had. He shrunk back from the woman and lowered his head, and wrapped both his arms around Julia.

Once the crowd saw that it was safe, once the first protestor had safely made her attack, there was a surge toward us. Taunts led to shoves that led to punches. I was struck in the jaw, then I heard Suzanne scream. My mind went blank. I wasn't really seeing anything. And so I just started flailing with my fists. I hit what felt like three different people before I was pinned down on the ground by retaliating protestors.

I was lying on the ground, struggling for breath under the weight of I didn't know how many people, when I heard someone yelling: "Get outta here; move back; come on, get up, get off 'a there." Once the pile of protestors started to peel off of me, I saw the policeman's uniform.

He was pulling bodies up from the pile, and pushing others away from himself. They were shouting "pig" back at him, but he seemed to relish the opportunity to shove the protestors around. Then he spotted Will. "Oh, it's you," he growled. "It figures. Go on, get outta here before I throw you back in jail."

We walked obediently through the still-taunting crowd. As we approached the gazebo, I saw Sharon engaged in a finger-pointing argument with the man holding the megaphone. We slowed to a stop, but the policeman quickly pushed us from behind. "Keep moving," he yelled. In the time it took us to pass the gazebo, I overheard only a fragment of Sharon's argument.

"...And how do you justify your violence?" I heard her yelling.

"We reject violence. We're for peace."

"Then what do you call this? What do you call what you're doing now?"

"You bust in here like pigs, and then you blame us for defending ourselves?"

At the far edge of the park, once we were well past the crowd of protestors, we stopped and waited for Sharon. When she joined us a few minutes later, we all silently walked to the car and drove home.

We were almost to Corcoran before my own anger began to poke out from the stunned haze that had clouded me ever since the fight. I wanted to wait until I was alone with Will, but then Julia invited us all to her house for a drink.

We had just sat down on Julia's porch when someone said something about the incident in the park. It was then that I confronted Will.

"How could you do that? How could you just take it? You didn't even stand your ground. Is that how you were in Vietnam too?"

I kept my eyes riveted on Will. I just couldn't figure it out. I knew he was disgusted by privileged college kids whose radicalism made them media darlings, while kids from poor families went obediently to Vietnam and got labeled as war criminals. So he must have been afraid of the protestors; that was the only explanation.

"You don't fight just for fighting's sake," he said, without any emotion.

"Yeah, well, it doesn't seem as if there's anything you'll fight for."

"You have to pick your battles, Glen. You just can't fight without reason."

"And there wasn't reason tonight? My god, we were under attack. They spit on you."

Will laughed. "I guess spitting doesn't seem like much of an attack to me."

And The Band Played

We had moved Ardelle's piano into the ballroom; and while Suzanne practiced her music up on the patchworked stage, I found some quiet job in the back — far enough away to keep from being noticed, but close enough to hear.

"I don't want to be practicing while you're working," she had said, when I first suggested she practice during the day.

I pretended to be motivated by altruism, but it was simple selfishness that had prompted my suggestion — I didn't want her to have to practice at night; I didn't want to wait until ten o'clock to sit outside and have a beer with Suzanne.

"But that would be so rude of me — playing my music while you were doing all the work," she added.

"I'm used to working alone; besides, I like music while I work." Lucky for me, Suzanne didn't simply replace the batteries in the radio to which we had been listening.

Watching her play from the back shadows of the old ballroom, I wished that I had kept up with the piano lessons my mother had started me on when I was nine years old. I wished I could be a part of something that so completely consumed Suzanne. But all I could do is watch. And become jealous — jealous of how intimate she was to her music.

I soon learned that it didn't matter from where I watched her or how much noise I made while I worked. Once she started playing, Suzanne was no longer sitting up on the stage of a rundown ballroom in an abandoned little town. Not that I knew precisely where she was — I just knew she wasn't in the same place in which I had spent the last nine summers of my life.

She had a look of serene mastery when she played. As if, without the slightest exertion, she could simply command the piano keys to create the harmonies they did. As if the enticing poise of her slightly parted lips simply seduced the piano into playing.

My jealousy intensified after the other musicians began joining her in the practice sessions. Ardelle had hired five musicians, all male, from the musicians' union in Millerton. "Let me do that," she had told Suzanne. "I know about these matters," the former entertainer had boasted.

"She's hiring them with her own money," Suzanne later told me.

"I didn't think she had any," I answered, without thinking that my remark would only heighten Suzanne's worries.

"Glen, I feel awful about that."

"Look, there's no reason to feel awful," I answered, thinking more clearly. "Ardelle is having a great time. And besides, she's reliving all her old memories. If you ask me, she's doing it more for herself than for you."

✧

Maybe it was just the Corcoran effect that was making Suzanne and I seem more alike, more compatible; but I didn't care. All I cared about was that we seemed headed in the same direction.

I was making more visits to the Church of the Sagging Roof, though I made sure my visits did not coincide with Lorraine's cleaning schedule. And I was praying — something I had never done before. I had always just sat and brooded, and felt sorry for myself, and fantasized of someday living a different life. To me, the church had always been a dart board, at which I had pinned my disappointments. But during the summer of 1970, I prayed...and for very specific wants.

The priests and nuns at the Catholic school preached that people found God in their moments of greatest agony. But for me, during the summer of 1970, the path toward God did not wind through the province of despair — it didn't follow the roadmap of desperation, but of hope.

Or maybe I was just used to talking to someone who didn't talk back.

During one of my visits to the church, I saw Suzanne sitting in the front pew. Instinctively, I froze and started to backpedal. But the church wasn't that big, nor were there any other noises to camouflage mine.

"Hi," she said, turning around. "I didn't know you came here."

"I was just...looking for Grandpa."

"He went into Millerton, didn't he?"

"Oh yeah, but I thought he might be back."

"I think he left only about twenty minutes ago."

"I guess I lost track of time."

Suzanne stared for a moment, and then turned more fully around, resting her arm on the back of the pew. "You want to sit down for awhile? — it's nice and cool in here."

"It's because of all those shade trees outside," I answered, as I started walking up the aisle.

"I like having a church so close by like this."

"It's a good hideaway."

"No, because it seems so natural, so much a part of things. Out in the outside world, churches seem like some far-off errand you have to run. Like one of those distant antique shops my mom is always driving to but never buying anything at."

Suzanne, I noticed, was using more and more the phrase: 'out in the outside world.'

"You ever just sit and think about God?" she asked. "About whether he really exists?"

"I'm not that religious."

"Neither am I — or at least, I've never been before. But just before you came in, I was thinking: you ever watch science-fiction movies?"

"Sure."

"You ever see flowers or beauty or even vibrant colors in their depictions of the future? Never. It's always just bleak and stark and so unlife-like. Human beings can't even imagine something like a rose, much less create one. Isn't that proof of God's existence?"

"I think it's proof that science fiction directors have a morbid view of the future."

"It always takes you awhile to warm up, doesn't it?"

"Warm up?"

"Yeah, warm up to being serious with me."

She smiled, and I laughed. And over the back of the pew she crossed her arms and rested her head upon them.

"I've come to the conclusion that God might be contagious," she said, still smiling.

"You mean being in here?"

"No, I mean belief. Belief can be contagious. Once you start believing, even it it's in something small, you learn how to believe — and then you can believe in the really big things."

"So faith is a paint-by-the-numbers deal? I always thought it was a matter of revelation."

"Right, the bolt of lightning scenario. And maybe that's what it is. All I can say is what I've been feeling. You know, there's nothing but belief around this place — Ardelle believing in Interlachen, Julia and Lillie believing their husbands will come home, your grandfather...well, on and on I could go. But it makes me want to believe. And not just in that creaky old building."

"Doesn't everyone want to believe, in something?"

"I don't know," she chuckled. "Sometimes I think the world is too strangled by doubt to even want to believe. I mean, my parents — they're too consumed with their shallow notions of freedom to even believe in love. And my sister — she's too addicted to rebellion. You say the world wants to believe? I don't think so."

"Suzanne, I wouldn't take this place all that seriously. Granted, there's a lot of belief here, but I think it might be just a substitute for reality."

"This almost scares me to say, but I really think Ardelle believes in me. And I think your grandfather does too, although you'd know better than me. I've never felt anyone believing in me before."

The way she spoke, with her lips uttering the words that brought a slight glistening to her eyes, made me want to rush out an exclamation that I too believed in her, even if I wasn't completely sure that I did.

"I feel like I'm always laying a lot of stuff on you,"

she said, exhaling a long breath. "And maybe you can't understand me — you don't seem like a doubter."

"Are you kidding? With a retarded brother?"

"That's just what I mean. You had to believe in him, unconditionally."

"I don't want to talk about it," I said. But after a few silent moments added: "You're wrong though — it was Ricky who believed in me." And as I spoke, I could feel a sharp edge to the words. But maybe Suzanne thought it was an edge directed at her, because she turned away and looked down at the pew. And we sat for awhile in silence.

"I suppose I better get back to work," I said, feeling that one of us had to do something.

"No, I'll go; you stay," she answered. "After all, there aren't too many time slots when Lorraine and Valerie aren't here." And then her smirk broke out into a full-facial smile.

And as she walked toward the door, I felt a kinship that was deeper than any I had ever felt with Ricky. The thing about having a retarded brother as your best friend is that you don't have a lot of two-way conversations.

✧

The next day, I ran into Myron, limping his way to Julia's, forty-five minutes early for dinner.

"Hey Glen, I got a job for you," he called out. "Carl Hubbard — you know, from Hubbard Implement — says we can use one of his trucks for harvest if I fix it. But we got to go pick it up. It'll drive okay, though you're gonna have to take it easy. So will you go in and pick it up? You have to take someone with you though, to drive the pickup back."

"You want me to go in now?" I asked.

"There's no rush — anytime this week is fine. It won't take me that long to fix it. You on your way to dinner?"

And in that instant, an idea flashed in my mind.

"Actually, I might go in right now. I've got a big project at the ballroom that's going to take up the next few days. I'll see if Suzanne can ride in with me. Tell Julia we'll grab something in town."

Suzanne was alone at the piano when I walked into the ballroom. She was one-handedly pecking out some variations of a melody I had heard her playing earlier. I told her I had to run into town on an urgent errand for Myron, and asked if she could help out. Since we'd probably miss dinner, we could get something in Millerton, I said.

Hubbard Implement, as I'd suspected, was closed when we pulled up to its door. (And I was glad, because now Suzanne and I wouldn't have to split up.) So we went for a pizza, at a restaurant located on the same block as the movie theater.

"It feels strange not to be eating with the gang," Suzanne said, as she picked up the menu.

"Yeah, we've been kind of locked away in Corcoran all summer."

"I'm awfully sorry about that," she said, dropping the menu from in front of her face. "Working on Interlachen has pretty much soaked up every free moment you've had. I appreciate it, I really do. I know you're not doing it for me, but I still want you to know I'm grateful."

"Hey, if it weren't Interlachen, it would be something else. Some beaten-down old house, or maybe the church — or worse yet, patching up the cracked gravestones in the cemetery."

"But you've hardly been away from Corcoran all summer."

"Well, there's a lot of work to do," I said, letting her think what she wanted to think.

She nodded and set her menu down on the table, and I felt us trapped in a straightjacket of niceness. I wanted to say something honest.

"They're setting up for a concert," Suzanne said, looking out the window at the band shell in Memorial Park.

Men and women in white shirts were moving chairs and setting up music stands for the weekly city band concert — a cultural anomaly in the age of rock and roll. Once a week during the summer, the sound of Sousa marches brought to the park gray-haired couples with folding chairs and parents with young children. Once a week, for an hour and a half, Memorial Park returned to an increasingly distant past.

"They have them every Wednesday," I said.

"I heard from my mom yesterday," she then said, staring back down at the menu laying on the table. "My sister's in the hospital. She had a drug overdose."

"Is she alright?"

"Yes. Luckily for her, she overdosed in some public park and some passerby called an ambulance."

"How long's your sister been in San Francisco?"

Suzanne laughed a snide, mocking laugh. "Three years now. Who knows? — maybe she's still even enrolled at Berkeley."

"Were you and she close?"

"I don't think you could say my family was ever particularly close."

Maybe if Suzanne's eyes had been focused on me, I might have said that the only thing that bound my family together was a retarded brother who was now dead. But instead, I just asked: "So what did your mother say on the phone?"

"She blamed my father, naturally. And she complained about how everyone has left her to do their own thing. Of course, she couldn't talk long — she was late for her yoga lesson."

✧

We ordered a pepperoni, mushroom and black olive pizza, along with a pitcher of beer. Then we settled into some casual gossip about the gang back in Corcoran.

I didn't care what we talked about. I just wanted to watch Suzanne and listen to her voice. Even when she took a sip of beer or a bite of hot pizza, her face retained its smoothness, like a pool of water that ripples but never splashes. And even when she frowned, her eyes looked as if they could laugh at any moment.

The band concert was into its second piece when we finished our pizza. I waved Suzanne off when the bill came, claiming that it was a business trip that had brought us into town.

"Okay, then how about you let me treat you to some popcorn over at the concert?" she suggested.

We found a spot of grass, under a linden tree, off to the side of the park benches that were lined up in rows in front of the band shell. The city band was struggling through a march, but the audience didn't seem to mind. They had come just to sit in a park on a summer's night and have a band full of white-shirted musicians attempt to play a familiar march. I thought Suzanne would belittle the band's musical talent, but I was wrong.

"Tell me about your family, Glen," she said, when the band finished the march. "Your mother is your grandfather's daughter, right?"

"Yes."

"So is she a lot like your grandfather?"

"The farthest thing from him."

"How so?"

"If Grandpa sees hope, my mother sees danger," I began. And it was true: while Mom constantly walked a tightrope over the abyss of expected doom, Grandpa seemed to stroll obliviously across the topography of his life.

✧

To my mother, life was a never-ending process of preparing for the worst; and the Four Horsemen were forever pulling an extra horse. Consequently, she overreacted to the slightest hint of danger. When a newspaper article reported a possible link between a certain preservative and the occurrence of cancer in laboratory rats, Mom staged a Boston Tea Party, dumping down the sink the contents of every box and can of food stored in the cabinets of her kitchen. The next day, a medical group urged people not to panic.

Even the dinner table was infused with the drive to avert doom. Whenever we ate fish, we had to follow a strict eating procedure. Each bite had to be chased with a mouthful of spongy bread — the thought being that the bread would coat the fish bones and prevent them from puncturing the throat. Like everything else, eating was a dangerous activity.

Mom was even suspicious of good luck, thinking of it only as God's cruel way of weakening one's defenses to life's looming tragedies. Once, during one of the many fundraising events at the Catholic school, my ticket was picked as the winner of a fifty dollar gift certificate at Crowley's Hardware. But my mother refused to let me keep it. "I'm not going to let fate buy me off with a mere fifty dollars," she said, as she donated the gift certificate back to the school.

My mother was a little retarded that way.

Or maybe it was all Ricky. The thing about having a retarded brother is that you have to keep child-proofing everything.

It often seemed that their belief in insurance was the only point of compatibility between my mother the pessimist and my father the optimist. Mom was always looking for insurance against the bad things that would inevitably happen, and of course my father sold it.

Dad owned an insurance agency. He was a good salesman; he was drawn to people like ants to spilled watermelon. Whenever we went out as a family, my father disappeared for long stretches of time. It was just assumed that Mom would pick out our table at the restaurant and that an appetizer would be immediately ordered, since Ricky became very impatient at dinner time. Eventually, after greeting everyone he knew, my father would join us — no sooner sitting down and laying a napkin across his lap than he'd begin looking around the restaurant again. I think he was always a little irritated at my mother for not being as gregarious as he was. But someone had to look after his retarded son.

My father couldn't fathom silence and solitude. In

some ways, he understood Ricky better than he did me. As I was growing up, one of the most subversive acts I could commit was reading alone in my room. It didn't matter if it was Charles Dickens or D.H. Lawrence or even the Bible. Not that my father was opposed to education — just that in his mind, reading, like everything else, should be done out in the open, at the kitchen table, in the midst of people. My father couldn't imagine any normal person not wanting to be constantly in the middle of a conversation. It was as if inactivity and silent contemplation were the catalysts to genetic deformity, as if one's genes were just waiting for a moment of quiet passivity so they could slip into that blissful state of retardation. As if Ricky's problem was that he hadn't been busy enough during those first few months of life.

Sometimes I saw it as a sickness or an addiction, my father's uncontrollable need to talk. As a family, we were all retarded in our own way.

✧

"Your mom's not close to your Grandpa then?"

"Well, if resentment is the emotion we're talking about, she's damn close. I don't think I've ever heard her say anything good about her childhood."

"Aren't you curious — I mean, about how everything got so bad?"

"We never talk much about things like that. Maybe because all our attentions were focused on my brother."

It hadn't been an accidental reference. I wanted to talk about Ricky.

"Ardelle's told me a lot about your brother. She says you were..."

"I was a lousy brother. I was ashamed of Ricky. I never stood up for him."

The words just flowed out, as if they were water rushing out from an opened faucet. There, I thought, it was out. No more pretending. No more deceit.

"You shouldn't be so hard on yourself," she started to say. I knew she felt she had to say something. "That's pretty young for having..."

"You don't really know me, Suzanne. I'm a lot different back home than I am here."

"I was a lot different in Seattle."

"I've never gone to a dance....or even on a real date, alone that is."

"Are you thinking that's some kind of flaw...?" — I was staring up at the band, but I could feel her leaning closer to me — "...How I'd love to have not had many of the dates I've gone on. Glen, you had a...special brother..."

"Special brother?" I sneered. "Yeah, that's the official label. That's what everyone says — 'special brother.' But they don't mean it, not in the way special is supposed to mean. They mean retarded — they just don't have the guts to say it."

"I can say retarded if you want. I can say moron or dimwit. But if you want the truth, if you want the way Ardelle and your grandfather describe Ricky, then I'd say he must have been an absolute joy. And I wish he was here right now. I think if Ricky was here, we wouldn't have spent so much time fighting."

Even as I stared into her eyes, they didn't turn away. But I didn't know if she was really saying what I thought she was.

"To me, there's a beauty in...well, flaws," she added,

"and there's something beautiful about a person who can love the flaws in others."

The band had stopped playing, and scattered applause had replaced the music. A dog ran by, just a few feet away from us, chasing a frisbee. And I thought Suzanne may have deliberately brushed her hand across my leg.

And as the balding conductor was announcing to the audience, "Ladies and gentlemen, that was John Phillip Sousa's immortal 'Washington Post,'" Suzanne leaned over and kissed me, half on the check, half on the lips.

When my eyes finally regained their focus, I saw Suzanne with a smile that seemed a little bit like a question mark. "No one's ever kissed me before," I confessed.

"Well, kisses can be like people," she answered. "They like to be put into pairs."

With children shouting and dogs running by, Suzanne and I slid our bodies closer. I put my hand around her neck, and she placed both hers on my thigh. We kissed, even as the students were starting to arrive for their nightly protest of a war thousands of miles away.

I sat up against the trunk of the linden tree, and Suzanne moved in between my legs and leaned her back against my chest. We sat like that for the rest of the concert — she turning around every once in a while to say something, me smelling her thick dark hair as I rubbed my nose against it. I always thought Ricky's acceptance was more unconditional than anyone else could ever give, but Suzanne's acceptance of me seemed more real, more conscious.

"Won't it be fun when it's ready?" I heard her ask, in a voice somewhat muffled by the music.

"When what's ready?"

"Interlachen. Won't it be fun to have all those people there? For everyone to drift outside during the break? Hot and sweaty from the dancing; and cooling off in the night air. I used to play in a band in Seattle, and I loved the breaks as much as I loved playing. I loved wandering outside and being in the midst of all those people."

I muttered a "yeah," or something like that, but I was glad Suzanne couldn't see my face, because it probably had a look of skepticism on it. Deep down, I had always presumed that Suzanne was just playing along with Grandpa's and Ardelle's dreams for Interlachen.

"You really think we'll get that big of a crowd?" I asked, dipping my toe into the waters of her conviction.

"Why not? Interlachen's a great old place — a big place. Even if my band isn't the greatest, everybody love dances. And Ardelle has someone who's going to do the promotion for it. Don't you think it will work?"

What I thought was that if Ardelle had found someone to do the promotion, he or she was probably more experienced in promoting vaudeville acts than rock'n roll bands. But then, I had been wrong about so much.

"Sure," I said. "Maybe this summer is a time for things to work out."

She tightened her grip around my arms that encircled her. "I think so too," she answered.

There was something in her tone that gave me the feeling, even after all that I'd said, that Suzanne still had an inflated view of me.

✧

That night brought little sleep to me. It was as if I

couldn't wait for the next morning to come, as if I stayed awake just to coax the sun out of its slumber.

And yet, even after the morning light filled my room, I pulled the sheet over my head and burrowed deeper into the pillow. And I replayed once more all the memories of the night before.

Grandpa sent me back to Hubbard Implement, but this time he wanted me to take in an old tractor that Myron had managed to get running. It could make it into town, Grandpa told me, but it needed a new power take-off system that Myron couldn't install. Grandpa spoke apologetically, since driving a tractor that couldn't go any faster than 10 miles-an-hour wasn't exactly a sought-after job. But on this morning, it was a job that suited me perfectly.

Corcoran never looked as good to me as it did that morning when I steered the old tractor onto the shoulder of the highway. It never looked so good because I never before had such an intense desire to come back to it. On that day in July of 1970, Corcoran was, to me, the most exciting place on earth.

Taking Sides

We were cleaning up the dinner dishes when we heard the pickup truck rumble down the road and pull into Grandpa's driveway. Julia had held dinner a half hour for Will, before finally giving in to group pressure.

"I hope he ate in town, because there's hardly anything left," Julia snarled, as she opened the refrigerator door.

We continued with the dishes: Lillie and Suzanne at the sink, while I cleared the table and Julia put the refrigerated items away. Lorraine and Valerie rearranged the chairs, as Myron and Ardelle brought out the cards, and Grandpa took out his pipe. We carried on with our customary tasks, all the while waiting...for the door to open and Julia to scold Will for being late. But when it didn't, and when after our waiting had grown stale, Julia wandered out to the front porch. I heard her footsteps stop for a moment, and then the slam of the screen door. When it opened again, Julia was at the tail end of a sentence: "...put something on that," she was saying.

I looked around the corner of the kitchen and saw Will in the living room, leaning gently on Julia's arm. He had cuts across his face and on his arms. His shirt was torn, and there were stains all over his clothes. Julia led him to a chair and then went to get a washcloth.

"What happened to you?" Grandpa asked, squinting his eyes in vicarious pain.

A fight had broken out at Sisseton Heights, Will said. It was the park along the river where he was trying to get Craig Schlomberg's monument built.

As Julia dabbed at his cuts, Will looked more humbled than hurt. And when Sharon began questioning him, he looked even more so.

"It was just you? There wasn't anyone else on your side?"

Will shook his head.

"Doesn't that tell you anything? Doesn't it sink into that stubborn skull of yours?" Sharon's face was getting red.

"It doesn't tell me anything I didn't know at the beginning."

"You're making a mockery out of everything we're trying to do," she exclaimed. "Whether you intend it or not, the rest of us are getting tagged with this craziness of yours."

"Look, I don't mean for..."

"The people at the VA are beginning to think we're forming some kind of radical commune here. And contributors to our spousal support network are starting to have second thoughts."

"Then I should move out of here."

"Maybe what you should do is abandon this ridiculous crusade of yours."

"Actually, Sharon, I don't think the people at the VA are very upset at all about..," Lillie started to say.

"Well, there's also the matter of Eamon," Sharon continued. "Martin Schlomberg is one of the strongest supporters of that development project. And you can bet he's using this spectacle of Will's to stir up public antagonism to Corcoran."

"Don't worry about me, son," Grandpa interjected, looking at Will. "I can handle this."

There was a long pause during which Will stared at Sharon. But it wasn't a stare of hurt or anger. It seemed like one of calculation. And as I watched him, I wondered what kind of guilt could make a man who had acted so cowardly in Vietnam walk into a hostile crowd and single-handedly stand up against them.

"Like I said before," Will started to say, as he stood up, "I gave my word to your husband. He knew how his father would react, but he still made me promise. But he didn't know how it would affect you all..." — Will was glancing around the room, but it seemed obvious that he was speaking strictly to Sharon — "...So if you want me to pack up and move on, just say the word."

"Hey, no matter what you do, I don't want you packing up. You got a home here," Grandpa pleaded.

"I don't want you to leave either," Lillie added. "There are a lot more people supporting you than you think."

"And we couldn't be doing to Interlachen what we're doing if you weren't helping out," Ardelle said, following Lillie's lead.

"You haven't even got to the roof on the church yet," Lorraine complained.

"I'd like you to stay," Julia said, still holding the wash cloth in her hand.

"Hell, what do we care what people think?" Myron barked. "There's no way we can bring in that crop without help, and I want to get a new truck."

It was then that everyone looked to me.

"Yeah, I'm for you staying," I said to Will.

Sharon then stood up and walked toward the door. On her way out, she said: "Fine, stay if you want; what do I care? If that's what you've come here to do, I'm not going to stop you."

The News

The story on the "incident" at Sisseton Heights involving the "disgraced veteran" appeared on the front page of *The Millerton Observer*. Witnesses stated that when Will Kramer arrived to conduct his daily vigil, he began taunting and verbally abusing the anti-war demonstrators who were gathering for a speech by Martin Schlomberg. Being "outnumbered and obviously frustrated," Will Kramer then began shoving and slugging the peaceful protestors. "No injuries were reported, but a court order has now been obtained barring Will Kramer from Sisseton Heights."

On the inside of the newspaper, where the article was continued, an editorial described Will Kramer as "symbolic of all that's gone wrong with this country: disgraced in Vietnam, and violent at home."

Will's arrest, according to the article, ended up being the warm-up act for a rally organized by the Schlomberg for Congress campaign. When Martin Schlomberg finally appeared and stood behind the microphone, his words were greeted with "raucous cheering."

"I hereby dedicate my campaign to speaking out for all the courageous men and women, like yourselves, who will never be given medals for their bravery," the newspaper quoted him as saying. "And your bravery is an even more admirable one than the bravery of the battlefield, because you have faced ridicule and rejection by your family and by your own government. Maybe there is little I can do to have this country recognize your courage, but at least I can fight to stop this park, this communal gathering spot of yours, from being turned into a monument of war in the name of my son."

✧

Schlomberg received lots of coverage in that day's *Millerton Observer*. After his speech in the park, he attended a union meeting to talk about the need for jobs in Millerton. He promised that if the proposed development west of the city went through (west being Corcoran), there would more than a thousand new jobs created. So he urged his listeners not to give up on a project that was "being temporarily held up by a greedy and belligerent land owner." The alternative development plan, being proposed for the area around Sisseton Heights, was a much less ambitious project; and if that plan was adopted, instead of the Corcoran plan, far fewer jobs would be created, candidate Schlomberg warned. "We must be steadfast," the article quoted him. "We cannot let the selfishness of one person deprive an entire community of progress."

✧

But I still couldn't see how Grandpa's revered Corcoran was in danger of being put to any financially profitable use. I still assumed that there was no one on earth who would actually take out a bank loan to buy any Corcoran real estate.

Star-gazing

After Julia had sent us all away so that Will could lay down quietly on her couch with an ice pack to his bruised head, Suzanne and I were sitting on the grass outside of Interlachen, with the sun still more than an hour away from setting, when Grandpa came walking down the street. I gave him my seat on the bench, next to Suzanne, while she went to the cooler for another beer. It took only one question about Sharon's earlier statement concerning the developer's pursuit of Corcoran to get Grandpa talking.

"Oh this is nothing," he said, taking a sip from his beer. "We've faced much rougher times in the past. Why, there was a time when I honestly doubted whether Corcoran could survive."

That was just like my grandfather, I wanted to tell Suzanne. In his mind, Corcoran had indeed survived all these years.

"It was about a year after the explosion at our grain elevator. We were close to finishing all the repairs, but then some kids from Millerton snuck into the elevator late one night and decided to climb to the top. The last one up was the one who fell. He died instantly, the coroner said. And then came the lawsuits. That's when I actually thought Corcoran might fold, especially after my sister decided to sell all the land she owned. I had to mortgage everything to buy it. Now those were the tough times."

Even this story, which I had heard many times before, felt like a brand new one to me. Grandpa's stories were so much easier to listen to when Suzanne was present. She had a way of making him pick up the pace; and I just enjoyed the chance to watch her without having to say anything.

"So, your ballroom here is starting to take shape, huh?" Grandpa said to Suzanne.

"My ballroom?" Suzanne answered, with a kind of self-conscious chuckle.

"Of course. If it weren't for you, this place would never be getting a second life. You know, I always think of my wife when I look at Interlachen; and you remind me a lot of her."

"Really? How so?"

"Grace, that was her name, used to work at the ballroom — she sold tickets. And I had a job back in the kitchen. That's how I first got her interested in me. The orchestra usually played four sets in a night, and the help always got off for one of them — and I always took my break whenever I saw Grace taking hers. Then I'd ask her to dance. She always kidded me that I courted her on the cheap."

My grandmother died the year before I was born. Whenever my mother's sisters would come to visit, they'd stay up and talk late at night, at the kitchen table, usually with a bottle of wine. The conversation always came around to the same subject, and I often heard them express a back-handed sympathy toward their mother. They felt sorry for what she was put through, yet they also blamed her for not saving them from what they had to endure.

"So why do I remind you of your wife?" Suzanne asked.

"Well...she was full of energy, like you, and she was talented...and she loved Interlachen," Grandpa answered, tentatively at first, and then picking up speed. I could tell from the first part of his answer, the generic part, that Suzanne probably hadn't at all reminded him of his wife. At least not until now, not until he hit upon the Interlachen angle.

✧

When Grandpa finally left us, I asked Suzanne if she wanted to go for a swim down at the beach. There was very little breeze, and the lake water would be as smooth as glass; and just enough of the moon was shining to help us see the dock and the shoreline...and whatever else. And it was still hot from the cloudless day. A swim would feel great, I told her. It was maybe the only benefit of living in Corcoran during the summer — a private beach just steps away.

"No, I don't want to," she answered.

"What's wrong? Don't you know how to swim?"

"Well, that's...No, I never learned."

"We can just stay in the shallow part. You have to go out a long way before it's over your head." It wasn't strictly the swimming that I was so interested in.

"No, I just don't want to go in. I, I don't want to get wet." But then she said: "How about if we go down to the lake and sit on the bank and watch for shooting stars."

"Was your heart really set on a swim?" she asked, after we had sat down on the blanket we had brought with us.

"No. Was yours on watching for shooting stars?"

As she shook her head, she leaned against me and reached her arm across my stomach. When she lifted her head from my shoulder, it was an easy step to kissing her.

She slid down on the blanket until she was laying on her back. But her lips seemed to reach up toward me, not wanting to let go, coaxing me down next to her.

The longer Suzanne's soft lips pressed up against mine, the more my senses became numb to everything else around me. I didn't hear the crickets; I didn't smell the lake; I didn't feel the grass under us.

We had fallen asleep sometime during the night, and we awoke when the birds began their morning chorus. For a moment, my mind was confused, and I didn't know where I was or what day it was. And I was unsure if my memory of the night before was a dream or reality. Until Suzanne drowsily pulled me back to her.

The Empty Room

Grandpa was still asleep when I tiptoed up the stairs and down the hallway.

Several times each day for the past six weeks, I had walked that hallway. I had climbed the stairs, turned to my left, and walked the length of that hallway to my bedroom, located at the far end. I had walked past Grandpa's room, past the bathroom, and past the door that was now always closed. Not once had I opened that door and gone inside and sat down on the bed. Not until now.

Maybe it was Suzanne's comment that made me open the door to Ricky's room — the comment about how if Ricky had been here this summer I wouldn't have quarreled with Suzanne as I did. And she was right. The thing about Ricky was that he made pretensions pretty much impossible.

The thing about Ricky was that he would have made me see the truth about Suzanne right away. She would have smiled at him, and hugged him, and I would have known it was safe.

The thing about Ricky was that he made you forget about probabilies and caution and common sense.

✧

Inside Ricky's room were all the shelves and piles of books — Grandpa hadn't touched a thing.

I always thought Ricky collected books and magazines because, like aliens, they were a mystery to him. Just as some kids bring home stray animals, Ricky was always toting him some thrown-away book or magazine. Some had syrup stains on them — a sure sign that he had rummaged through someone's garbage — and others were all crackly and wrinkled from sitting out in the rain.

Whenever the public library had its ten-cent sale of falling-apart books, Ricky was the first one in the door. Then, after he spent all his money, the library volunteers told him to come back at the end of the day and they'd give him a free bag of books. Mom saw this as exploitation — using a retarded boy to cart off the unsold junk. But more generally, about Ricky's acquisition of books, my mother felt as if she were being mocked and ridiculed by life — the piles of books constantly reminding her that she had borne a son completely incapable of understanding them.

That was another difference between Mom and Grandpa.

✧

When I was nine years old, our parents moved Ricky and I into separate bedrooms. It was their first attempt to insulate me from the retarded fall-out. But Ricky hated it. He hated being alone. At night, even after a dozen attempts by Mom to get him asleep, he would sneak into my room and fell asleep on the floor next to my bed. That's where I'd find him in the morning, sometimes after stepping on him as I climbed out of bed. In the end, we became roommates once again, and Dad got a study.

I never told Mom; I never told her that Ricky slept in his own room in Corcoran.

✧

"The Three Corceteers" was what Grandpa called us. "She Shree Corceteersh," Ricky said, whenever the three of us went to The Fieldstone.

In the Shadows

It stayed with me. It grabbed a little spot in my mind and kept flashing itself — that look everyone had given me at Julia's, after they had all asked Will to stay. And I found myself listening more carefully to those offhand comments that I had never paid any attention to before. Like Ardelle's "What would we do without your summer visits?" and Myron's "Don't worry about me, I've just been restin' up all these years, gettin' ready for when you take over;" and even Lorraine's "You know, it's not too early to start planning for the church's centennial." I noticed that when they asked at dinner about how the crops were coming along, they all tended to look at me. And when Sharon or Lillie or Julia wanted to use one of the abandoned houses for something, they came to Grandpa, but they always wanted my assent too.

That's when I started trying to see myself in terms of expectations. That's when I started worrying more about the development project and Martin Schlomberg. And that's when I started having second thoughts about the statement I had made at Julia's house when Will had offered to pack up and leave.

"I read in the paper that you can't go back to Sisseton Heights, that there's a court order against you," I said. Will and I were working alone, putting a new door on the ballroom.

"Yeah, there's a court order," he acknowledged, not straying his eyes from the hinges.

"So, is that the end of it? I mean, there's nothing more you can do, right?"

"I have a signed codicil to Craig's will. It's witnessed, and it's legal."

"But why cause all this trouble for the living? Just to fulfill some promise to a guy who's dead?"

Will laughed an impatient laugh — one of those laughs you make when you've been asked the same question for the tenth time.

"There's a lot I can't see and don't know," he started to say. "Sometimes I feel like I've been living in the shadows for years. I never saw what Vietnam was all about, and I don't know how it will end, but I did what I thought I was supposed to do. And no, I don't know everything about Craig Schlomberg or why he asked of me what he did. All I know is that sometimes you just have to follow your own code of rules, and then hope for the best. It seems to me that, when you're in the shadows, you've got to rely on your own light. And my only choice is whether I live up to my word or I don't. Maybe that's a simplistic formula for life, but it's the only one I have."

Then he raised his screwdriver back up to the hinge and continued where he left off. He worked with the screws for awhile, until he stopped and stared blankly at the hinge, his screwdriver not moving. "But I don't want to hurt anyone else," he said in a tired-sounding voice, "so if you ever think I'm doing that, you tell me and I'll be gone, okay?"

"Sure," I nodded.

I had begun the conversation intending on issuing an either-or ultimatum: either forget about that monument stuff, or leave Corcoran. It was up to me to make the decision no one else wanted to make. It was up to me to protect everyone else from Grandpa's delusions. It was up to me to think of the future — that was how I had begun the conversation.

Up From the Foxhole

On an overcast Saturday in late July, Interlachen Ballroom hosted its first public event in eleven years. I doubted it could have passed even the casual eye of any building inspector, but that was one of the benefits of Corcoran — building inspectors had completely forgotten about the place.

The event was a party for the entire post-combat recovery unit of the V.A. Hospital — staff, patients, and friends and families. There were more than 200 patients alone, and both Julia and Ardelle had opposed inviting friends and families as well. They did not think they could prepare enough food and beverages for such a huge crowd. But Sharon and Lillie reassured them that almost no family and friends would attend.

"That's the problem with these men," Lillie had said. "They've withdrawn from the rest of the world. We'll be lucky if we get a third of the patients."

But we did much better than that. One hundred sixty two men came to Corcoran on that humid afternoon. It wasn't food that was in short supply, it was ice.

This Interlachen party marked the next stage in Lillie and Sharon's outreach program. The Sunday picnics had gotten too big. They had become too much of a chore to host every week. So Lillie and Sharon had decided to put on bigger and less frequent affairs.

Corcoran, I imagined, was like a foxhole for these men. A place to duck while the artillery fire of the world passed overhead. A place to venture into the combat without getting shot. To the men of the PCR unit, Corcoran was part of the real world only insofar as it wasn't part of the hospital grounds. It was the shallow end of the pool to someone who wasn't sure they wanted to go swimming.

Perhaps in an upper-class neighborhood of elaborate homes and neatly manicured lawns and shiny new cars, these men would have felt too inferior. They would have felt hopeless, as though they were too far down the ladder of opportunity to have any real chance at a happy or normal life. But in Corcoran, they seemed to feel just the opposite: that they could only improve on the lives we led, that they weren't too far behind in the race of life. If misery loved company, I figured, the patients of the PCR unit had to feel content in Corcoran.

Although it had been hectic getting ready for the party, the actual event was less challenging than our picnics had been. There was no pressure to make conversation, nor any fear that the wrong thing might be said. There was no circle on the grass, where everyone could see everyone else. And there was no feeling of confinement, that once you sat down you were there to stay.

At our Interlachen party, the vets and their nurses kept their own company. They divided themselves up into their familiar cliques; and it was our role, as hosts, to serve the guests, not to keep them company. The size of the gathering conferred an anonymity, at least for those who wanted it, that hadn't previously existed at our picnics.

Grandpa had said beforehand that he intended on talking to every single person who showed up. Never before had such a large contingent of potential residents come to Corcoran, and Grandpa was not about to squander the opportunity: "Getting them here is the difficult part; now all I've got to do is give them a reason to stay."

Nor did Myron embrace the new anonymity. He designated himself as the official greeter, and sat down with whomever would have him, and with whatever mechanics there were who wanted to engage in some friendly shop-talk.

At the other end of the social spectrum was Will and myself. I worked behind the bar, where the three beverage choices were beer, lemonade and water. I poured the glasses and pitchers that Lillie and Sharon and Julia carried to the tables. Occasionally, one of the guests came up to my makeshift bar, and we'd talk for as long as it took to fill the requested glass or pitcher. But generally, I was on my own.

Will had volunteered for the worst job — tending the big vats of boiling water in which the ears of sweet corn were cooked. Ardelle, Lorraine and Valerie also worked in the kitchen, but their job was to get the sandwiches and cole slaw that had been prepared earlier ready for serving; and they made regular retreats from the hot kitchen, primarily to get a cold glass of water or lemonade; and Valerie took even longer breaks, wandering frequently over to the table where Seth was sitting. But Will never once came out of that kitchen.

As the men ate and talked and drank their beer, or as some of them just stared blankly out across the open space of the ballroom, Suzanne's band had its musical debut. It had been Ardelle's idea. "That's what they do on Broadway, you know," she had told Suzanne. "They test out the act on a safe, out-of-town audience." And in Ardelle's mind, the patients of the PCR Unit at the V.A. Hospital definitely qualified as a safe, out-of-town audience.

My beer-and-lemonade bar was off to the side of the stage, but just far enough in front of it so that I could see Suzanne at the piano. I had heard her sing and play many times; but now, up on the stage, playing for an audience, Suzanne seemed far-away and untouchable. Behind the piano, hers was like a face in an impressionist painting. And though the words of the songs were familiar, the voice singing them was like the distant voices of the radio — a voice that could never be confined to Corcoran.

During each of her breaks, while the four members of her band grabbed a pitcher of beer and headed outside, Suzanne came over to the bar. And she would ask over and over how the band sounded, and I would say over and over that it sounded great.

It was during Suzanne's final break when we heard someone shout from up near the front door that the protestors had arrived. Suddenly, the tense sound of anxious curiosity replaced the relaxed buzz of casual conversation; and those who could move went immediately to the windows.

Outside, a long column of cars and vans was parked along the road; and their occupants were gathering around a man who must have been the leader. After receiving their instructions, they lined up on the road, one next to the other, and sat down. Those who weren't holding signs held the hand of the person sitting next to them.

Then the leader, standing up and facing the ballroom, raised a megaphone to his mouth and began speaking.

"On behalf of People for Peace, we have come here today to register our opposition to the government war machine that you symbolize and support. We must confront the mindset of war wherever we find it; and today, that mindset is here."

Around the bar had gathered most of the Corcoran crew. It was the most central and visible spot.

"What are we going to do?" Julia asked.

"This is the last thing these men need," Lillie said.

"It must be damn hot sittin' out there on that asphalt," Myron remarked. This was the closest he had come to the kitchen all afternoon.

"As long as they stay there, we'll be all right," Sharon said. "Let's not panic. Suzanne, why don't you start playing."

"Should we call the police?" said one of the nurses.

"Oh hell no," Grandpa exclaimed. "If they want to hang out here, let 'em. They look peaceful enough. In fact, let's ask them if they want some lemonade — we got gallons of it, right Glen?"

Grandpa — his mind must have been brimming with thoughts of how he could make his pitch.

"Oh my, the church isn't locked," Lorraine said.

"...1-2-3-4, We-won't-tolerate-your-war," came a chant from the sitting protestors.

"Shouldn't we say something to everyone?" Lillie suggested, looking at Sharon.

"No, let's not make a bigger deal out of it than we have to."

"How did they ever know we were here?" the nervous nurse asked.

"Who knows?" Sharon said. "But we had notices all over the hospital..." — and then, suddenly, her face became draped with the look of second thoughts — "... Or maybe they're not even here because of the party, maybe they're here for..."

She didn't have to finish the sentence; we all knew what she was going to say. Will Kramer. They were here to fight Will Kramer on his home turf.

"Don't they have any compassion?" Julia scowled. "After all these men have been through?"

"It's political," said a woman whose name badge read 'Flora Linson, V.A. Public Relations.' "To them, these aren't wounded men who've suffered the horrors of war, they're just symbols of a cause."

"I'm surprised there aren't any television cameras," Sharon said.

"Just wait," answered Flora Linson.

"You want me to go out and talk to them?" we heard Will's voice from behind us. "I'm familiar with most of them, and I expect they know me too."

"And what could you possibly say to them?" Sharon asked, in an irritable tone.

"I don't know. But if they're here because of me, I might be able to get them to move, or maybe even to..."

"Listen, we'll take care of it," she snapped. "Why don't you go back to the kitchen?"

He stood and stared at her, with eyes that flashed a look of defiance. But it was a momentary flash, and then he pivoted and retreated to the hot kitchen.

As it turned out, all the debate about whether to call

the police had been unnecessary. Before Suzanne's band could start playing again, two sheriff's cars turned off the highway and drove down the road leading up to the ballroom. The cars pulled up to within inches of the protestors, and then sounded their sirens. But the protestors did not move.

One of the officers brought out a hand-held loudspeaker. In a staccato voice, he told the protestors that they had to remove themselves from the road, that they were violating section something-or-other of the state penal code, and that they'd be arrested if they didn't disburse immediately.

When it became apparent that no one was about to move, the lead officer radioed in for a police bus to transport all the protestors to the county jail. But they didn't seem the least bit frightened. To the contrary, they displayed a look of triumph. (I had seen enough television news programs to know that, in the protesting community, getting arrested was like receiving the Medal of Honor.)

Grandpa was the only one who looked frightened. He ran outside to the uniformed officers and begged them to leave the protestors alone. No one had called to complain, he told the officers. There was no harm being done, he pleaded. Corcoran was a very friendly and hospitable place, he announced to the chanting protestors.

But someone had complained, the officer told Grandpa. And that someone, it turned out, was the one Corcoran resident who wasn't at the party (although Julia had dutifully invited him). A complaint had been called in by a Mr. Harold Nelson, the officer told Grandpa. Besides, the officer said, blocking a public road was a criminal violation — the sheriff's office didn't need a complaint.

A television camera crew beat the police bus by several minutes, just in time to get set up for the main event.

The protestors followed the script perfectly. They refused to stand, and then went all limp when the officers tried to pull them up. It took two (and sometimes three) men to carry each protestor to the bus. And sure enough, once in the bus, the protestors began their songs and chants of peace. Grandpa couldn't watch — he came back into the ballroom and tried to interest everyone in more food.

In the next day's newspaper, Corcoran was called "a little nest of hypocrisy." Everyday it sent one of its own into Millerton to picket and demonstrate in Sisseton Heights, the editorialist wrote, but when anyone else went to Corcoran to protest they were herded up like animals.

✧

That night, after all the protestors had been hauled off and all the guests had returned to the hospital and all the clean-up had been done, Suzanne and I carried the leftover food to the big freezer in Grandpa's basement. When we finished putting it all away and were walking out through the front porch, we heard Grandpa's voice call out from the far corner. He was sitting in his favorite rocker.

"If you two don't have any plans, how about sitting with me awhile?" he asked.

Suzanne sat down in the chair closest to Grandpa, and started rehashing the day's events with him. But I was distracted by something else — by Grandpa's use of the phrase "you two." And the more I dwelt on it, the more I began recalling how other people had been speaking to us lately.

"Why don't you two stop by tonight and listen to the game with me?" Myron had asked.

"If you two are going into town, could you pick up some groceries for me?"

"One of my suppliers gave me some movie coupons, and they're yours if you two want to go to a movie," said Ardelle.

(Later, I would ask Grandpa how he knew that Suzanne and I had become a couple. "Oh hell, haven't you two always been?" he snorted.)

"It's been a long time since there were so many people in Corcoran," Grandpa was saying. "It was kind of exciting, don't you think?"

"And I get the feeling it's not over. I think those protestors will be back," Suzanne replied.

"We'll handle it better next time — I'll win them over. Everyone's skeptical when they first see Corcoran, remember?"

"Don't get your hopes up, Eamon."

"That's what I've been told about every person living here right now."

"At any rate..."

"I used to take all this for granted," he interrupted, sweeping his eyes out over the darkness of his Corcoran. "Every Saturday night we had something going on at Interlachen; and there were so many cars there wasn't room to put them all. Our front yards were parking lots. Oh, the sights we'd see."

"Maybe things will get so busy around here that you'll miss the quiet times," Suzanne said. She didn't really want to encourage Grandpa, I could tell, but she felt as if she needed to say something.

"We were all in the same boat, so to speak. It was nothing to be called out of school because your father needed to round up some cows that had strayed out of a broken fence. We had a one-room schoolhouse, and we all wore the same kind of clothes, and our families all lived in the same kind of houses. But it sure wasn't like that when my kids went to school. They had to go into Millerton, into the city, and I think they always felt self-conscious about where they came from. I think they always felt like outsiders..."

Grandpa then reached down to the floor and picked up the glass from which he was drinking. It looked like his usual.

"...But I figured their distaste would turn to fondness, just as it had with me. Hell, I knew how they felt. I never told them, but I'd felt the same way once. When I was a young kid, I dreamed of leaving. I dreamed of cities and excitement, and of building things, like those skyscrapers that were beginning to go up..."

He leaned way back in his rocker — so far back that the creaking of the wood legs became almost a screeching.

"...But then, I was kind of like that. I always came to appreciate things too late. There was a Mr. Benton who ran the feed and hardware store. A tough nut he was; he never gave credit, ever. And yet, after my father died, he carried me and my mom for three years, until we got straightened away. He gave me a job in his store on weekends and after school; and every Friday night he gave me an extra dollar. But all the time I worked there, I couldn't wait till the store closed and I could go home. He had nobody. No family. I think he wanted to marry my mom, and I think he wanted to be like a father to me. But I never let him. And I didn't find out until after he died that he was the one who had kept the school open. A town couldn't afford to lose its young people, that's what he used to say."

"And it didn't," Suzanne said, filling in the silence when Grandpa again reached down for his glass. "You stayed, just as Mr. Benton had wanted you to."

"Well...I don't know if I did much good," Grandpa replied, but with a voice that showed the effect of Suzanne's remark. She had a way of bringing a punctuation of satisfaction to Grandpa's face.

Then the rocker screeched again as Grandpa built up the momentum to stand up. "I guess I'll go to bed and let you two be. Young people should only have to put up with so much reminiscing."

"So where do you want to go?" Suzanne asked, after we'd said goodnight to Grandpa and were walking out toward the street. "We could head over to The Fieldstone, have something to eat and watch television. I've got the key; Ardelle doesn't mind."

"I couldn't eat a thing, and I don't feel like television."

"You want to build a fire on the lake bank?"

I wanted to make out, that's what I wanted. But I was also occupied with another thought — a realization of sorts. As we walked down the dark road, I suddenly felt as if we owned it all. Suzanne and I. Everything around us was ours. When the sun set and the darkness sent everyone else to their lighted windows, the rest of the town became ours. The beach at the lake. The benches outside Interlachen. The road. The Fieldstone. Every inch of Corcoran outside the lighted windows of the houses that sheltered everyone but us — it was ours, mine and Suzanne's. Ours until the rising sun would once again briefly interrupt our reign.

"Let's go to the ballroom," I said. "I want you to play for me, that one song you did this afternoon — 'Can't See That Far.' I want to hear it again, with just you playing."

"Glen, I played all afternoon. You've got to be kidding me."

"No, I'm not. I want to hear you, all alone, playing for just me. I want to sit next to you, at the piano."

Maybe she thought I was just trying to flatter her. Maybe she even thought I was being patronizing. So I had to ask again, and finally beg.

We walked slowly through the darkened ballroom, holding each other's hand and trying to remember the placement of all the obstacles. A half moon shone through the windows and provided enough light for us to climb the stairs to the stage and find the piano. I told Suzanne not to turn on any lights, because someone might see them and panic. They might think the protestors had returned to seek their revenge. No, I said to Suzanne, it was best to forego the lights.

She laughed nervously as we sat down together on the piano bench, and reminded me once again that "we really don't have to do this." Then, just before she started to play, she leaned over and kissed me. Suzanne's kisses were a lot like her music, so filled with possibility.

Afterward, we walked down to the lake and let the breeze cool us off, the ballroom having had retained the heat of the afternoon.

Allure

At dinner, Lillie told us about the funeral and asked us all to come. It was for a former patient of hers. He had attended one of our first picnics, and shortly before he died he told Lillie he wanted to be buried in Corcoran. (We all presumed he had no home or family — except for Grandpa, who considered the request to be a deathbed tribute to the specialness of Corcoran.)

"I think it's just so sad when no one goes to a funeral," Lillie had said.

At the gravesite, I stood on one side of the coffin — I was serving as a pallbearer. And Suzanne was on the other side. She wore a navy blue blouse — it was the closest she had to black.

I didn't have to turn my head very much to see her. She didn't have her hair pulled back into a ponytail; she said it wasn't dignified enough. But a wind was blowing, and her hair was swirling about her face. And her hand kept trying to pull it back, away from her eyes. She didn't even seem to notice what she was doing; it all seemed so automatic with her. But I kept watching. Even when her eyes disappeared, I could still see her mouth. I'd never noticed before how it too had its expressions.

It wasn't a long service, but I still didn't really hear anything that was said. I thought Suzanne looked so alluring, with her hair like that, and her tongue always wetting her lips because of the all the dust the wind had kicked up, and the way her legs stood so straight and tall the whole time. I thought it was alluring the way she actually seemed to look sad. And I thought about being with her, later that night, and kissing her, and running my hand along her leg.

As we walked over to The Fieldstone, for a post-funeral lunch, I thought that anyone who could make you think about kissing in the midst of a burial was probably someone you loved.

The Scent on the Pillow

When I came down for breakfast, I heard Grandpa talking on the telephone.

"He's been in there all night?" I heard him asking.

"Is that it? Is that the charge?" he then asked.

"Hell yes, get him out. Will there be any problem?"

"Then let me know what the bail is."

"Yeah, I'll hang around the house this morning. But you think you'll be able to call me by ten?"

"Alright, Robert. Thanks for the call."

"Will was arrested last night," Grandpa told me, after hanging up the phone. "He spent the night in jail."

"He didn't mention anything about going into Millerton," I said, as if Will should have announced his plans to get himself arrested. "What happened? Was it a fight?"

"No. Destruction of public property. Apparently, he was caught digging up Sisseton Heights."

"What for?"

"Don't know. That was all the information my attorney had. You want some bacon?"

"What the hell was Will thinking? Was he just going to start building that monument, out in the middle of plain sight?"

"Like I said, don't know. Damn, we're out of cereal."

"Grandpa, don't you think Will is going too far with this crusade of his? I mean, the whole thing is so pointless."

"Pointless? Let me tell you something about pointless — it's a lazy word. Used by people who want an excuse for not trying. I don't know what Will is up to, but the boy's got guts and stamina, and I respect that. So, you want to give my pancakes another try?"

The last time Grandpa had fixed pancakes, they had to be scraped off the skillet. But I was too lethargic to propose anything else. I was not looking forward to the day. On our agenda was one of the worst jobs on the farm — baling hay. It was part of an arrangement that had existed for years with Ambrose Kowalski, a farmer who lived several miles to the south and who raised cattle: Grandpa gave him hay in return for a year's supply of beef.

Baling hay was one of the jobs that made you feel, after just twenty minutes, that you'd been slaving away at it all day. The eighty-pound bales came out of the baler as if they were on an assembly line. There was no let up, not as long as the tractor pulling the baler kept moving. And you only had a matter of seconds to pull the unwieldy bale from the baler and then stack it on the hay wagon. If even one bale was missed, the whole operation bogged down.

But the worst part wasn't just keeping up with the baler, it was the dust and shreds of hay that collected on the sweat of your skin. And when it got under your shirt, it was even worse. Not only did the dust and straw itch like crazy, but it seemed to add another covering to your skin, making you sweat even more. Yet you couldn't remove your shirt, because then the stalks of hay sticking out from the bale would cut your skin raw. And so it went, the worst job on the farm.

Normally, Grandpa drove the tractor and I stood on the wagon, behind the baler, stacking the bales. His job was to keep the tractor going straight, at a steady pace, and of course to occasionally yell back to me: "Are you managing okay?" But today, Sharon would be driving the tractor. She had volunteered; and Grandpa, citing what he thought were "developing allergies," immediately assented. There was never any discussion over whether my job was up for negotiation.

✧

The mid-morning sight of Ardelle driving up was like a glimpse of paradise. Ice water, gallons of it, she'd be bringing. And a nice long break.

But when I climbed down off the wagon, I found that Ardelle had brought more than ice water — she had brought news. Will wasn't being released from jail. Another charge had been made against him, a much more serious charge. Sexual assault. A woman was saying that Will Kramer had taken her to a motel and tried to rape her. There were witnesses who saw them going into the room. The judge had set bail too high for Grandpa to do anything.

Sharon then rattled off a quick interrogation. Who was the accuser? What motel had it been? Who were the witnesses? Ardelle had no answers, except for the motel — it was the Blue Bell Motel.

Our break wasn't nearly as long as I had hoped. Within minutes, Sharon was climbing back on the tractor. I tried to involve her in a conversation, but she didn't seem to hear me.

✧

When I went over to Julia's for dinner that night, after a very long shower, I expected Sharon to be reveling in her "I-told-you-so's" about Will Kramer. But she wasn't there. Nor was the television on. Instead, everyone was sitting around a bare table, with Grandpa telling them everything he knew about Will and what the lawyer had said about his defense.

I was glad when Suzanne volunteered herself and me to take dinner into Will.

"Now, I'm going to send enough food for all of you," Ardelle told us. "Will shouldn't have to eat alone — I want you to keep him company, okay?"

"Of course," Suzanne said.

"Make sure to tell him not to worry about us. Tell him we're all A-okay," Myron added.

"I'll make sure to tell him," I replied. "But I think his worries might be focused elsewhere right now."

Lorraine and Valerie reminded us to tell Will that they were praying for him, and had lit a candle for him in the church.

✧

To my surprise, I did tell all these things to Will. I told them to him because I was desperate for things to say.

While we sat at a table in the visitors' room, eating the dinner Ardelle had prepared, I watched Will and tried to figure out if he was acting like a guilty man.

It was a phrase I'd always heard: "acting like a guilty man." I had heard my mother saying that her best friend's husband was "acting like a guilty man." I had heard my father say that some man on the evening news "looked like a guilty man." And as I watched Will, I came to the conclusion that he definitely did not look innocent. He seemed too embarrassed, too ashamed; and he didn't once proclaim his innocence. Even after we had finished eating and it became obvious that there was nothing to say, Will didn't do anything to try to make us stay longer. It was my assumption that innocent people would want to be in the company of other innocent people, that they would do anything to keep from being sent back to their guilty cellmates.

I couldn't wait to get to the car. I couldn't wait to shake off the sleazy air of that dinghy, foul-smelling visitors' room. I didn't even stop at the reception desk when Suzanne paused to ask about visiting hours. But it wasn't just the jail. I really wanted to get out of there because of the plans I had made for later that night. (Before going over to Julia's house, I had hidden a couple of blankets and pillows, a candle, and a bottle of wine behind a tree at Porter's Point.)

"You didn't seem very talkative in there," Suzanne said, once we got to the car.

"What was there to talk about?"

"You could have been a little more supportive. The poor man is going to have to spend the night in that place."

"I'm not even sure he wanted us visiting him. I think he was embarrassed and..." — I was going to say something like "acting guilty," but I stopped myself.

"You don't believe in him, do you?" Suzanne asked, with a question that sounded more like an interrogation.

"What do you mean?"

"You don't believe he's innocent, do you?"

"How could I have an opinion? I don't know anything about the evidence..."

"That's right, the evidence. That's the first thing you think about, the evidence. Not the person, but the evidence." She spoke those words, "the evidence," with such disdain.

"I don't know what you're getting at. You want me to just blindly go about believing anything, willy-nilly?" I had never seen her like this before.

"Do you even believe in me?"

"What do you mean, believe in you?"

"No, you wouldn't know what I mean, would you? You don't believe it'll succeed, the Interlachen opening, do you?"

"Suzanne, are you forgetting that I'm the one who's been working day after day on that old ballroom?"

"Oh I know you've been working, but that's not what I'm asking. You're quite used to working, I can see that. But your sweat isn't accompanied by faith, is it?"

I kept looking over at Suzanne as we drove through Millerton on our way back to Corcoran. Her voice sounded so aggressive, so taunting, that I expected to see anger in her eyes. And yet they were clear. They were quizzical and persistent, but they seemed strangely free of harshness. Still, I couldn't tell if she was upset with me or unsure of me. I couldn't tell if she wanted to goad me into a quarrel or into a confession.

"Well...I hope it all works out," I said.

"Just as, I suppose, you hope Will beats the rap against him? But you don't believe in him, do you? And you think the idea of me starting up a band and playing at Interlachen is crazy, don't you?"

"Did I ever say that? Did I ever once say that?"

"But you've thought it, haven't you?"

"Look, just because I think something's crazy doesn't mean I abandon it. I've lived with crazy people all my life. Maybe I haven't always done right by them, but I've never abandoned them. And isn't that what counts?"

"It's not faith."

"Hell with it then. I guess I'm incapable of your so-called faith."

What seemed like a long silence ensued.

"Well...at least you don't just tell me what I wanted to hear, and heaven knows I gave you plenty of chances," she said, in a much gentler voice, as if to signal the end of the interrogation. She reached her hand over to my leg and patted me a few times, but in a gesture that seemed more patronizing than affectionate.

By the time we pulled into Corcoran, I had dismissed the plans I made earlier. There was no way I was going to act romantic now. I had my pride; and besides, I wasn't about to make a fool of myself.

After parking the car, I coldly suggested that there were still a couple of hours left to work on the ballroom. I wanted Suzanne to feel guilty, to feel selfish about having me work on her crazy dream that I didn't believe in.

"Sorry I even brought the subject up," she snapped, turning away from me.

But her reaction had overshot what I'd intended. I had only wanted to dish out a little guilt — I hadn't wanted her turning away from me in such a sharp way.

"You want to check in with the others? Maybe they're still at Julia's. We could see if they met with the lawyer," I said, trying to steer us to a neutral site where we'd do no further damage to each other.

She replied: "Let's go down to the lake and watch the sunset...that is, unless you'd rather go over to Julia's." Her voice, I thought, sounded...careful.

"Alright," I said.

We walked in strained silence down to the lake. The water was tinged with a reddish orange from the sun that was just about ready to drop out of sight. It was Suzanne who suggested we sit on the edge of the dock, and it was she who first took off her shoes and hung her feet into the water.

"I thought you had something special planned for tonight," she finally said, keeping her eyes riveted on the ripples her feet were making.

I forgot I had told her that. The morning suddenly seemed like such a long time ago.

"Well, I don't know if tonight is such a good night. Maybe we should just call it quits for the day."

"Why not? Why isn't tonight such a good night?"

"Are you kidding? I mean...." It seemed so obvious to me.

"You mean just because of our discussion in the car? Why does that make any difference?"

"Am I missing something, or didn't we have a fight? You seemed upset with me; and frankly, I'm...sort of upset with you. And with that kind of mood between us, tonight's probably not the best time for what I'd planned."

"Glen," she said, shaking her head, "even if we did

have a fight, maybe that's exactly why tonight's the perfect time."

I had heard arguments all my life, but I had no experience with the protocol of resolution. To me, quarrels were never temporary. But before I could say anything, Suzanne grabbed a fistful of my shirt and pulled me toward her. And within moments, she had resurrected the mood that so often existed during our nocturnal visits to the lake.

I kissed her with an urgency to escape the strangeness and tension I had just moments before felt. And she seemed to welcome it. She even seemed to encourage it. As if she too wanted to cement our bond, and to squeeze out any solvent of separation.

When we walked off the dock, the sun had already disappeared. I went to the hiding place and retrieved the blankets and pillows and wine. I had no interest in opening the bottle, but Suzanne was marveling at how thoughtful I'd been — so I went through with the whole ritual. Yet all I wanted was to return to the urgency that had occurred on the dock.

I wanted to do something that would change us, that would express everything I hadn't said. I wanted something to happen that would make it harder for us to come apart. I wasn't thinking, I was just reaching and grabbing and yearning. But when I started pulling her shirt out from her jeans, she stiffened and started to pull away. And when I tried to press her closer to me, when I tried to slide my hand under her shirt and against her skin, she suddenly jerked away, with an abrupt and willful force.

By the time I propped myself up on my elbow, she

was at the other edge of the blanket, sitting up, tucking in her shirt.

"I'm sorry," I muttered. "I thought it was okay. I thought it was what you wanted." There really was nothing to say. I felt like a fool.

"No, it's okay. I mean, no, don't be sorry. I'm...you just startled me...I'm...I got confused." She wasn't even looking at me as she fumbled with her words.

"I just...I don't know...Let's take things slow, okay?" she added, in a voice that seemed so false and concealing.

"I thought we had been taking things slow," I said.

"Look, maybe we should...call it a night. I'm sorry... I...Let's just call it a night, okay?"

She was busily folding up the blanket when my embarrassment turned to anger.

I'd pick up everything, I said. I didn't want to delay her in "calling it a night." I'd walk her home right away, and then I'd come back. I grabbed her hand and started pulling. She said I didn't have to walk her home. I sort of threw her hand away and said "fine." I didn't even look at her as she walked away.

I went to bed right away. Not because I was tired, but because I just didn't know what else to do. And I thought sleep would make everything disappear. But of course I couldn't sleep. All I could do is twist and turn and move restlessly in my bed.

I should have followed my earlier instincts, I thought. Tonight hadn't been the right time. Suzanne hadn't forgotten, or forgiven, my comments about believing in her. I should have trusted my instincts: quarrels can never disappear so easily. Or maybe it was more than that. Maybe it was a culmination of everything I had never done. The apologies that had never been given. The emotions that had never been acknowledged.

I thought about how indecisive I had been with Suzanne. How guarded and stationary I had been. How I had simply floated on the waves that some outside wind had created, never raising my sails and setting my own direction.

✧

After what seemed hours of sleepless self-reproach, I heard my bedroom door open. I sat up with a jolt — Grandpa was not one to wander the house at night.

Without a moon shining in through the window, I couldn't see the person opening the door. But after my initial shock wore off, I knew who it was. I knew even before I smelled her familiar scent.

"Glen, it's me," she whispered, as she felt her way to my bed.

I waited in stunned silence as she stumbled over some shoes and ran into the edge of my bed. She touched my face with her outstretched hand and sat down beside me. Then, without saying a word, she wrapped her arms around me and held me. She held me until my stoic reserve melted away and I returned her hug. Finally, she unwrapped her arms, backed away slightly, and placed her hands on either side of my face.

It was a soft kiss, a sympathetic kiss, a pleading kiss. It was a kiss that put all my questions and confusions at ease — a kiss that seemed to say all I wanted to know.

She gently pushed me back down onto the bed, and then laid down next to me. She nuzzled her face into my neck, and we laid together without saying a word. Finally, when my breathing had slowed almost to the point of sleep, she whispered: "I'm sorry about earlier. It wasn't you, and it definitely wasn't how I feel about you. There's something I need to tell you, first. And I just couldn't let...well, anything happen...without having told you. So...I will tell you — maybe not now. But... later, okay? Okay?"

"Sure," I whispered back, feeling her arms tighten around me. Feeling every worry and reproach suddenly vanish.

I fell asleep, without moving my position at all. It was easy to do. The sound of her breathing was like a hypnotist's watch.

When I woke up awhile later, we were still locked in our hold. My face was resting up against Suzanne's head, her hair cushioning my mouth and brushing up against my nose. I loved the scent of her hair. I loved the feel and taste of it against my lips.

From the sound of her breathing, I figured Suzanne was deep asleep. I laid perfectly still as I listened to her and gently twirled a strand of her hair with my tongue. It was like I had snuck into her private world. It was like I was invisible to her, and yet she was completely open to me. And then, remembering my earlier thoughts, the ones about all the emotions I had never expressed, I whispered, almost inaudibly, "I love you."

I meant it as a dress rehearsal of sorts, for when I might finally work up the nerve to deliver the line to a live audience. I thought it was safe. I thought I was invisible. So I didn't expect the voice that then spoke.

"I love you too," came the words that were partly muffled by my chest, from someone I thought was sleeping.

Our arms tightened around each other, and our faces pressed closer together. But we said nothing more, nothing that might dampen the echo of what already had been said.

When I next awoke, with the sun just beginning to light my room, Suzanne was gone. I thought for a moment that it had all been a dream, but then I breathed in the scent she had left on my pillow.

✧

Normally, the second day at the baler was the toughest day. The back was sore, the muscles were fatigued, and the skin was chafed. But this time, the second day was a breeze. I didn't feel the weight of the bales nor the constant stabs of the sharp-edged stems. All I thought about was the feel of Suzanne's body next to mine — her leg between my legs, her hair against my face. And of course the words she uttered when I thought she was asleep: "I love you too."

Grandpa and I finished the baling late in the afternoon. (Sharon had some business in town, he told me.) And while I was in the shower, Ardelle stopped over to ask Grandpa if I could take Will's dinner in to him. She had driven in to see Will over the noon hour and had seen the food served in the jail. "It ought to be taken in right away, before Will eats any of that slop they serve," she was saying to Grandpa when I came downstairs with my hair still wet.

"Oh good, you're finished with your shower," she said. "Will you run this into Will right away?"

I could tell that Ardelle wasn't going to leave until she saw me drive away with her food basket in the front seat of the pickup.

"I'll tell Julia to hold your dinner," she shouted, as I drove off.

I was just going to drop off Will's dinner and head back to Corcoran, but he asked me to stay. He wanted to talk to me.

"I need to ask you for a favor," he said, after we sat down at one of the visiting tables. "It's important, very important."

"What is it?"

"I need you to get a soil test done for me. It's for a sample I put under that big weeping willow in Sisseton Heights. It's already in a plastic bag — all you need to do is get a chemical analysis of it. Will you do it?"

"Why do you need a soil test?"

"I can't tell you. I just need that test done. And quick."

"Why are you asking me?"

Will looked away. I could see the impatience on his face. But when he returned his eyes to me, he spoke in a calm and deliberate voice. "Because I trust that you'll do it and keep quiet about it."

"You don't want me to tell anyone?"

"No. Get the test results and bring them back to me."

"Why did you put a bag of soil under the tree?"

Will's impatience returned and he chuckled a nervous laugh.

"Glen, I'll tell you everything once I see the test results, okay? I might be heading down a dead-end, but it's my only chance. Will you just do it for me?"

Maybe it was the way he was pleading with me, or the unquestioned obedience he wanted from me; but I didn't even think twice about asking a question I never would have asked before.

"Did you assault that woman?"

"No," he answered, staring at me with eyes as flat and direct as the question I had asked. "I'm sorry you felt you had to ask me that," he said, "but I guess we don't know each other that well."

"Can I ask you something else, not related to your arrest?"

"Are you going to get that soil test for me?"

"Yes, I promise."

"Okay, ask away."

"Why are you really going to all this effort and taking all this abuse? It can't be just because someone asked you to."

Will leaned back in his chair and took a long, deep breath. Then he sat up straight, braced his elbows on the table and leaned out over it.

"It was a couple of months after Lt. Schlomberg came to the platoon. We were patrolling the Caiphong Highlands. Around midnight, all hell broke loose. The NVA came at us in a full-scale assault. There was fire all over the perimeter, and mortar shells were being lobbed into our command bunker. I grabbed the radio and called for an air strike — I was giving the map coordinates for the strike when Lt. Schlomberg grabbed the map and yanked the mouthpiece out of my hand. In all the confusion, I'd forgotten that we'd sent a small patrol out to another position — a position smack dab in the middle of the coordinates I'd given for the air strike. If Schlomberg hadn't corrected it, I would have slaughtered those men. Their deaths would be on my conscience still."

"Then how could you have shot yourself just to get out of combat? You let your platoon go off and get massacred. Isn't that worse than accidentally calling in the wrong coordinates?" I asked.

"I can't answer that," he said, though without the shame and remorse I had expected. "But yes, I do feel responsible for them in a way..." His voice trailed off and his eyes looked away, and then he didn't say anything more.

✧

I drove straight to Sisseton Heights after leaving the jail, and the small plastic bag of black dirt was lying under the big weeping willow tree, just as Will said it would be. On the way back to Corcoran, I stopped at Farmland Fertilizer: it was where Grandpa had soil samples tested every year to determine what kind of fertilizer to apply. It was the only place I knew of to take Will's bag of dirt. And the man behind the counter wouldn't ask any questions: he'd seen me many times before.

✧

From the highway, I could see the line of cars and vans parked along the road that led into Corcoran. I slowed to a crawl as I inched my pickup truck between the vehicles parked on either side of the road. Up ahead, the protestors were marching along the road's shoulder, carrying signs that were no longer just in protest of the war. (The new ones called Corcoran the home of hate-mongers and rapists.) I turned off the road before I came to them, and took a back way to Julia's house.

The dishes were being done, but everyone wanted to hear the news of Will. I had the feeling that no one really wanted to leave, that they were a little leery of going out into the world of the protestors; and so the whole crew crowded around me, except for Sharon who was once again absent (and Suzanne, who was over at the ballroom rehearsing with her band).

When I asked how long the protestors had been there, thinking they must have just arrived and that the sheriff had not yet been able to respond to Harold Nelson's complaint, I was told that the sheriff had already come and gone, but had been unable to do anything. It was perfectly legal to march along a public road, as long as no obstruction to traffic was made, the sheriff's officer had announced.

But at least Grandpa had abandoned any delusions about the protestors. In fact, he had completely reversed his attitude, likening them now to the locust plague of 1939 that devastated thousands of acres of crops.

"That's the trouble with them protestors — they got no anchor in their life; they're just roving like a swarm of locusts," he said, looking out Julia's window. It was one of Grandpa's favorite sayings: "a person's got to be anchored in life."

As I relayed the news of Will, except for the part about the soil sample, I saw how my audience kept darting their eyes out to the protestors. Every sign was being studied, every chant was being deciphered. It was as if a great and ominous enemy was massing for an attack. "I saw on television what happened during those riots in Detroit,"

Lorraine warned. "Or how about Watts?" Myron added, showing that he too kept up on current events. It was a great day for Corcoran, I figured: to be compared to cities like Detroit and Los Angeles.

While I was still eating the leftover dinner, Julia took charge of things and announced that it was time to discuss Will's legal defense. The lawyer had suggested that the areas around Sisseton Heights and the Blue Bell Motel be canvassed for any witnesses who could help Will. On her tablet of paper, Julia began making a schedule of canvassers. She put people together in pairs, except when it came to me. (I had requested mornings; if possible, I wanted to preserve my evenings.) "No, you're needed at the farm," Julia said.

"Yes, definitely," Grandpa added. "Someone needs to keep the operation here going." His eyes carried an unfamiliar, though not entirely unexpected, look of worry. Just yesterday he had told me that a good harvest was needed this year to pay off the bank loans that had been called due, coincidentally by the same bank that would be financing the Lakeview Development Project.

When our meeting finally ended, I went over to the ballroom, after walking Lorraine and Valerie home. They were feeling a little threatened by the protestors, having seen those television images of urban riots with their burning and looting. That night, I thought, all the doors in windows in Corcoran would be locked, maybe for the first time ever.

Suzanne was up on stage by herself, sitting at the piano and testing out a new arrangement. But instead of going up to her, I went right to work on some of the light fixtures that were being replaced. I was intent on showing Suzanne how dedicated I was to the Interlachen reopening, and how much I believed in her. In fact, I became so absorbed in my work that I did not hear Suzanne walk up behind me.

As soon as I turned around, I felt a nervous self-consciousness come over me. As if I should say something about last night, about her late-night visit to my bedroom, the things we had said, and her disappearance sometime before morning. I felt as if we were different, after last night, but I didn't know how to go about acting different or recognizing that difference.

Suzanne gave me a quick, casual hug and asked if she could help me with the fixtures. For almost two hours, we worked side by side, talking only about the day's events and the difficulties of getting the old lights off the wall. Outside were the sounds of the protestors. Their chants had long since given way to singing and guitar strumming; and they were now sitting in circles in an empty lot about fifty or sixty feet down the road from the ballroom. I enjoyed the constant background sounds — they gave Suzanne and I something to talk about when our own conversation lagged.

When the sun went down and the light went from dim to dark inside the ballroom, Suzanne suggested that we stop for the night. She didn't feel like turning the lights on and being seen by all the protestors outside. She even asked if we could lock the ballroom, but I told her that locks hadn't yet been installed.

"Well, I'm going to cover up the piano then," she said, walking up to the stage and pulling out a large canvass from where it sat in the corner.

"You think that's going to do any good?"

"It might, if they come in here and start partying."

"They seem pretty content outside."

"Don't you think you ought to put away some of these tools? You don't want them stolen." The comment made me smile and put my arm around her. It seemed to reflect a neurosis I hadn't noticed before — a neurosis which made her seem more compatible with Corcoran, and with me.

We went out and sat on one of the benches just outside the front door of the ballroom and debated what to do. I sensed that Suzanne seemed a little edgy. From the sounds of splashing and shouting, I figured some of the protestors were down at the lake. Perhaps she was put off by the realization that, at least for tonight, Corcoran was not all ours.

I proposed going into Millerton, now that our hideaway had been invaded, but then remembered that I had given Grandpa the keys to the pickup. But it made no difference, because Suzanne didn't feel like abandoning Corcoran in this time of crisis. "They might need us; you never know," she said.

Then she suggested watching some television. "We could either go to my place or yours," she said. (Ardelle's and Grandpa's houses had become her place and my place.)

But I dismissed that option. I wanted to say something about last night, and I didn't want to lose this opportunity. I didn't want to get caught up in a card game with Ardelle or a story of Grandpa's. And I didn't want last night to drift too far into the past before we acknowledged it.

Finally, I just blurted it out. With no lead-up, no introduction, no segue.

"Why...?" I started to ask, "why did you say that thing last night?" I felt a red-hot flush fill my face.

"You mean why do I love you?" she replied, so easily.

"Yeah, I guess," I said, laughing with embarrassment.

Suzanne slid over and circled my neck with her arms. "I love you for everything you try to do, and everything you try to be," she whispered.

I felt an urge to interrogate, but her pause was brief. And as soon as she resumed speaking, I knew I didn't want to interrupt.

"I love that you're not afraid of disappointments and setbacks and flaws and imperfections. I love that you're so unpretentiously different. I love you because I trust you and because you're strong enough to be such an anchor for everyone here. And I love the way you look in a sweaty T-shirt."

Two phrases of hers kept echoing in my mind: "not afraid" and "strong enough." They were exciting to hear, almost as exciting as the words, "I love you too." I didn't believe them, of course, but it didn't matter what I thought. All I cared about was how Suzanne saw me.

"So, your turn," she then said, in a perky voice, as she sat up and crossed her legs under her.

"What?"

"It's your turn to tell me why you love me."

She seemed so unafraid of that question, as if she was free of all the insecurities that had prompted mine. And my answer flowed without thought or edit.

"Because you're like this curtain that lifts up and shows a whole new world. You're like that to me; you're like a brand new life that's even better than any one I could have dreamed up. And of course, I love the way you look...in everything."

✧

It wasn't as good an answer as the one she gave. But then, the thing about having a retarded brother, you learn that love doesn't have to be explained.

Everyday when I went to Room 305 to pick him up, Ricky grabbed my hand and said, "I love you, Brosher Glenn." He said it even though I had told him hundreds of times not to say that anywhere outside of our house. But Ricky's urges were always stronger than his memory.

I used to think it wasn't really love I felt toward Ricky, or he toward me. I used to think it was just pity, or responsibility. I used to think only certain kinds of people could love, and only for certain kinds of reasons. The thing about Suzanne, she taught me that I was all wrong about love.

✧

We sat there, together, on that old, worn bench, listening to the sounds of strangers singing, laughing, swimming and shouting — strangers who had come to express their outrage at us. We sat there listening to it all, and yet not listening. It felt like the most peaceful moment of my life.

Spoiled

It happened quite by accident, or perhaps it happened so gradually that I never recognized it coming. During the day, after school, Mom would briefly leave me alone with Ricky while she took Clare to do errands. In the evening, if Dad had to work late, Mom would have me look after Ricky while she went to a meeting at the school. And then, one night when Dad was being given some honor by the Chamber of Commerce, I volunteered to baby-sit Ricky.

Our babysitter had canceled at the last minute. It happened all the time. Ricky had acquired a reputation among Willow Bend's babysitting corps: no one ever came back a second time, and new ones were always canceling at the last minute. In their defense, Ricky was more than a little unmanageable with them. But what they didn't realize was that Ricky needed routine. He had to sit in a certain chair and eat with a certain fork and wear a certain bib and have his hair combed a certain way. The routine seemed to keep him from getting confused; because when he became confused, all hell broke out. Ricky may have had the mind of a 5-year-old, but he had the body of a healthy teenager. He didn't just throw a tantrum, he could throw the entire kitchen table.

I wasn't even asked to stay home and baby-sit Ricky

that night — I just volunteered. I volunteered as soon as I sensed my parents start to slide down their trough of bickering. My mother asked me if I was sure. (Maybe Ricky was retarded, but he was a lot better than the Chamber of Commerce.) And my Dad patted my shoulder and said, "You're a good son." (Actually, his look was more of relief than gratitude — Dad, I thought, was sometimes embarrassed by Ricky.)

I was asleep on the couch when they arrived home that night. Dad carried Ricky upstairs, and Mom gave me a piece of cake from the dinner. We were one big happy family.

At first, my parents made a big deal out of me taking care of Ricky. Mom would ask days in advance if I could stay home with him on a particular night, and Dad would always make sure I received some reward. Not only would he pay me, but he'd give me an afternoon off from working at his office. As for me, I liked feeling indispensable. But most of all, I liked the silence that had come over our house.

Pretty soon, my parents were fighting over me. Mom wanted me as a babysitter, while Dad thought I should be down at the office doing "man's work." But Mom usually won out, especially since my Dad seemed to like rejoining the social world.

Maybe I enjoyed being the one who could handle Ricky, but it was much more than that, much more than I ever let on. Unconditional love from another person is a powerful thing, even if it does come from someone who is retarded. Ricky spoiled me — he spoiled me because I never even had to make the slightest effort.

And I kind of liked all Ricky's routines. It seemed

a luxury to me, to know exactly what to do to have someone act a certain way, to know that all I had to do was make some popcorn and sit next to him on the sofa while we watched television.

✧

The thing about having a retarded brother was that he took the blame for everything that was wrong. The other thing about having a retarded brother was that I got used to having someone take my insults and then forget all about them a minute later.

Vindication

Going to work the next morning was like being the first one to leave a campground. The protestors, most of whom had camped down by the lake, were all still asleep.

My job that day was to deliver the hay bales, and I was planning on having to make four or five trips with the hay wagon. Even before I left the house, I could hear Myron in the machine shed, revving the tractor's engine. He had never raced the motor like that before; and it wasn't until I saw the devious look on his face as he asked if I could see any movement among the sleeping protestors that I understood why he was doing it now.

When I climbed onto the tractor, Myron shouted to me to run it at full throttle as I drove past the slumbering campers. And when I was about a hundred feet down the road, I heard Myron start up the old grain truck that was missing a muffler.

After returning from my second load of hay, I saw Myron limping around Porter's Point, bending over every two or three steps to pick up some trash and then drop it into the plastic bag he was dragging along. I shut off the tractor engine, leaned over the steering wheel, and just sat and watched. It wasn't like Myron to be voluntarily picking up trash — he didn't even like to walk that much. Although, he seemed to be doing more bitching than walking. I could see from the turned and mocking faces of the protestors that Myron was grumbling out loud as he walked among them.

There he was, an old man with a limp, cussing nonstop as he picked up the litter of people fifty years younger than him. I found myself cheering for him. And then, as if the spotlight of the whole summer suddenly shined upon me, I climbed down off the tractor, walked into the garage, picked up a garbage bag, and headed toward Porter's Point.

The closer I got the more nervous I felt, but I didn't let my legs slacken in their pace. I figured the protestors would confront me, just as they had that night in the park. I figured they'd taunt me — I figured they'd treat me as they had Will.

I called out to Myron when I was still a hundred or so feet from him — I didn't want to be tempted to turn back. He swung his head around and broke out into a beaming smile. And then I started talking loudly, about the tractor and the hay delivery and all the trash that was littering this beautiful spot by the lake. I wanted to show them that I wasn't afraid; or maybe I just wanted my own voice to drown out theirs.

We kept talking the whole time; and the more we talked, the more we disparaged the litterers. But they did nothing. They just laid in the grass, listening to their tape decks and soaking up the sun. Protesting must be like a job, I concluded, and this group's shift hadn't started yet.

After about fifteen minutes, and with plenty of trash yet to be picked up, both Myron and I decided we had made our point; and with just a nod of the head between us, we headed home. But as we walked, we spoke with voices energized by victory. And I was sure that later on tonight we'd each tell our tales of triumph to our own private audiences.

"Glen, I want to show you something before you go back to work," Myron said, as he turned toward his workshop.

"It's a new gift I made for you to give Suzanne," he said, opening the door.

"What do you think? — she'll love it, don't you think?" he asked, holding up a miniature woodcarving of Interlachen. "I carved it out of an old piece of driftwood, to give it that aged look."

"Actually, I think she will love it," I replied.

"What do you mean, 'actually?'"

Myron was sometimes suspicious regarding reactions to his handiwork. And most of the time, he had reason to be.

It had started a couple of weeks ago — when Myron began giving me romance advice.

"Forget that damn 'Dear Abby' Valerie is always quoting, I'll tell you how to romance a girl," said the man who, as far as I knew, had been a life-long bachelor. (But what worried me for days afterward was the fact that even someone like Myron saw me as needing help in this area.)

"Women like gifts," he told me. "Lots of gifts. And if you make them yourself, it's even better."

At first, I figured Myron had come up with his gift theory from one of Ardelle's magazines. But later, after I saw how enthusiastically he worked on things for me to give Suzanne — things like wood carvings of animals, and candlesticks made from scrap iron, and little knick-knack shelves to hang on a wall — I concluded that it was purely self-interest that had prompted his advice. Myron may not have known much about how to pursue love, but he did now how to turn a lathe and use a chisel. And he did love the reaction he got from Suzanne every time I gave her one of his gifts.

She pretended to go along with the official story — that I had made the gift — but she told Myron that she knew I could never have done it by myself, that I had to have had a lot of help from an expert craftsman. She pretended that she and Myron were sharing their own little secret. In that whole gift program, I was just the middleman, the delivery boy.

✧

When I returned to Corcoran after delivering my third load of hay, the place was a beehive of activity. A "Schlomberg For Congress" bus was parked just down the road from Interlachen, along with a couple of television news vans. Crowded around Martin Schlomberg, who was giving a speech in front of the most dilapidated house in Corcoran, were about sixty men and women in suits and dresses. The protestors were being kept off to the side by a cadre of young campaign workers. A large banner hanging behind Martin Schlomberg read: "Schlomberg For Peace and Progress."

Even over the noise of the tractor, I could hear fragments of what the candidate was saying. "...We cannot stand by idly while opportunity knocks...I ask the voters: is the preservation of this abandoned, decrepit old house worth depriving a whole community of its economic future?" And when Schlomberg got to the part in his speech about opposing the war, he was interrupted by loud cheers from the protestors.

As I came to the road that led directly past the well-dressed crowd gathered in front of Martin Schlomberg, I felt the devious urge that had possessed Myron earlier. But the cars were parked too close together, and I couldn't maneuver the tractor any closer to the microphone or the television cameras.

✧

When I returned from my final load, it looked as if everyone was back from Millerton. Grandpa's pickup was in his driveway, and Julia's and Lillie's cars were parked in front of their houses. I even saw Sharon's car. It had been since Will's arrest that I had last seen her.

I pulled the tractor up to the machine shed, but I didn't unhook the hay wagon, nor did I sweep it clean. And I didn't gas up the tractor so that it would be ready for the next person to use. I just shut off the motor and ran home — I wanted to get in a shower before dinner.

I bounded up the front steps in one jump, and I swung open the screen door so hard that it hit the wall. I was a couple of steps into Grandpa's living room before the door slammed shut behind me, and before I noticed everyone silently staring at me.

Lillie looked worried, Julia seemed ready to slide off the edge of her chair, Sharon had a tormented look on her face, and Grandpa was strangely subdued. My first thought was that bad news had come from Vietnam.

"Glen, if you've got a minute, maybe you could sit down — I need to tell you something," Sharon said. Her voice had a preparatory tone — a tone ready to deliver serious, and probably unpleasant, news.

No one else said anything. There was nothing friendly or casual or relaxed about the mood in the room. It was the kind of mood that kept people from sitting back in their chairs and crossing their legs.

"I think you deserve to hear this too, Glen, because of...well, because it affects you too. Anyway, what I was saying is that..." — and then she took a long and labored breath, but still no one made any attempt to speak — "...what I was saying is that I'm a fake. I'm not at all what..."

"I won't have you saying that," Grandpa interrupted.

"Yes, you're only punishing yourself," Lillie added. "You don't have to be telling us this."

Another silence ensued, and Sharon flashed a tense smile at me. And then she took another deep breath, as if to muzzle any further interruptions.

"You see, I've let everyone believe that I'm someone I'm not: the innocent factory worker who married the son of a prominent family; the grieving widow who becomes a kind of role model for other Vietnam wives. But it's not true; not really. None of it."

She reached for the glass of water on the table beside her.

"I suppose I never said anything before because I didn't think it mattered, I didn't think anyone needed to know. And I liked what I had become — I liked how people thought of me. But now...well, maybe it's jeopardized...I mean...I think I know why Will's in jail."

And with that introduction, Sharon went back to the

beginning: to her marriage to Craig Schlomberg. Actually, to before her marriage.

She had gotten a job at the Schlomberg factory; and soon after, she started getting invited to parties. They were small parties, thrown to entertain important customers. There was a large suite at the Blue Bell Motel, connected to a couple of private rooms, located at the very back of the motel, with a parking space and entrance that were hidden from view — this was where the parties were held.

Sharon was staring down at the floor as she spoke about these parties. She was quick to add that she was expected only to flirt with the men and "keep them company," but the way she glossed over the details of those parties suggested that she may have sometimes exceeded expectations.

Martin Schlomberg was almost always there, Sharon explained, and it wasn't long before he embarked on an affair with Barbara Benley — the woman who had first invited Sharon to the parties. Barbara lived by herself, ever since her husband was drafted and shipped out to Vietnam.

"Barbara and I were going to live together, but once her affair with Martin started....well, she no longer had to worry about expenses," Sharon added.

The first time Sharon met Craig, Martin's son, was at one of those parties. Barbara had mentioned to her ahead of time that his father wanted Craig to "have some fun." It was well known around the factory that father and son were in no way two peas from the same pod. Craig was quiet, studious and shy. He didn't drive around in the convertible his father had given him, nor was he ever seen racing his father's boats in the lake on which his family had a cabin. For the past three years, Craig had been attending a religious college, and there were rumors he was contemplating the ministry.

It was the only party Craig ever attended, Sharon said. And he was so uncomfortable that he left after less than an hour. Sharon, who had been "requested" to "loosen him up a little," left when he did and suggested that they walk downtown where the 'Pepper Days' festivities were being held.

"It really was a pleasant evening," Sharon recalled. "We wandered through the food booths, stopped to watch some jugglers, and ended up in the beer tent. And I think even if he wasn't who he was, I still would have wanted him to call me again."

But it was Sharon who made all the calls and did all the initiating. She had been promoted to an office job, and Barbara continually told her how much Martin Schlomberg (who apparently didn't relish the thought of a minister in the family) would appreciate her "keeping company" with his son.

And then came the night when Sharon was awakened by the phone call from the hospital. After arriving almost unconscious at the emergency room, Barbara had mumbled Sharon's name when asked whom should be notified. As it turned out, Barbara was experiencing toxic shock from an abortion performed earlier that evening in her apartment by a doctor arranged by Martin Schlomberg.

"I don't know how it happened," Sharon told us, "but somehow Barbara's husband learned about the abortion. I think he found out she was in the hospital; and then when he called her, someone told him what had happened. But I don't know for sure."

What she did know, however, was that several days later Barbara's husband shoved the muzzle of a rifle into his mouth and pulled the trigger.

It was a statement that made me cringe: I could almost feel the cold metal in my own mouth. And I saw Lillie nod with a pained look of recognition, as if she was now remembering the news of that suicide.

About a week later, Craig unexpectedly showed up at her apartment, Sharon said. "He'd never done that before, and he was obviously upset and agitated. He kept muttering snide remarks about his father — about the affair and the suicide, and even something about how his father was killing people. And then he made his proposal. It wasn't romantic or affectionate or even endearing. But it was a proposal; and he argued so fervently in its favor that he must have actually thought I'd turn him down. But after all, an opportunity like that rarely comes around to women like me."

So they were married the next day, in front of the justice of the peace, with no one present except two strangers who served as witnesses. Craig was depressed that night, Sharon remembered. But as she told herself then, everything had happened so fast.

Craig dropped out of school and moved into Sharon's apartment. They talked, though only superficially, about a house. And then, two months later, Craig came home with the news that he had enlisted in the army. Three days after that, he left for basic training. She was positive, Sharon told us, that he volunteered because he regretted having married her.

Never once did Sharon set foot inside the Schlomberg house. In fact, the day after Craig left for the army, she was fired from her job. "It was a lie about me refusing to inherit any of Craig's share of the Schlomberg wealth," she said. "Hell, Martin said he'd expose everything in my past if I tried to collect even one dollar. You see..." — and then she stopped and looked away with a regretful blush — "...Martin had photos of me with some big customer who I think was being blackmailed to do business with Schlomberg Manufacturing.

"I'm so ashamed of how I lived then," she said, her voice carrying the emotional ring of confessions. "Everything was such a mess. It seems so obvious now, but back then I just didn't see it. I just went with the flow, but the flow was all downhill."

"You don't have to tell us all this," said Lillie, who reached her hand over to Sharon's.

"That's right. This is none of our business, and you have no reason to...," Grandpa started to say.

"But I think it does concern you, Eamon," Sharon interrupted. "I think Martin Schlomberg wants to bulldoze Corcoran so as to get rid of me. I'm a horrible reminder to him, as well as a potential scandal for his campaign."

"Nonsense," Grandpa barked. "They've been trying to move me out long before you arrived. And I never told you this, but one of the reasons I wanted you women to move in here was to make it harder for the county to condemn Corcoran. I thought if people lived here, particularly wives of servicemen, it would be harder to condemn the place."

I could see that Grandpa expected his revelation to

have a stunning effect, but no one seemed even mildly surprised. Except me. I never thought Grandpa had any logical reasons for trying to fill up the houses in Corcoran.

"That's right," Julia added. "You can't just assume that all this development stuff is happening because of you."

"But even if you're right about that, what about Will?" Sharon replied, persisting in her own prosecution. "I know the woman who is accusing him of assaulting her at the Blue Bell; and I think Martin Schlomberg put her up to it. He's paranoid. He thinks Craig put Will up to some vengeance scheme. And I know Craig despised his father — God, the things he used to say about him."

"But you can't prove any of this," Lillie said. "So what good is it going to do to air your private life and then...."

"Maybe I can't prove it, but I know it's true. I just know it. And maybe if I come forward, someone else who knows something more specific might do the same. You don't understand — there was a lot going on at the Blue Bell. I think Martin was letting the union run some kind of drug ring out of there; I think it was his way of paying off the union for some..." But then she just stopped, as if her revelations had raced too far ahead of her intentions — as if she had to remind herself what to focus on.

There was a long silence before Sharon spoke again. "I know something else about Will Kramer that I've never told anyone before, not even Will. I know he didn't do what the army said he did — shooting himself in the foot just to get out of combat. I received a letter that Craig wrote to me that night. He was depressed, I think, and had to confess to someone. It was Craig who was trying to shoot himself, not Will. And it was Will who tried to stop him. But in the scuffle, the rifle went off and hit Will. I still have the letter. It's true. And sometimes I even suspect that Craig might have deliberately, or at least distractedly, led his platoon into that ambush. He wasn't suited for the army, or for combat. He was scared to death — in fact, I think he was so scared he wanted to die."

Lillie's and Julia's mouths were hanging open. Even Grandpa looked stunned. And I felt torn between Sharon and Will. I felt sorry for her, but I also felt a respect, and even a pride, for Will. I wanted the world to know that Corcoran wasn't a hideout for cowards.

"When Craig died, and I became his widow," Sharon continued, in a voice that cracked, "everything changed for me. It was like I was given a fresh start, a chance to throw away my old life and step into a brand new one. Suddenly, people were looking up to me. I didn't care that Martin Schlomberg didn't give me anything from Craig's estate. His son had already given me a second chance. I never meant to try to be someone I wasn't — it was just that, after Craig's death, all the people from the VA and American Legion started treating me as someone special. And I guess that's why I hated it when Will showed up here, even though I knew the truth about him being falsely accused in that court martial."

As her head slumped, pulling her shoulders down with it, everyone started telling her how strong she had been for all of us, and how much help she had been to so many people. But it was Grandpa who addressed the issue of whether she should go to the district attorney with what she had told us.

"Listen, Sharon, before you do anything, let me think awhile on this, okay? Let's just sleep on this for tonight, okay? There's no rush to do anything, okay? Will you promise me you won't do anything until you talk to me first?"

She nodded, passively. And then Grandpa tried to change the subject. "Well, what do you say we all have some dinner? I'm starved," he said, rubbing his hands together with a forced smile on his face. "What's for dinner tonight, Julia?"

"If you'll excuse me, I'm not very hungry," Sharon said, as she started to stand up. "I'm going to go home and rest awhile."

After Sharon walked out of Grandpa's living room, the rest of us seemed edgy and uncomfortable, as if trying to pretend that nothing had happened. It was almost as if we were afraid to be alone after she left, as if we were afraid of appearing to be gossiping about her.

"Oh Glen," Julia said, as she opened the door to leave, "I think Ardelle probably has Will's dinner ready to go. Could you run it into him quick? We won't be eating for at least another forty-five minutes yet."

"Yeah, sure," I answered. "I'll just hop in the shower and..."

"Can't you do that when you get back? It's getting late," Julia snapped.

"You look fine," Grandpa said. "Run it in now, before he has to eat that slop they serve."

Suddenly, I felt everyone's impatient eyes upon me. They wanted me gone, and they wanted me gone now. As if all the wrongs committed against Will Kramer could be righted if I just got his dinner to him on time. I couldn't help but feel that, in this one moment and in this one act, everyone watching me wanted to show their loyalty and concern for the man now sitting in jail.

As I was leaving for the Millerton county jail, I saw a television van parked across the road from where the protestors were gathered. It looked as if the news crew was getting ready to do a live feed for the six o'clock news. The protestors were the most energetic I had seen them all day.

✧

Will shook his head with a disbelieving smirk when he walked into the visiting room and saw me sitting at the table with Ardelle's picnic basket.

"You know, for three years I ate army C-rations," he said, as he sat down, still shaking his head. "The food here isn't going to kill me — you can tell Ardelle that. And besides, I'm getting a reputation in here as a dinnertime prima donna."

As Will's curious but still smiling eyes studied the picnic basket, I noticed how calm and relaxed he appeared, especially in contrast to how I felt. I was having to devote all my energy just to corralling the stampede of words that was rushing toward my mouth. There was so much I wanted to tell him, and not just about what Sharon had said — I even wanted to tell him about Suzanne and me. But when he casually asked me for the news of Corcoran, I couldn't hold back the stampede — I blurted out everything that Sharon had told us. And I spoke so rapidly that I left out facts and had to backtrack and clarify.

What seemed to surprise him the most was the fact that Craig had written a letter to Sharon telling her about the incident with the gun. There hadn't been that much time for letter-writing, Will kept repeating. "First thing the next day, the platoon went out on patrol," he said, with a far-off stare in his eyes.

A few moments later, he looked squarely at me and said: "I should have kept him from taking the platoon out on that mission — that's what I should have done."

"You tried to save his life, you couldn't have done anything more than that," I said, suddenly feeling quite protective of Will.

"Oh, I don't know that he would have actually committed suicide. Maybe he would have wounded himself, and maybe that would have been the best thing for everyone. Even if he had killed himself, maybe that would have been the best thing. Maybe all those guys would still be alive today."

"Do you think he deliberately led them into that ambush?"

"I don't know if it was deliberate, or just the recklessness of too much depression and fear, or just an unavoidable occurrence. I should have blown the whistle on him, but I felt I owed him. And I thought I could fix it later, more quietly."

"How could you have known?"

"Yeah, that was the problem in Vietnam. You never knew where anything was going, or how anything would work out. But there's still the regrets, and the doubts."

"You can't succumb to them; you had no control over what happened; you couldn't have known...." And suddenly the hypocrisy hit me, and I instinctively looked around, to see if anyone was waiting to call me on what I'd said.

"So, did everyone seem surprised by what Sharon said?" Will asked, in a more eager voice.

"Yeah, I guess...I mean, of course. Absolutely. Although, I mean, not that they ever believed you were a..." And then I realized that I wasn't entirely sure of what Will was asking, and I didn't want to utter the word 'coward.'

"Did they seem surprised to learn the truth of what happened?"

"I'm not sure they ever really believed the official story," I said.

"You can tell me now, but did they think I attacked that girl?"

"I can honestly say that they never did."

For a moment following my answer, and while Will's face shown with a look of relief, I was afraid that he was going to push his luck and ask me a direct question: whether I had believed in him. But he didn't. He just sat there and enjoyed the vindication. He looked like a man who hadn't experienced that kind of enjoyment in awhile.

Will was not too interested in discussing what I thought would be of utmost concern to him: how and when he was going to get out of jail. Instead, he seemed to want to dwell on Craig Schlomberg and all the details of a past that up until now he had been forced to keep secret. And eventually, his focus turned to Sharon. He said he didn't want her to do anything to embarrass herself, but I could see how relieved he was that she had broken her silence.

"He, Craig that is, didn't go to Vietnam because of Sharon," Will said. "I think he wanted to hurt his father, and I also think in some way he wanted to make up for what had happened to that husband of his father's lover. There's more too, but I won't go into all that right now. Like I said though, those reasons just couldn't sustain him once he got to Vietnam. All those resentments, caked over by a naive idealism, left him too weak, I think."

When the guard yelled that visiting hours were over, Will asked me to tell Sharon what he'd said about Craig's reasons for going to Vietnam. Then he walked across the room toward the door that led back to the cells. I had never seen the look in Will Kramer's face that I saw as he turned to smile at me. He looked contented and serene. He looked like an innocent man, like a man who wasn't afraid to go back to Corcoran, or to the rest of his life.

Not once, I realized as I drove back to Corcoran, had he mentioned to me anything about the soil test.

Revelations

I awoke suddenly, as if sensing that someone was standing over me, watching me. But there was no one. Yet I had awakened so abruptly that I could not go back to sleep.

I went to my door and opened it, half expecting to find someone outside of it. But all I saw was a light coming from downstairs. I tiptoed past Grandpa's room and saw that he was not in his bed. Then I went down to the kitchen, to where the light was coming from.

He was sitting at the table with a cup of tea in front of him and his head propped up by his hand. I couldn't tell if his eyes were open or closed

"Grandpa, what are you doing?"

"Oh, Glen, you startled me," he said, jerking his head up.

"Can't you sleep?"

"I thought I'd just get a cup of tea and....No, I guess I couldn't sleep." His face was sagging with fatigue, and his wrinkles looked especially deep.

To me, Grandpa had always been ageless. He had always looked the same, for as long as I had known him. But now, sitting in that dimly lit kitchen, with his tattered robe wrapped around his tired body, my grandfather looked old.

"Are you feeling okay?" I asked, afraid that something had happened during the night to make all the ills and weaknesses of old age suddenly catch up with him. And for the first time in my life, I thought of Grandpa as being susceptible to things like heart attacks.

"Oh sure, I'm fine. Strong as a horse," he said, trying to conjure up his usual bluster. "I'm just trying to figure out this thing with Sharon."

"Well, do you really have to figure anything out? Isn't it all up to her?" I asked, pulling a chair out to sit down. "You shouldn't worry about that. It's her responsibility. She has to tell what she knows."

"Yes, but what will it do to her? Have you thought about that?"

I could tell it wasn't a question to which Grandpa was looking for an answer, and for that I was glad — because I wasn't thinking much about Sharon. It wasn't her troubles that were on my mind.

"She's built a new life here," Grandpa continued. "Corcoran's given her a fresh start. And that's how I've always thought of this place — as giving people who come here a fresh start in life. Glen, I don't want to sacrifice any more people's happiness for the sake of this decaying old town."

I had never before heard him refer to his beloved Corcoran that way. Maybe he really was old and tired. Maybe he would never be the same again. Maybe my grandfather had finally fallen victim to resignation.

"On the other hand...hell, I don't exactly feel like giving up either," he added, with a little more energy in his voice. "After all this time, and all this blood and sweat, I don't want to be the person to give up. I feel responsible to the sacrifices they all made to work this land, and to the dreams they all had. Do you understand what I'm saying, Glen?"

I nodded. Grandpa always asked me that whenever he talked about his responsibility to the past. It was his way, I figured, of trying to pass that responsibility on to me.

"Oh, what am I doing," he said in a huff, shaking his head and sliding back his chair. "It's the middle of the night and you're in no mood to hear all this. Let's get some sleep, okay?" Then he forced out a smile, and I followed him upstairs.

At his door, I stopped and watched him walk to his bed. I wanted to say something that would relieve his anxiety. But all I could come up with was a trite cliché that I had never believed myself. "Things will work out, Grandpa," I said. "It'll look better in the morning."

✧

Grandpa was still in bed when I left the house the next morning. I walked over to Myron's; we were going to spend the day preparing the machinery for harvest. But instead of being bent under the hood of a truck, his head was glued to a telescope.

It was set up in the loft, which had once been used to store hay back before Myron turned the old barn into a garage, and which Myron now used as a makeshift planetarium. But at eight o'clock in the morning, Myron wasn't doing any stargazing, especially with a telescope that wasn't pointed up.

When I yelled up to him, he waved me off and told me to be quiet, all the while never taking his eyes from the telescope. So I climbed the ladder to the loft and walked up behind a bent over Myron, who I found to be spying on a couple of female protestors, skinny-dipping in the lake.

"I'm not letting you look, no matter how much you beg," he growled, keeping his head perched at the telescope. "Besides, you're young — you don't need to be a voyeur. But this is the first time I've seen any naked women in Corcoran, and I doubt the opportunity's ever going to come again."

I laughed and patted Myron on the shoulder. His head must have bumped up against the telescope, because he barked at me not to do that again. Then I left him to his indulgence and went back down to the garage.

An hour later, after I had just finished changing the oil in the tractor, Myron was still at the telescope. Occasionally, he yelled down to me with an update on what was happening. The two swimmers had, unfortunately, come out of the lake and gotten dressed. But Myron was hoping that where there was smoke there would be fire: that more protestors, preferably female, would decide to go for a morning swim.

It was probably near ten o'clock when I heard Grandpa yelling to me from his back door.

"Glen, what's with the soil sample you took in for testing?" he shouted.

The first thought that came to me, as I remembered my vow of secrecy to Will, was that I had forgotten to tell the man at Farmland Fertilizer to contact me, and only me, about the test results.

"Glen, you hear me?" Grandpa shouted again.

"Uh, yeah. It was just a sample I took in for a test," I yelled back, trying to think of an answer as I spoke.

"From where?"

"Huh?"

A few moments of silence passed, and I hoped that Grandpa had given up. But then I heard his voice at the door of Myron's garage. "Where's the sample from?"

"Oh, it's just something I was curious about — just wanted to check how..."

"And I'm curious about where the sample came from? You think we got a problem in one of the fields?" Grandpa's voice was ornery; he probably wasn't used to sleepless nights.

"You know, I'm not exactly..."

"Good god, Glen, I asked a simple question, and I want a simple answer. Now where's the sample from?"

Even though Grandpa was yelling at me, I couldn't help but feel sorry for him — the way his voice sounded so troubled. And it was this sympathy, along with a reluctance to actually lie to my grandfather, that made me tell him about Will.

"Why in the hell didn't you say so in the first place?" he snorted, his voice no cheerier than before. "You got some kind of secret you're keeping from me?"

But Grandpa wasn't really interested in Will's request, I told myself. He was only concerned that something was happening in Corcoran without his knowledge.

"I'll finish up here and then go into Farmland for the results," I called out to Grandpa, who had already started walking back to his house.

But when I finished replacing the belts on the tractor and went over to get the keys to the pickup, I found that Grandpa had taken it. And not until late that afternoon, after he had returned to Corcoran with Will in the passenger seat, did I learn where Grandpa had gone. He told us all about it when we gathered at Julia's for dinner.

The soil sample had contained astronomical levels of tetrachloride — a hazardous chemical that had killed seventeen people four years ago when it seeped into the water supply of a Pennsylvania town. The man who did the testing was positive that something had contaminated the sample. "Eamon, there's no way any of your land could have this chemical in it," he had said to Grandpa, who did not correct the man's mistaken belief as to where the sample had come from.

"But when I told Will about it, he wasn't surprised at all," Grandpa said, as he winked at Will.

"I just always assumed Craig wanted that monument in Sisseton Heights to be a constant, irritating reminder to his father," Will interjected. "Then, a few days ago, something made me think that perhaps he had a more spiteful motive. During the time I knew him, he told me lots of things...about his father."

It was during that brief pause before saying "about his father" that Will glanced over at Sharon, who was quietly sitting off in the corner of the room, as far from the center of attention as she could get. It seemed like a glance meant to reassure her that Craig had only talked about his father.

"There was a lot of ill feeling there," Will continued.

"You know, I do remember Craig once saying something about his father cutting corners at the factory... and something about gambling debts," Sharon said from the back of the room, snapping out of her silent shell. "Everybody kept it quiet, even the bankers, but Craig said that was why the factory was going broke."

"So, am I missing something, or how does this all relate to that chemical stuff?" Myron asked.

"The day before I got arrested," Will replied, "something made me remember a comment Craig had made when we were on leave in Saigon and a truck hauling big chemical drums practically ran us over. He said something about that truck making him homesick — he was being satirical, of course. He said it reminded him of the trucks hauling hazardous waste out of his father's factory, to dump in a place that his father later donated as a park. I think it was his father's donating the land to the city that really galled Craig — because that way his father would never get caught. I suspect that was the reason Craig made me promise what he did — it was the only way he knew of to nail his father on..."

"But of course we didn't know for sure, that Sisseton Heights had really been a dumping ground," Grandpa interrupted. "We could only guess."

"But it was a pretty solid guess," Will said, as he went on to describe the next step: the blackmailing of Martin Schlomberg.

"So you went to him with the pollution evidence and forced him to back down?" Ardelle asked. She had the same eager, gloating smile that Myron and Lorraine and Valerie had. They seemed to be enjoying this tale of Corcoran's counterattack against the outside world.

"He had no choice," Will said.

"He's guilty alright," Grandpa said.

"So what's going to happen to Sisseton Heights?" Sharon asked.

"Well, we didn't push our luck," Grandpa said.

✧

Out in the boondocks of Corcoran, we were distant observers of the events that transpired in the wake of Grandpa's and Will's blackmail of Martin Schlomberg. We may have known why certain things were happening, but we were completely in the dark as to how they were happening. All we knew was what we saw and heard.

No explanation, other than "insufficient evidence," was given for the charges against Will Kramer being dropped. And two days later, the developer announced that it was no longer considering Corcoran as a development site. We also learned that Corcoran had not actually been the first choice of the developer — Sisseton Heights had been. But Martin Schlomberg had swayed them away from that location. Besides, his gift of land to the city carried the condition that no building or development ever be done on the site.

But not everything was good news for Grandpa. The reasons given for abandoning the development project was the high cost of pursuing legal action against a belligerent land-owner. To everyone hoping that the Lakeside Development Project would provide the jobs that were being lost in the factories, Eamon O'Shea was the person to blame.

The protestors likewise left, though I never really noticed their actual departure. It was like waking up to a sunny day after a week of rain — sometime during the night the clouds had just floated away. And like puddles on the sidewalk, the trash left behind by the protestors was the only reminder of their presence.

And once again, Suzanne and I had Corcoran to ourselves.

✧

It was a little more than a week before Suzanne's band would christen the renovated Interlachen; and just three days after that, Sharon and Lillie were going to hold their first daylong retreat for families of Vietnam vets. So no longer were Suzanne and I alone in the ballroom after dinner.

The presence of the protestors had put a hold on things between us; but now they had left, and now things could get back on track. And in a way, I thought, maybe the hold had been good — maybe it had come at just the right time. That night, up in my room, when Suzanne had explained her reluctance and said we needed to talk "sometime," I figured it was just a delay tactic. But now we'd had our delay. And now we could pick up where I'd wanted us to be that night down at the lake.

But the more I tried to push things along, the more Suzanne seemed to be retreating. I didn't notice it right away — maybe because we were so busy, or maybe because I just assumed she was getting nervous about the opening. Yet whenever I tried to flirt with her or make late-night plans, she became edgy and irritable; and her face would tense up and she would invariably find a reason to put me off.

After a couple of days of this, I decided to have the talk.

✧

Long after everyone else had gone home, Suzanne and I continued to work. I was painting benches, and she was replacing broken floor tiles. I kept waiting for her to say something, but she just kept working on the tiles.

Nearly two hours passed before I finally went up to her. She was on her knees, scraping out an old tile.

"It's getting late. How about wrapping it up?"

""I want to finish this first," she answered, not looking up. "But you go ahead."

"What's going on, Suzanne? Don't you think we should talk before we just drift off into total indifference? I mean, has something happened?"

She stayed kneeling for a few moments, with her head down, and then looked up at me and said: "Let's walk down to the lake, okay?"

We walked in a silence that continued even after we sat down on the bench Myron had just built. (He had waited for the protestors to leave before he put it out — he didn't want them tearing it up for firewood.) Suzanne kept her eyes glued on the nervous motions of her interlocked fingers. And the longer she went without speaking, the more alarmed I became at what she needed to talk about.

"Look, if you want to say something, just blurt it out," I finally said, impatient with the wait.

"I didn't exactly plan on having this talk in this kind of way," she said.

And then another long silence followed, until she finally turned to me and rested one hand on my shoulder. It was dark now, with just a sliver of a moon shining. Maybe the darkness made it easier on her. Maybe she had waited for it.

Off in the background, I could hear a blur of voices, sounding as if they were coming from Julia's porch. That was the thing about a place like Corcoran: even though there were so few people around, you never felt alone.

Depending on how the wind was blowing, you could hear dishes being washed in a sink or a toilet being flushed.

"Remember, earlier? when I seemed kind of reluctant to...get physical?" she started.

"Yes?"

"Well, I need to tell you why."

Then she folded one leg under the other, wrapped both her hands around mine, and told me about the accident that had occurred less than two years ago.

She was alone in the kitchen of her home. Their housekeeper had just gone to the grocery store to pick up some ingredients for the donuts she was making in the deep-fry cooker.

"I was grabbing a drink out of the refrigerator; and as I was shutting the door, the edge of it caught my pearl bracelet. The pearls came loose and scattered across the floor. I don't remember much after that. I've gone over it a million times in my mind, wondering how I could have been so careless and stupid..."

I could feel Suzanne's jaw tense up on my shoulder. And her hands were tightening their grip.

"....Anyway, I was down on the floor, trying to find all the pearls — and I was in a hurry. I shoved a kitchen chair out of the way, and it must have caught the cord to the deep-fry cooker. That's the last I remember, until I was at the hospital. I had tipped the cooker over, and the boiling grease poured all over my back."

I cringed as her chin dug into my shoulder. Hearing her tell that story was like listening to fingernails run across a blackboard. I shivered as I thought of what had happened. And I could tell Suzanne was shivering too.

She had never before told anyone about that incident. She had never before needed to — everyone in her school heard about it; the months of absences had, in itself, made the announcement. She had never described the weeks of operations and skin grafts, and the months of lying stiffly on her stomach.

Suzanne told me that her back was a quilt of scars, and that the scars ran down onto her upper arms. (So that was why she always wore long sleeves.) She was ashamed of it, she said, beginning to cry. She was ashamed of the ugliness. And she was terrified of having someone see her and instinctively wrinkle their face in revulsion.

"That's why I stopped you the other night. That's why I wouldn't go swimming. I don't want you to see it, or even feel it."

I shifted my position so that I could put my arms around her, but I found myself being very careful in how I touched her back. We sat like that for a long time, with me giving Suzanne a one-way hug. She was all curled up, her own arms held tightly to her chest, her face buried in my neck. And as I held her I stared out over the dark water.

I tried to come up with something to say that would relieve all her fears, but all I could think about was the scars that were just beneath the shirt my hands were touching. I tried to imagine what they looked like, and whether I would be repulsed if I saw them. I wondered if I would lose all attraction to Suzanne.

I pressed my hands slightly tighter against her back — not enough to make Suzanne take notice, but just enough to try to feel the scars. It was all I could think about — her scars. And suddenly, all those nights I had stayed awake, fantasizing about Suzanne and about being with her, seemed so far away. My instincts had been right — it had been too good to be true.

I was sure I would find her repulsive. How could I possibly be attracted to a body full of scars? I didn't even want to see it. Besides, what could be worse than having her see the revulsion in my eyes? But it was so tragic. She was so beautiful. Her soft, elegant face framed so strikingly by her thick, wavy hair. Her eyes so wide and full of energy. Her legs so alluring.

As I was immersed in an analysis of my probable reactions, Suzanne swung one of those legs across my lap and then moved over to straddle me on the bench. She placed her hands on either side of my face and brought her lips to mine. But I was reluctant. There was no desire, only speculations of scars.

"I shouldn't have been afraid to tell you," she whispered, when she finally released me. Her face, even though just inches from mine, was like a black-and-gray sketch in the dark night air. "I knew you were different, as soon as I met you, but I was still scared. It's just that, since the accident, I haven't trusted that anyone could see my scars and not look on me as some grotesque monster. I guess I was so afraid of people pitying me that I just dropped out...of everything. I just withdrew into my own little shell."

I was glad our faces were blurred in darkness, because I didn't know how I looked, and I didn't want Suzanne to see into my eyes.

"Sometimes I think I was brought here just so that I could meet you," she added, before she kissed me again.

This time, as she kissed me, the desire returned. But it felt like a different desire — the desire to live up to her faith in me. And then it came to me, like the jolt of an electrical shock, as if all the chaotic electrodes of my confusion were suddenly aligned perfectly. Suzanne's scars weren't an ugly deformity, they were like an imprint from God, designating us for each other. They were what had brought her to me. They were what had made it possible for her to love me.

On that moonless night at Porter's Point, I suddenly saw clearly. I saw everything...even Ricky. Even the grief that I had seen only as guilt.

I had never believed in him. And because I'd never believed in him, I never saw him for who he really was. And I never trusted that my love for him was anything more than pity or responsibility. The thing I should have learned from my retarded brother was that love requires courage, and that courage only comes from faith.

It was like what the nuns had told us about faith — that you had to believe in God before you could love him; and what inspired faith was not the tidiness of perfection, but the turmoil of imperfection. It was the suffering and death on the cross that demanded faith, not the desire for an eternity of paradise.

Maybe the only way to deal with retardedness and craziness and scars was with faith. And maybe the only way to faith was through retardedness and craziness and scars.

Without her scars, maybe I could never really love Suzanne. Maybe it was her scars that would give me the courage to love her in a way I had never before known possible.

As we kissed, I moved my hands down to the middle of her back. I didn't hug her; I just held them there, gently touching her shirt.

"I'm all healed. I'm not going to break," Suzanne

whispered through our kiss. Her lips were curved up into a smile — it was her first smile since everyone had left us alone, hours ago.

"Does it hurt?" I asked.

"No. It's sensitive, but once I get used to your touch I'm okay."

"So, are you used to it?"

"Yes, but...I mean, I don't want you to be grossed out."

"How about if I just touch your back, while we're kissing. I'll be gentle."

"It's going to feel...weird. I don't want you to be surprised. I..."

"Shhh. The only thing that's going to feel weird is if you don't relax," I answered.

I eased her shirt out of her jeans, slipped my hand underneath it, and then softly touched her back. As I skimmed my fingers across her skin, I felt a continuous series of uneven ripples and ridges. I moved my hand all over her back. It felt like wrinkles, but without the age. Suzanne had her hands around my head and was holding me in an uninterrupted kiss. She seemed afraid to stop — afraid that any momentary break would cause me to realize what my fingers were feeling.

Despite her resistance, I moved my lips down to her neck. She shivered as I pulled her collar down and kissed that part of her upper back that I could reach. I felt her freeze and start to pull back, but I held tight. With my lips, I could feel the quilted skin that my fingers had been caressing. In between the dimples and ridges, there were glassy smooth patches — the centers of the skin grafts.

After a while, she pulled my lips back to hers. "Are you sure you don't find it disgusting?" she asked.

"I'm absolutely positive," I answered, surprised at how unaffected I had been by the feel of her scars. Although, perhaps the physical feel of her skin was being overshadowed by my yearning to fulfill her trust in me. There was, I discovered, something very sexy about a person who trusts. There was something very sexy about the moment in time when the perfect mixture of love and desire combusts into trust.

"You're not going to shut me down this time, are you?" I pleaded, half-teasingly. "After all, I've always heard that the front is even more interesting."

"I guess I'm just an opposite kind of girl — it's the back that I'm protective of. Once you make it there, the rest is a cinch."

"Will you let me take off your shirt?"

"Oh God," she said, her body tensing up, "I don't know. Do you think you're ready for that? I mean, seeing is so much different than feeling."

"How about if I don't look?"

"Do you think we're going too fast? Don't you want to take some time to get used to...everything?"

"I've been doing nothing but taking time. You don't know how many times I've thought about you, and..."

"Yes, but you just found out about my scars tonight. That's not enough time for you to..."

"Suzanne, I don't need any more time."

I coaxed her into turning around and sitting on the bench between my legs. Then I undid a couple of buttons and slide her shirt down over one shoulder. Maybe I was a little afraid or uncertain, because I didn't open my eyes until I had been kissing her back for a minute or two. And when I did open them, I felt as if there was an instant welding of our fates. And maybe I felt a tinge of selfishness, as if that terrible day when the scalding oil poured down on Suzanne's innocent back was the day God gave me the chance to break out of my passive and self-pitying past.

"Your scars are all mine, do you know that?" I said, my breath more gasping, now that my hands had moved to the other side of her body.

"How do you mean?" she asked, more lazily — more comfortably.

"Because they saved you for me."

"Funny, that's how I've felt about your brother," she said, reaching back with one arm and pulling my face down to her neck. "He made you what you are — able to love abnormality. My scars needed someone like Ricky."

I moved up to kiss her cheek and I tasted the salt from her tears.

"I wish I could have met him," she said. "I wish I could have thanked him."

And as she said this, I thought of the eulogy the priest had given at Ricky's funeral. It didn't mean anything to me at the time; in fact, it seemed just another typically Catholic pronouncement — the priest's statement that "God put Ricky on this earth to show us something, and now he's taken him away to see what we can do on our own." It made Ricky sound like those training wheels I used when I first learned how to ride a bike. But now, with Suzanne's skin against mine, I felt as though I understood perfectly what the priest meant.

✧

We sat silently holding each other for a long time, with our eyes cast out across the dark water. "I don't want to go home tonight," Suzanne finally said. "I don't want tonight to end, not until the sun says it has to. Will you stay with me?"

"Of course."

"Can we stay here? Will people see us in the morning?"

"Yeah, maybe. Myron gets up pretty early, and so does Grandpa."

"Where can we go? I'd be a little nervous about taking you to Ardelle's."

"Hell, I'd be a little nervous going."

"Hey, what if we go up to the cemetery?" Suzanne suggested. "Nobody goes by it in the morning, right? And we could still see the lake. Do you think Eamon might wander up there yet tonight?"

"Not..if..he..hasn't gone there by now," I answered, feeling that a cemetery just didn't seem to fit the occasion.

But it was to the cemetery that we went, after stopping at Grandpa's house to sneak out a couple of blankets and pillows.

It was a warm night, with the slightest of breezes. We had to walk slowly to navigate around the headstones. I took Suzanne to a spot toward the back of the cemetery, past the gravestones and yet still within the soft, mowed grass. And there, among the dead generations of Corcoran, we made love.

I had been wrong. A person didn't need to be perfect to be loved. And maybe love was just a blessing, completely beyond the realm of human control.

Hudson Joad

During the time between the protestors leaving and Interlachen opening, I decided not to go to college in the fall. Suzanne and I would spend the year working and saving up, so that we could both go to the same school. Actually, the money wasn't the real reason, for either one of us. After having worked all summer on her music, Suzanne didn't want to put on just one or two performances. And I didn't feel like leaving Suzanne. I didn't even feel like leaving Corcoran.

I not only succumbed to my grandfather's delusions, I began extrapolating beyond them. Maybe Corcoran could indeed experience a grand rebirth. Maybe it could have a prosperous future. Maybe those developers were onto something. Maybe Grandpa and I could do what they had planned on doing.

And it wasn't just Grandpa and me who were having dreams of Corcoran. The V.A. had agreed to fund Sharon's proposal for a counseling and support center for veteran's families; and both Sharon and Lillie had devised a strategy for recruiting wives of men who were serving in Vietnam to come live in Corcoran. Something had to be done, Sharon said, to counteract the loneliness and alienation into which society was forcing veterans and their families.

It hadn't taken long for Sharon to snap out of her melancholic funk. It was a triumph of inertia, I concluded. She had gotten involved in too many projects; she had made too many commitments. Pulling away took too much work. Retreating required too many casualties. So after a couple of days of sullenness and unending telephone rings, Sharon went back to her life. The inertia of it had saved her.

It seemed as if everyone was uniformly excited about Corcoran's future. Even Will Kramer was showing no signs of leaving.

Will was like a lifeboat trailing behind the leaky, listing ship that was Corcoran. He seemed to know how to do just about everything. He could re-wire the electrical circuits in the ballroom, and assist Myron with a valve job on one of the tractors, and then accompany Lillie and Sharon to the V.A. to promote their ideas for a retreat center. And in between all this, he helped Julia with her renovation projects.

Two adjacent chairs were always left for Suzanne and me at the dinner table. (We were eating a half hour later now, and skipping the evening news programs altogether; it was primarily for Will's sake — he'd had enough of Vietnam, he said.) And Ardelle constantly lobbied for her house to become the venue for our romance. She was always urging me to come over in the evening, after our work on the ballroom was finished. She even promised Suzanne that she'd start going to bed earlier, that she was a very sound sleeper.

And Myron was busy building a bench swing to put down by the lake. "You folks need a swing," he pronounced. "All young couples should have a swing to sit on and watch the sunset." In Corcoran, needs were simple.

It was an odd feeling, realizing that Suzanne and I had become such a center of attention. But maybe, to them, the most important thing was that love was still alive, that it hadn't been completely strangled by the war and their exile to Corcoran. Maybe their image of us helped them to remember what they were waiting for, what they were hoping for.

Yet what surprised me about all this was Suzanne's reaction – her easy embrace of the future, and of our place in it together. "Why don't we plan something big for next year's Memorial Day," she once said. "I think Eamon would really like it. And I think it would be great to see the cemetery all blooming with flowers."

✧

There were the occasional disturbances. Nothing major, not like those few days with the protestors; just little, isolated acts of vandalism, probably by unemployed factory workers who had obviously been convinced that the Corcoran hold-outs were responsible for the dismal economic outlook facing Millerton.

They came late at night — their goal, probably, to wake up everyone and draw them angrily to their windows. But unknown to these noisy intruders, Corcoran was fairly immune to the effects of late-night honking and shouting. Will was accustomed to sounds a lot worse than honks. Sharon, Julia and Lillie were not old enough to let mere honks rile up within them a sleepless rage at the younger generation. Grandpa, Myron, Ardelle and Lorraine were hard of hearing. And Suzanne and I were never sleeping.

It wasn't until the next morning that we would discover whatever pranks the drive-by vandals had pulled the night before. Eggs splattered on cars was the most frequent occurrence, but sometimes the chosen missiles were tomatoes. A couple of windows in the ballroom were broken, and Sharon's car tires had the air let out of them. But that was about it. And yet, these petty pranks seemed to ignite within Grandpa an anger he had not previously displayed toward either the developers or the protestors.

"They fouled their own land, and then they expected to take mine," he grumbled one morning, staring at the egg-splattered windshield of his pickup. "They rant and rave about grand social ideals, and yet their own individual ones have been smothered by self-indulgent greed."

It was a theme on which he seemed to be dwelling lately. One night at dinner, after the subject of the protestors was raised, Grandpa started in on one of his tirades. "That seems to be the thing now — this idea about just living for the present. Well let me tell you," he said to everyone, and yet to no one, "the present is momentary. In a fleeting moment, time passes from the future to the past. It's the future and the past that occupy the vast majority of our time here on earth. Imagining and remembering — that's what life is."

✧

All during that week preceding the reopening, Suzanne and I trudged around Millerton putting up fliers. They advertised the grand opening of the county's largest dance floor, with a special appearance by a Seattle band called "Hudson Joad." It was Ardelle's idea to use the term "special appearance" ("In show business, every appearance is a special appearance," she said), as well as to identify the band as from Seattle. "It's like fishing, honey," she told Suzanne. "Nobody wants to go off their own dock; they always want to trek clear across the lake. Same thing with entertainment — the further away the act comes from, the better it's bound to be."

But the name of the band was Suzanne's creation. "It comes from the 'Grapes of Wrath,'" she told us one night at the dinner table. "Hudson was the make of the truck the Joads drove to California."

"But why the 'Grapes of Wrath'?" a puzzled Ardelle asked.

"I don't know," Suzanne said, "I guess because this place kind of reminds me of that novel."

Will was the only person who laughed and nodded his head in a big, rocking motion. I wasn't sure anyone else knew what to make of Suzanne's analogy.

The fliers went up everywhere — on telephone poles, in the entry way of bars, on community bulletin boards in the parks. They were our last ditch effort to entice a crowd to drive out to some unknown ballroom in some blink-and-you'll-miss-it town. Ardelle had already taken out advertisements in the local newspapers, and had hounded radio stations to announce the event during their listings of entertainment happenings. Still, none of us had any idea as to how many people would actually show up. Ardelle, who had long since become the de facto producer, as well as financier, decided to cut the admission price to one dollar. "It's more important to lose a little money with a big crowd than to lose everything with a small crowd," she said — a strategy with which Grandpa wholeheartedly agreed.

But all of Ardelle's planning and financial support only increased Suzanne's nervousness.

"What if it's a flop? I'll never be able to face Ardelle again."

"Don't worry. If there's one thing everyone around here is used to, it's flops."

But what a stupid thing to say. Contentment and happiness had dulled my sense of self-vigilance.

✧

No farm work was done in that week preceding Interlachen's opening. But Grandpa did have me mow all of Corcoran. Every yard of every empty house. He even wanted me to paint the fronts of some of the houses, and maybe plant some petunia beds, but Ardelle vetoed those ideas. There were enough real jobs to do, she fretted.

Ardelle was a lot more anxious about Interlachen than Grandpa was. But then, he had seen failure so many times that he no longer had any fear of it. In Grandpa's world, failure was a fact of life.

On the day of the opening, we all gathered at Julia's for breakfast. As Ardelle gave out the work assignments, it finally sunk in that there was actually going to be some nightlife in Corcoran. People were actually going to drive to Corcoran to have fun. Suzanne was actually going to perform up on a lighted stage in front of hundreds of people.

This last realization left me jittery. I wondered how tonight might change things between us. Up on stage, she'd be in the spotlight — she wouldn't just be someone who was hanging out in a ghost town, having run away from home. Suddenly, my tolerance for scar tissue didn't seem sufficient to single me out from all the men who would flock to her. And suddenly, it seemed inevitable that she would soon tire of everything that had been Corcoran.

✧

I didn't see much of Suzanne throughout the day. Ardelle had designated me for errands, and I spent the morning and most of the afternoon in the truck, making trip after trip into Millerton. When I came back after the last one, I helped Will move the tables and chairs into place. From there, we carried all the plastic cups and paper plates from the storeroom into the kitchen. Ardelle had decided to sell hamburgers, chili dogs and french fries. ("Way out here, where else are they gonna eat?") What she undercharged on the admission tickets she was going to make up on the food prices. "When you're hungry, you don't think about price," she said. And I had to wonder if she ever applied such economic strategy to The Fieldstone.

But at least on this day, all her strategies made perfect sense. Julia was assigned to be the ticket-seller — it being good business to put an attractive woman out front, to lure inside the indecisive; just as it was a wise decision to put Valerie and Lorraine behind the kitchen counter, way behind the kitchen counter.

Will and Sharon were to handle the beer and beverage bar — Ardelle's theory being that the most authoritative should be placed in the spot that had the greatest potential for disturbance. I was slotted as the errand boy, in charge of keeping in touch with all stations and getting whatever they needed. And Grandpa and Myron were asked to watch the exit doors, just in case someone tried something funny. It was one of those jobs that was given just so that the two men didn't feel left out, but we all knew there wasn't a chance in hell that either one of them would sit still for more than five minutes.

✧

I was helping Valerie pry open a stuck window in the kitchen when Suzanne arrived, about forty-five minutes before the band was to start playing. She was wearing a long-sleeved black dress, short in the hemline and tight in the fit. She wore a lot of makeup, or maybe it just seemed like a lot because she never wore any; and her hair had some extra waves in it. She was stunning, in a way I had never noticed before — stunning in a distant and untouchable way.

It was only eight o'clock, and already there was a steady line of people at the ticket booth. Ardelle, whose eyes were starting to sparkle with the look of success, insisted that Suzanne have something to eat. "You shouldn't be up on stage with an empty stomach," she advised.

Then she turned to me, handing me two chili dogs, and said, "Here Glen, both of you need something to eat. Take Suzanne out back and sit yourselves down on the bench."

I did as I was told, and Suzanne followed me. We sat on the same bench on which we had sat dozens of times before. But this time a flurry of noises were streaming out of the windows. A parade of cars were filling the empty lot across the street. And next to me sat a nervous Suzanne who took one small bite out of her chili dog before she set it down on the bench.

"You're going to be great," I said.

"I don't know. I just don't know."

"You've practiced a hundred times — you'll do great."

"And what if I don't?"

"I'm thinking more about what happens when you do," I muttered.

"What's that?"

"Nothing. You'll do great. Don't even think about anything else."

"There's a lot of people showing up."

"I think we're going to have a full house."

I knew she was nervous. And I knew I shouldn't expect anything from her, not now. But still, I felt as if we were suddenly strangers, trying so hard to make conversation, to pass the time.

I couldn't say anything, because I knew I was being petty and jealous and selfish. Yet as I looked out over a bustling Corcoran, I was plagued with the feeling that everything was different. I had come to love Suzanne in the isolated, predictable cocoon of Corcoran. And I couldn't help but feel that Suzanne and I were so inextricably linked to the place that any change in it would immediately translate to us. I was more like Ricky than I thought — I too obviously thrived on routine.

With my half-eaten chili dog in my hand, I wanted to reach out and break the bubble of change that was separating us, and touch Suzanne with the familiarity of our past. I wanted to hug her, to have her hair pressed to my face, to tell her something that would make us both look forward to later that night. I wanted to tell her something that would make her smile, something she would remember as she played her music. I wanted to...

"Hey, Suzanne, we gotta check the mikes," her guitar player yelled out from the back door.

"Okay Mitchell," she answered. Then she turned to me with a forced smile. "Will you destroy the evidence?" she asked in a whispered voice, looking down at her chili dog.

"Sure, good luck," I said, rushing to say something. Rushing to hide beneath a sterile platitude any evidence of how I was feeling.

"I'm nervous," she said.

"Don't be, you'll mesmerize them; and that's before you even sing a note."

"I suddenly wish it was just you and me here, like it was for so many nights. It'll be like that later, right?"

"It'll be the longest wait of my life, but you just try to keep me away." My smile, I felt, was so much more forced than hers had been.

"Let me see you every now and then, okay?" she whispered. Then she kissed me, lightly and quickly, and disappeared into the ballroom.

✧

As it turned out, Ardelle proved to be quite the promoter. She had hoped for a crowd of two hundred fifty. We stopped counting at five hundred.

I saw Suzanne perform only her first two songs. After that, all my time was spent in the truck. More chili dog buns were needed, more bags of frozen french fries, more plastic glasses, more kegs of beer. I even missed seeing Suzanne during the break between her first and second sets.

Maybe I could have timed it to be there when she took her next break, but I didn't. Maybe I even deliberately missed her — maybe I didn't want a repeat of that scene on the bench.

A cold feeling of estrangement came over me as I watched her up on that stage. And I couldn't ignore the comments that buzzed around the edges of the dance floor like irritating mosquitos. Comments from gawking men.

"She's hot."

"I'd like to have those legs wrapped around me."

"She's driving me crazy."

"What a babe."

But the comments didn't make me angry as much as they made me feel irrelevant. Actually, they seemed to reignite all those feelings I'd had when walking Ricky through the crowded, gawking hallways of Roosevelt High.

But I knew I was overreacting. I just needed to adjust to Suzanne in this new light, I told myself as I ran my errands. That's all I needed, I thought. Everything would be alright once the lights went on and the cars drove away and Suzanne and I could be alone.

✧

It was near the end of Suzanne's second set when Ardelle asked me if I could pick up twenty more bags of ice. She said I didn't need to go right away, that Suzanne had been looking for me during her first break. But I insisted on going; I wanted to keep busy. And I told Ardelle that I'd be back in time for the break.

On my walk to the truck, I wondered if it would be better for both of us if I didn't make it back for her break. Suzanne didn't need my insecurity, and I didn't think I could take all the men who would be approaching her as we tried to talk. Or maybe I was afraid.

I saw a group of guys huddled around the open trunk of a car. They looked like they were up to some kind of mischief, but I didn't stop. I heard them laughing, in a scheming, nervous sort of way, but I just kept on walking to my truck. Maybe I was afraid of them too.

✧

The fire trucks passed me as I pulled off to the shoulder on my drive back to Corcoran. It was not unusual to see fire trucks speeding out of Millerton and into the surrounding farm country. Hay fields would sometimes catch fire during the dry summer months, as would old barns and gasoline tanks. But when the third and fourth trucks passed me, I knew it was no ordinary fire to which they were heading. I knew it was Corcoran.

The road into Corcoran had been blocked by the sheriff's patrol cars, but from the highway I could see Interlachen ablaze. The fire department never even attempted to save the old ballroom. Apparently, it was too far gone by the time the trucks arrived. All they could do was hose down the surrounding buildings to prevent the fire from spreading. And of course they did what they could to administer first aid to those who had been injured. But there were no attempts at rescue — whatever rescuing there was to be done had already taken place by the time the Millerton Fire Department arrived.

According to reports, Will Kramer had personally pulled more than a dozen people out of the burning ballroom. When he went back in the last time, despite Julia's attempts to stop him, he went in after Suzanne. Ardelle had just run up to him and Julia in a panic and said that she couldn't find Suzanne, that she thought Suzanne was still in the building.

In Cemetery's Shadow

Sixteen people died in the fire that destroyed Interlachen. Will and Suzanne were among the sixteen.

It was a mystery as to why Suzanne didn't get out, but it was no mystery as to how the fire started. As a prank, or maybe even as an act of vengeance on a place that had denied so much opportunity to so many in Millerton, a group of young men had set off a cachet of fireworks just outside one of the ballroom's back windows. It had achieved its desired effect; a shrieking panic immediately erupted from the crowd inside. There was a rush for the doors before Will was able to calm down the stampeders, and before the fireworks had spent themselves. Within minutes, order was restored. Unfortunately, it was this false alarm and the ensuing sense of relief that may have later caused the indifference to the smoke that was beginning to seep into the ballroom from some roof timbers that had started to burn.

I went to the court hearing in which the fireworks-lighters were charged. I was fairly certain that they were the same men I had seen huddled around that open car trunk. But I never found out if they were convicted, or whether they served any jail time. They never even really registered in my consciousness. Because when I thought about Suzanne's death, I could only think about the fact that I wasn't there when she needed me. I had run away, leaving all the bravery to Will.

✧

What a waste it was, I so often thought. What a waste to spend those last moments on the bench as I did, holding a chili dog — so gripped with the silence of jealousy and doubt. What a waste.

✧

Everything that subsequently happened in Corcoran came to me second-hand. A week and a half after the fire, I went down to the army recruiting center in Millerton and volunteered. Enlistments at that time were almost nonexistent. So the recruiter was surprised when, after telling me all about the wide range of options available in the army to an enlistee, I chose a combat assignment to Vietnam. I wanted to go right away, I told the sergeant. My one bag was lying at my feet — I was ready for boot camp.

✧

After the fire, Corcoran started to disband, slowly but steadily, just as the charred remains of Interlachen slowly but steadily crumbled. Julia went to see her husband in Honolulu when he was on leave; and during that visit, he convinced her to move in with his parents until his tour of duty ended. Lillie transferred to a VA Hospital in San Francisco where her husband was being treated — he had been injured by a bomb blast in the Saigon cafe in which he was eating. Sharon moved to Washington, DC when she was given a management job with the Veterans

Administration. Valerie married Seth and moved with him to Pittsburgh, where his family owned a paint manufacturing business; and Lorraine was given an apartment in Seth and Valerie's big house.

For the first few weeks I was in the army, letters came almost every day from Grandpa. He begged me to return. He said he could get the army to annul my enlistment, given the trauma that had preceded it. But as the days went on, his letters returned to his usual themes. He wrote about how good the crops looked, about what a bountiful harvest the fall would bring, and about all the uses to which the money could be put. He wrote about how the harvest would boost the morale of Myron and Ardelle. But he never mentioned how he was going to bring in that big harvest.

When Ardelle wrote me in October, she said Grandpa was working day and night. It turned out to be an extended autumn that year — the first snow didn't come until Thanksgiving, so Grandpa had almost two full months of harvesting. When it was all over, he had harvested every acre of his land, all by himself. He had never done that before.

In December, the only letters I received were from Ardelle. She wrote that Grandpa was resting up. It had been a tough harvest. He had a cold. She was taking his meals to him.

Grandpa didn't send me a Christmas card. In February, he went to the hospital. On March 3rd, Grandpa died of complications from pneumonia.

✧

Ardelle moved back to the retirement home from

which Grandpa had once rescued her; and she took Myron with her — a man who had never lived in a city or in the confines of one room; a man who had never not had a garage in which to work. But they had no choice. They didn't own their houses, or the land, or even The Fieldstone. Everything had gone to Grandpa's children when he died.

✧

I never did see Vietnam. I didn't even leave the boundaries of the United States. By the time I finished basic training, the only troop movements were those leaving Vietnam. America was in the process of pulling out. Although, even if my company had been sent to Vietnam, I'm not sure my commanding officer would have taken me. I had acquired a reputation of being skittish and jumpy and even hysterical. It was a result of my nightmares, during which I'd scream and sometimes jump out of my cot. There were times I would wake the entire company. But, contrary to what so many of my fellow soldiers thought, it was not because I was terrified of the prospect of combat. My nightmares were all the same — they were of scars and burns and flames and searing heat.

When I got out of the army, I went to college. I majored in business and then went to work for an investment banking firm. Just as my father had always wanted, I became a businessman. Not only that, but I doubled the money he invested with me. My father was proud of me; but making money was easy. It was a lot easier than trying to sleep at night. It was even easier that babysitting Ricky.

I married a woman who sold real estate. We bought a house and had beautiful furniture. My parents came for Christmas, along with my sisters and their families. We had finally become a normal family.

But I was a lousy husband: indifferent was how my wife described me. And it was during my marriage when I learned the flip-side of the rule of emotional relativity that Suzanne had taught me: the more love involved, the faster the time passes.

When the marriage finally ended, I was thankful I had been too indifferent (or too afraid of the retarded gene) to have children. On the night I came home to her note, I packed my car and drove to Corcoran (or what was now a subdivision called Orchard Park).

Grandpa's house was all that was left of the Corcoran of 1970 — that and the cemetery. It had been given to me in the settlement of his estate. Grandpa had never gotten around to amending his will; but both Ardelle and Myron threatened to make trouble, to testify that Grandpa had not wanted his children to have any part of Corcoran. So as a pay-off, I was given the house and all the land designated for the cemetery (which was considerable, given Grandpa's belief that a large cemetery would be needed for a thriving and prosperous town). It was an easy concession for my mother's siblings to make, because they had suddenly become wealthy. Not only did a developer buy the land, but a bottling company bought the rights to the underground springs that were discovered to be feeding into the lake. According to the deal reached, my mother and her siblings received a twelve percent royalty on every bottle and jug of spring water sold.

Throughout my marriage, I often went back to Grandpa's house (which was what I still called it). I used it as a get-away; I took long vacations there. My wife called it my "cemetery house." I was the only person, she said, who went to a cemetery for his vacation.

I never told my wife much about that summer of 1970. I never wanted to tell her about the feelings she said I was incapable of having. But in a way, I was also embarrassed. I didn't think one summer in my eighteenth year should continue to haunt me as it did.

It was from Grandpa's house that I watched the Orchard Park development spring up. I watched all the oak and maple trees get cut down, and all the old houses get bulldozed. I saw big tractors scoop up the rubble pile that used to be Interlachen. I watched as the barn where Myron and I fixed furniture and worked on tractor engines was demolished. And even the church was torn down — a church whose sagging roof never did collapse.

The houses closest to where The Fieldstone used to stand were the first to go up; and the ones closest to Grandpa's house were the last. It was June — one of those rare occasions when I had brought my wife with me to Grandpa's house. We had gone to bed, fairly early. The windows were all open, it being a cool summer night. Sometime after midnight, I awoke; and in that momentary transition to consciousness, before I recognized the furnishing of the room around me and the woman lying next to me, I was positive that I heard Suzanne's voice singing one of those ballads that had so often lullabied us to sleep that summer. But when the moment passed, I realized that what I heard was a recording being played on a stereo in one of the new houses. It made me hate even more the houses and people that were moving into my memories.

✧

Only by accident did I find a means with which to survive in Corcoran after my divorce. The owner of the largest funeral home in Millerton called me one day; he said cemetery land was running out; he asked if I would be interested in opening up all that unused land in the Corcoran cemetery.

Violets

Maybe I came back to Corcoran for the same reason that Valerie kept writing all those letters to Vietnam servicemen. But Grandpa used to say that you couldn't dream without believing. And for a long time after that summer, I never believed in anything. I saw it all as delusions.

Once, when Suzanne and I were sitting alone in the church, I asked her how she could possibly believe in a God that had let her suffer like that.

"Actually, I didn't start believing until after the accident," she said. "I guess that was when I really needed it."

"But weren't you angry?"

"I think of it like this: if parents build a playroom and stock it with all their children's favorite toys, we don't blame them when the child falls and bruises herself on one of those toys. In fact, it's the parent whom the child goes to for comfort."

I used to tell myself that the thing about having a retarded brother was that you're always on guard, always suspicious. But that wasn't true. There was no way I could pin that on Ricky.

Maybe that's why I came back. Because, despite everything I thought when I was a boy, I really did want to be like my grandfather. And because I wanted to do something to make myself feel that I was starting over, that I hadn't given up.

✧

It was an easy business. The funeral homes basically handled the sale of the burial plots. All I had to do was maintain the grounds. Mow the grass and trim the trees and weed the gardens.

I built a small machine shed, where I stored the mowers and diggers and fertilizer spreaders. I thought I'd hire a landscaping crew; but I discovered that I enjoyed the work. I loved the gardens the best — I saved them for the afternoons. And in the evenings, I worked in the machine shed. I also built a greenhouse and began growing my own shrubs and flowers.

There were always visitors. Sometimes just a car or two, slowly driving through the cemetery before stopping at a gravesite; and sometimes a funeral procession so long that the line of parked cars stretched all the way to the front gate. Cemeteries seemed to bring out the best in people — there was never any littering, never any screaming, never any loud music, never any speeding cars. And there was something about funerals that seemed to open the windows to people's souls. I could sit on a bench a hundred feet away and feel like I knew the feelings and histories of the people standing next to the casket.

As with any place, there were the regulars. Some I noticed because of the drama of their emotions; others because they seemed as much at ease as if they were mailing a letter. I saw her maybe a dozen times before I picked up on her routine. She came at noon, every Monday, Wednesday and Friday. And every time, she brought a handful of violets. She crouched down, bending at the knees, and laid them on the stone. She stayed like that for five minutes or so, crouched down, touching the stone; and then she stood up and walked back to her car. The name on the headstone was Jennifer Dolan. According to the dates, she was twelve years old when she died.

It was Friday. A few minutes before noon. I had just cut some roses from up near the front gate. I had them in water, sitting on the golf cart I used to ferry things around the cemetery. I was planting some grass seed on a fresh grave, just twenty or thirty feet from Jennifer Dolan's grave.

Right on schedule, the car pulled up and the woman stepped out. She walked her usual path. She had the violets.

"Excuse me," I said, walking over, after she had stood up. "I just cut some roses; would you like some to put alongside the violets?"

"They're beautiful. Are you sure?"

"Here, you can keep them in the vase. We'll rest it against the stone."

"I didn't think that was allowed — to put vases on the ground. Won't the mowers hit it?"

"I'm the mower. I'll look out for it, and I'll keep them watered. They'll be in full bloom for your next visit."

She just stared at me, her face almost frozen. And then she started crying. I took a step toward her, and she leaned forward and put her arms around me.

Grandpa used to say that America was like a big venetian blind. Every now and then it opened and flashed opportunity. The opening might be small, and the flash brief; and that was why, Grandpa always said, you had to keep watching — because you never knew when the moment would come.

What I should have learned from my grandfather is that starting over is a state of mind, not a place.

CPSIA information can be obtained at www.ICGtesting.com
Printed in the USA
BVOW04s2256100314
347233BV00001B/12/P